Joshua 4.0 –

Joshua is everything a wc ',
and built with a body made f( ).
The problem is Joshua is a virtual reality comp   ne
isn't real...or is he?

Barbarian – Kate Douglas

Bryony believes her captive is the sex slave trader responsible for her sister's death. Holding him prisoner, she sexually "tortures" him for hours, getting him harder than steel but allowing him no release. Innocent of her charges and obsessed with Bryony, Jake hunts her down. Two years later he captures his prey. And payback is a bitch...

Manimal – Lani Aames

All Kelsey Locke wanted to do was get away for the weekend. She was sick to death of her ex-boyfriend and his irritating attempts to remain in her life. When a friend offered Kelsey the use of her secluded cabin for respite, she jumped at the offer. Kelsey was expecting snow, forest scenery, solitude to get some work done without interruptions, and not much else. Little does Kelsey know, someone – or something – is watching her. And his need to mate is strong...

A.D. 2203: Adam & Eve – Ravyn Wilde

Science has proven that Werewolves have but one genetic breeding mate, their mate who can be another Werewolf, a human female or possibly a warm-blooded Other. Male Weres can only detect their mate's scent during the full moon, so females of all warm-blooded species who don't want to be claimed make a habit of locking themselves in "safe rooms" where their scents can't be detected. For all of her 38 years, geneticist Eve Longtree, an independent human female through and through, has never forgotten to lock herself into her saferoom during Lupine moon. Until now...

At His Mercy – Doreen DeSalvo

Faith Hartely is a researcher in the field of metaphysics – she's also a psychic. She desperately needs Jake McIntyre's approval for grant funds in order to continue conducting research at the university. Jake, a university board member and skeptical to the bone of psychic "charlatans", is ruthlessly determined that Faith won't get that grant money. He wants her to prove her psychic abilities before he'll even consider it. He wants Faith to read his mind, and he arrogantly believes she cannot. Faith can read his mind, all right. But the idea of admitting what Jake is thinking aloud is a bit unsettling. He's thinking of Faith. In wicked ways that would make even a Lady of the Evening gasp in shock...

Time-share: Amelia's Journey – Lora Leigh

Determined to make Venus habitable for humans, a spaceship of scientists head to the veiled planet to work. An unexpected crash separates the crew, leaving Amelia alone with Mike and Saber. Strange things are happening in the biosphere, a primal, primitive phenomenon that affects not only Venus' organisms, but its 3 human inhabitants, too. The need to mate, to be impregnated, overwhelms Amelia, and the desire to be the one who impregnates her overpowers both men. Mike. Saber. Two hot-blooded males in their prime. But just like with any other species of animal, only one man can be the alpha male.

Need a more EXCITING Way to Plan your Day?

ELLORA'S
CAVEMEN
2005 CALENDAR

Coming This Winter

ELLORA'S CAVEMEN: TALES FROM THE TEMPLE I
An Ellora's Cave Publication, March 2004

Ellora's Cave Publishing, Inc.
PO Box 787
Hudson, OH 44236-0787

ISBN # 1-84360-813-8
ISBN MS Reader (LIT) ISBN # 1-84360-812-X
Other available formats (no ISBNs are assigned):
Adobe (PDF), Rocketbook (RB), Mobipocket (PRC) & HTML

ELLORA'S CAVEMEN: TALES FROM THE TEMPLE I edited by
The Legendary "Queen of Steam" *Jaid Black*.
Cover design by *Darrell King*. Photography by *Dennis Roliff*.

Ellora's Cavemen:
Tales from the Temple I

Joshua 4.0
By Sahara Kelly

Barbarian
By Kate Douglas

Manimal
By Lani Aames

A.D. 2203: Adam & Eve
By Ravyn Wilde

At His Mercy
By Doreen DeSalvo

Time-share: Amelia's Journey
By Lora Leigh

JOSHUA 4.0

Sahara Kelly

For my Partner...

Chapter 1

There he was.

Joshua 4.0.

Naked, arms outstretched, bald as a coot, and staring at her, eyes blank, waiting for her. For *her*. Andrea Jane Thompson, graphic artist *extraordinaire*. Waiting for her to turn him into Mr. Terrific, Mr. Make-Her-Mouth-Water, Mr. Yes-She'll-Cream-Her-Panties.

Andy grinned. Oh yeah, baby. We're gonna have *fun* with this one.

She was sitting in front of her monitor, hands encased in sensor mitts, a small headband resting around her ears, and wires linking her umbilically to her desktop. It was the culmination of several years of hard work, three rejected grant applications, and a final whimpering and begging letter to one of the largest Virtual Reality Graphic corporations in the country.

She'd finally been approved as a client to receive the beta version of the "Model Man" software—the 101X unit—for home testing. And now she'd gotten her very own Joshua 4.0.

She hadn't mentioned on the application that Joshua had haunted her dreams, of course. That was far too esoteric for the techno-geeks who'd be giving their approval. She'd merely cited her qualifications. Hot dreams about one's creations wasn't covered by the questionnaire. Thank God.

And that had been the standard 4.0 version.

But *this* one was different. This Joshua wasn't a render that required hours of morphs, textures and poses. This Joshua was hers to command.

Experimentally, she moved a finger. Joshua's arm responded.

Shit. The frickin' thing worked.

Once more she moved, a finger on the other hand this time, and selected some hair for him with her cursor. Bald men hadn't ever really done much for her, Captain Picard notwithstanding. And, of course, Vin Diesel wasn't bad. But Joshua…well, Joshua was going to get hair, whether he liked it or not.

A full head of long dark curls materialized, resting in a gleaming tumble on his shoulders.

Oooh boy. There's something about a guy with long hair.

She pulled a strand of hair over one of his shoulders and noticed the small bar at the top of the screen. It was flickering green, indicating that her usage of the 101X was being monitored and recorded by the servers in the home office of VRG Concepts, Inc.

That was fine by her. As a condition of her receiving this system, she'd agreed to allow her level of activity to be monitored. They'd find a hell of a lot of hours logged from her IP address, no doubt about it.

She was to report bugs, work the damn thing to death if she could, and put it through its paces. Not a hardship for someone whose life revolved around graphic arts. Her online artwork and freelance graphics now decorated some of the top websites, and she'd just put together a streaming video and a couple of Flash presentations for a very wealthy client.

It had given her the chance to take some time off for herself and when the approval for the 101X had come through...well, hell. All the ducks were lined up and quacking themselves sick.

She clicked her way through the texture selections, accepting and discarding, until her very own vision of paradise was looking back at her from rich teal blue eyes.

Funny, she'd never been much on blue-eyed guys, but there was something about the way these particular eyes glowed back at her that just grabbed her by the crotch and said "C'mon honey, let's play."

Mmm. Now that's something I'd like to find under my Christmas tree. Just like that. Naked.

She'd pegged the height dials to six foot three, and the shoulders and torso had expanded proportionately. So had everything else.

Fuck, this guy was built.

Andy selected her favorite texture...Joshua-Beach Male. His skin flickered and then turned a nice light tan, and hairs appeared. All over. Whorls decorated his chest in a very pleasing pattern, and...and...*oh yeah. There it was.* That super-fabulous moment when a girl could watch a guy's genitals come to life, without having to sit through dinner and a movie first. He'd gone from a flesh-toned wiener to a beautiful Louisville slugger in less than 2.3 seconds of render time.

There was some unique built-in specification with this particular texture. Some little peculiarity that turned Joshua's cock into a work of art. It grew, lengthening and thickening a little, and his balls filled out against the background of the dark pubic hair. Andy licked her lips.

His thighs were firm, his abs the perfect six-pack, although she could always change them later if she felt like it, and even his damn toes were ideal.

Shit. She was getting wet just looking at him. The thought of what she was going to do to him and with him made her sweat.

The program flickered and slowed down, and Andy rushed to hit the "save as" button.

Note to self. Don't sweat around the fucking cables.

* * * * *

Three miles away as the crow flew, or about fourteen miles away as the direct T1 cable traveled, Josh Miles sat in front of his flat panel monitor and stared at the numbers flickering across the indicator charts.

He had four 101X units out for beta testing, and his ass was on the line along with all of them. They were his baby, his idea, and had sprung fully-formed from his brain like some mythological creature.

He'd laughed when the art department had pinned up a photo of him from the last beach party and used it as a model for the original "Joshua". He'd chuckled when he'd tried the first interactive VR component that R&D had added. He'd grinned like a schmuck when he'd gotten approval for the board to begin testing.

Now…*now* he was simply nervous.

The concept of a fully interactive graphics system was so simple, he wondered why no one had thought of it before.

Of course, a concept is one thing. Anyone can have a *concept.* You don't need an education, an advanced degree in micro-processing and engineering, a multi-million dollar research company, or even a *dog* to have a *concept*. You could have one sitting on the toilet, doing the crossword puzzle in the back of the TV Guide.

In fact, Josh had. Mr. Whipple would have been flushed with pride.

Some clue, some inane six letter word, had triggered a series of cascading thoughts that had led to Josh's breakthrough. It ended with two simple words. "Why not?" And from that moment on, he'd been obsessed with the notion that interactivity via Virtual Reality would revolutionize the graphics scene.

In a few weeks, he'd know for sure if it had. But for right now, he had to sit and watch the usage bars log his four clients as they worked the 101X into a frenzy.

One dial flickered. Josh checked his records, pulling up the file that corresponded to unit three.

One Andrea Jane Thompson. Age 28. Graphic artist, experienced with...hmm. She *was* qualified. He leaned forward and clicked onto a couple of diagnostic programs and ran a remote systems check.

His robot pinged him back with the information that Ms. Thompson's level of resistance had dropped slightly, making her contact sensors fluctuate.

Josh frowned. What would cause that to happen?

He visualized her, sitting in front of her monitor—wired in to the system, and ran through the possibilities in his mind. Lowered skin resistance.

God damn! *Water*. Moisture on the skin.

Ms Andrea Jane Thompson was sweating. In March.

He wondered why.

Chapter 2

Andy shifted the small portable fan next to her desk and relaxed as the cool air blew over her. She'd shrugged out of her shirt, and now sat in her bra and shorts in front of the keyboard.

Not that she needed the keyboard, of course.

Uh-uh. One twitch and Joshua came to life. No clicking necessary, no mouse-overs, no nothing. Damn, this unit was superb. She could almost *think* him into doing what she wanted.

She blinked back a vision of Mr. Oh-So-Damned-Goodlooking's head nestled between her thighs.

Shit. She had to watch out for moisture. And *that* thought had certainly caused some. The time would come when Joshua got to play, but not quite yet.

She'd posed him casually, and he was now leaning up against an imaginary wall, arms folded, one leg slightly bent, and grinning at her with a real panty-warming smile. She loved that smile.

That smile had figured in a few of her more erotic fantasies lately. The ones that included a session with her "Super Sized Big Boy" toy. The pink one.

Well, hell. So she was horny. Most of the time that's what made her artwork so damned impressive. She transferred her unfulfilled lusts and desires into her images. She caught that yearning, that *do-it-to-me-before-I-die-here* feeling, and reflected it onto her figures.

16

Several clients had come up to her, cleared their throats and politely thanked her, blushing as they explained how their wives had *really* liked her work. She'd grinned and accepted their thanks. At least someone in this town was getting laid. *She* sure as hell wasn't.

Andy could, and probably should, have dated more. But she was tired of the bar scene, where she only drank beer since wine gave her a headache and mixed drinks gave her zits the next day. Beers were good, provided your date didn't mind you hitting the ladies' room every twenty minutes or so.

But the faces never changed, the jokes were old, and she'd quickly tired of the few guys who'd shown an interest. She'd brought one home as an experiment. The sex, to put it bluntly, had sucked. And he hadn't.

Yep. That was one relationship that had promptly developed a 404 Error. File not found.

It seemed guys could use their mouths for talking and drinking, and kissing too, but when it came right *down* to it, she'd picked the ones that lacked directions for anything below her navel. Sure, it was okay for *her* to use her tongue, her hands, ice cream, and whatever else was available. She just never got the favor returned.

She'd given up. Her "Super Sized" buddy did a better job, didn't mess with the sheets or leave the toilet seat up, and she could roll over and go to sleep secure in the knowledge that she wouldn't get the brush-off from it the next day.

Joshua was *always* there for her, however. His smile brightened her life, made her breasts ache, and so what if he wasn't real? He was her creation, and she could endow him with whatever virtues she wanted. And this one, this 4.0 version, was the best yet.

Time to *really* put this puppy through its paces.

Andy opened the file marked "AJ" and created…herself.

* * * * *

What the fuck was she *doing*?

Josh's curiosity was now thoroughly aroused. Unit 3 was functioning perfectly, but it sure was soaking up a huge amount of memory. It couldn't be all the 101X. He double-checked.

Aha. She was importing something from an older version.

Josh rolled up his sleeves and pulled his chair up to the keyboard. With a few quick commands he activated the 'view screen' function. As an integral part of the beta testing process, all beta units were equipped with this remote access feature. That way, his techs could figure out what the client was doing when something went wrong. *If* something went wrong.

It wasn't really an invasion of privacy, since the clients had signed on to the entire testing package. The fact that mention of this particular portion had been relegated to Paragraph 27, Subsection 3, (reduced-size font), was no fault of his. They were supposed to have read the whole damn thing…it was a case of *caveat emptor*, as far as he was concerned.

Without a qualm he pulled up Ms Andrea Jane Thompson's monitor screen.

And his eyes bugged out of his head.

There was Joshua…*himself*…looking pretty damn buff, even if he did say so. But he wasn't alone.

A woman stood next to him, wearing nothing at all. Nothing but her hair. Long, reddish-blonde hair. It fell down for miles and curled around a very lush pair of breasts. Her waist curved in, her hips curved back out, and Josh got dizzy as his eyes traveled the long road down her legs, and back up—to where a naked pussy was blatantly displayed.

He pulled his chin up off his desk, wiped a spot of drool from the return key and frowned. He knew just about every single model on the market for this particular application. *She* wasn't any of them.

His fingers flew over the keys as he requested information about "Figure 2".

Female. *Duh*. Frickin' computers were so damn logical at times.

Morph imports. Well, well, well. Wasn't that interesting? He typed on. File ID…"AJ".

AJ. Andrea Jane. She'd imported an image of herself.

Holy shit. She looked like *that*?

A man with a mission, Josh shamelessly rifled through the photo files on "AJ"'s hard drive. He was beginning to experience something of a hard drive himself. Ah. *There*. He'd found them. Three photos, full face, side face and full body. The body one was nude.

He swallowed. It looked like she'd taken it herself through her digital camera, since the original was lopsided and she had a remote mouse in her hand. But fuckin' *A*! It was her all right, down to the naked pussy. And she was one gorgeous chunk of pixels.

Josh's mouth began to water again.

The figures in the "Model Man" desktop began to move. First AJ assumed the classic standing pose, one leg slightly bent, knee pointing out. Her arms went up behind her hair. It was wanton, it was sexy, and Josh was getting stiffer by the second.

Then Joshua moved.

He fell to his knees in front of her and with a slight adjustment of his spine, his face disappeared into AJ's pussy.

Holy mother...board.

Josh watched, stunned, at the incredible job he was doing. Well, not *him*, his other him. Fuck. He wished it was him. The *real* him.

To his amazement, AJ's nipples were hardening. Andrea Jane had done an amazing job on this animation. He blinked for a moment and ignored his cock, which was now up to full speed and ready to party. *Down boy.* It's all virtual. *Shit.*

Josh's brain whirred while his cock ached. He double-checked the parameters Andrea Jane had entered for AJ. God-double-damn. She was good. They were as close as could be to the ones VRG had programmed into Joshua.

A very wicked idea crept lightly into Josh's mind and whacked him up beside the cerebral cortex.

So Ms. Andrea Jane liked to play sex games with her images, did she?

He reached for his virtual reality equipment.

Perhaps it was time to level the playing field and let the opposing team into the game.

Chapter 3

Andy squirmed a little on her chair as she manipulated the figures on her screen. She was looking for that one perfect moment, that image that would capture the essence of man giving oral sex to woman.

She'd run through this procedure before, getting aroused by what she was creating, and loving the experience. It was voyeuristic in a way, but she bypassed any guilt, since she knew she was in control.

These weren't *real* people, after all.

But with this new setup, her level of involvement had increased and now there was much less separation between her and the couple on the screen.

AJ's head fell backwards and her hands moved down to Joshua's head. Just as Andy had animated them.

Joshua's head moved rhythmically, in the pattern she'd established with the old Joshua's figure. But this one had muscles across his shoulders that flexed as he moved, and Andy couldn't stop the flood of moisture from soaking her panties as she watched how realistically he was working AJ's pussy.

She shifted position to try and unstick her underwear from various personal places. Her knee caught her can of diet soda, and she quickly struggled to stop it from slopping all over her connections.

Fuck.

A small puddle doused some of the wiring and there was a little fizzle and a pop and a mild tingle ran over her body. She ripped one glove off and mopped up the spill, cursing in an assortment of languages. Some of which she actually understood.

Settling back in her chair again she glanced at the screen. Joshua and AJ were frozen—AJ in a moment of pleasure, and Joshua with his head pulled back a little from AJ's crotch. Goddamn, the pussy lips were *gleaming*. How the hell had the programmers done *that*?

Impressed, Andy slipped back into her glove and tried to move Joshua back to his previous occupation.

He didn't budge an inch.

"Come on, Joshua. You know you like giving her head. C'mon, boy, let's get that tongue going…" Andy muttered quietly to the screen as she tried a few combinations of commands. The monitor flickered, and she held her breath. She exhaled on a deep sigh when it returned to normal.

Moving her fingers she tried to straighten Joshua's head.

She gasped. *AJ had moved.* What the *fuck*?

Christ. She'd switched the links somehow, and now she was moving AJ. Every twitch of her fingers resulted in a twitch from the woman on the screen.

No hours of plotting paths, no fidgeting with musculature, just a smooth glide.

She bit her lip and thought hard. *Hmm. Hoookay. Let's try this.*

Andy let AJ's fingers slide through Joshua's hair as he remained frozen between her thighs.

Holy shit.

The unmistakable sensation of hair transmitted itself through her sensory input devices to the skin of her fingers.

She jumped clean off her chair, un-sticking her underwear quite satisfactorily at the same time.

She was *feeling* what AJ was feeling. This was fucking incredible.

Her mind whirled. Hell, this was almost too good to be true. She could experience the best oral sex of her life. And no one would be any the wiser, since it was all virtual.

She settled into her chair again, and widened AJ's stance, shifting the image a little closer to Joshua.

Fuck.

The asshole didn't move. Like the rest of her dates, Joshua was apparently uninterested in doing anything more. *Crap on a cracker. It figures. I can't even get sucked by a computer program.*

* * * * *

Josh Miles was cursing his hard-on, and struggling into the virtual reality hookups. He probably should have added one for his cock, since it was pulsing inside his jeans and could probably have powered a router, a couple of servers and several ISP addresses from its heat alone.

He'd watched the power spike, the fluctuations and the odd transitions that were happening inside Andrea Jane's computer as he'd made the connections and snapped the links into place.

He knew what had happened.

He didn't know why yet, nor did he care particularly. That was what the techs were for. Let them earn their pay by figuring it out. Josh just wanted to play.

With Andrea Jane.

He bypassed the firewalls, created the connections, and felt a little zing as the final link dropped into place. He was in.

And he was *in* AJ's pussy.

He blinked. He could damn near taste it. Carefully he moved Joshua's head closer and slid the hands up the back of AJ's thighs to her buttocks.

Holy shit.

He could *feel* the smooth curves of her flesh. Since when had his VR system included a touchy-feely mode?

His palms itched for more, and he squeezed his fingers together, absorbing the sensation of firm, warm skin flexing in his grip. AJ's expression changed slightly, the eyes widening and her breasts rising on a breath.

*Christ on a crutch…*this was *amazing*.

The level of interactivity was astounding on a technical level, but Josh wasn't thinking on a technical level. He was thinking on a very fundamental level. He wanted that pussy. *Bad.*

He moved his hands again, letting them slip to the backs of her knees and gently smooth the sensitive skin where the joints flexed.

AJ's eyes closed and her lips parted.

Torn between his two heads, Josh began to lose himself in the action on the screen. His cock was about to explode through his fly like the alien creature through that guy's chest in a Sigourney Weaver film, and his mind tried to get itself around the fact that he was now connected to a woman sitting miles away.

Unable to stand the pain, Josh quickly slipped a hand to his pants and freed his cock.

Sure enough, on the screen Joshua 4.0's hand fell to his crotch, and the virtual image stroked himself. Blinking with relief, Josh noted AJ's downward glance and the tongue that flickered out between her lips.

Goddamn. He should have locked his office door. If anyone came in and saw him like this, they'd figure him for some kind of pervert.

He grinned. Well, if the shoe, or in this case the VR unit, fits...

* * * * *

Andy was panting.

She couldn't stop herself. Her quick glance downwards had translated itself onto the screen, and she just *knew* what her virtual self was seeing. One really fine piece of flesh, lengthening just for her.

She wiggled AJ's hips, just to give Joshua the general idea.

C'mooon, baby, put that mouth of yours on me.

Joshua was running his hands up and down the backs of AJ's thighs. And damn if she couldn't feel the same thing.

Ghostly sensations were tracing fire up and down Andy's own legs, and liquid was seeping from her pussy at the touch. She was getting one major case of the screaming sweats from this program.

God, I'm a pervert.

Her clit was aching now, on fire and throbbing. She spread her legs on her chair to ease the tension, and sure enough AJ also moved, spreading her virtual legs and adding a little thrust of her hips. *Shit, she IS me.* Andy realized she'd just done the exact same thing.

On the verge of disconnecting the whole shebang and diving for her Super Sized pink buddy, Andy licked her lips against the flood of arousal that was driving her slowly insane.

She had no idea why Joshua was moving, or why she was now activating AJ, but she couldn't have cared less. All she was aware of was the burning need between her thighs and the screaming desire to ease her tensions and just *come*, dammit, right there on her ergonomically designed computer chair.

Slowly, the image of Joshua stood up.

Oh noooo.

Andy slumped, shattered by the loss of his touch. Fucking *swell*. Now he'd probably turn, walk off the screen and go nail some virtual bimbo. He'd show up on www.bigcocksrus.com, coming all over the face of some plastic morph who wouldn't appreciate it. With an audio feed too.

But Joshua didn't turn and leave. To Andy's amazement, he closed the gap between the images and pressed himself against AJ's body.

She frowned. Usually the images merged. Now they didn't. They were definitely touching, since AJ's breasts were flattening slightly.

So were her own.

She felt the pressure against her nipples and gasped, pleasure sweeping over her and bringing her arousal up to the red line all over again.

Her eyes were glued to the screen as Joshua's hand lifted to AJ's face.

Andy's cheek throbbed.

Someone...*something*...was touching her. Or at least sending impulses to her brain telling it that something was touching her. Because of course nothing was *actually* touching her. She blinked.

Joshua's hand continued its caresses as his other one slid down over AJ's hip and disappeared between the two bodies.

Oh fuck me. Andy knew precisely where Joshua's hand was. She could *feel* the goddamned thing.

It was cupping her mound.

Andy couldn't help it. She moaned aloud.

Her twin image opened her mouth, mimicking Andy's expression. She probably would have moaned too if she'd been equipped with an audio track.

It felt so frickin' *good*.

It felt even better when a twitch in Joshua's upper arm muscle indicated that he was moving his hand. Covered by their bodies, Andy couldn't see what he was doing. She could only feel it. Feel the slight increase in pressure as the hand thrust against her. Feel a thumb search for the right spot...oh...oh...*there*!

She jerked, and so did AJ.

Ay ay ay...*the thumb was pressing, rotating, sliding over the most intimate of spots, and Andy's body was starting to squirm.*

So was AJ's.

Hell, this had to be some kind of electro-magnetically induced hallucination.

Dragging her mind off her aching clit for a second, she reached down. If *she* was feeling this good, maybe it was time for AJ to see what she could do to Joshua.

Her hands groped the air, and for a split second, she felt nothing. But then...*there* it was.

A very distinct sensation of holding a length in her palms. A throbbing length, smooth and hard, and...and...Andy let her fingers learn its shape...ridges and veins and whole bunches of fun stuff all in the right places.

Now *this* was what Andy would call a very nice cock.

She squeezed.

Chapter 4

Josh let out a strangled squawk as invisible fingers tightened around his cock. Thank God it was getting late and the building was emptying of employees. He couldn't begin to imagine what would happen if anyone peeked in and saw him with his cock out, squirming in the grasp of a bunch of cables and fondling thin air.

They'd have him in a padded room before he could say "download". And he could probably kiss off his 401K plan too.

The virtual sensation on his cock moved and all thoughts of discovery fled. The images on the screen were squirming now, much like Josh was, and he noted AJ's head tipping backwards as he moved his thumb a certain way.

He did it again.

Damn. He was losing his focus as the virtual hands moved slowly up and down his cock, learning its surface and tracing the long vein that ran from his balls to the head. He hadn't been this hard or this excited since…well, since he couldn't remember when.

He flashed back to his last date with difficulty—it had been quite a while ago. Nope. *Nothing* like this.

The figures on the screen moved in a carefully choreographed dance, their bodies hiding their hands. All Josh could see was AJ's expression, and Joshua's spine. But he could feel…ahhh, could he *feel*.

The hands released him, and he almost sobbed as his own movements found no soft folds of pussy.

What was she doing?

He stared as the image of AJ lowered herself to her knees and tugged on the arms of the image in front of her.

Oh baby. What now? What do you want?

Josh slid from his chair onto the floor watching as Joshua followed suit.

The images knelt, face-to-face, breast-to-breast, and AJ's head leaned against Joshua's as she reached between them.

With no real flesh to bar his way, Josh reached down as well. He moved one arm and saw his virtual self clasp AJ's buttock, pulling it close. With the other, he sought heaven.

There was nothing in his arms—it was all in his mind. All in some mysterious secret file that the VR unit had accessed from deep in the most miraculous of super-computers—the human brain.

And his was telling him he was getting the hand-job of his life.

He blew air through his lips as the sensation of fingers pulling on the hot skin of his cock made him crazy.

His hand pushed—*there*, fingers working fast now, seeking, thrusting, finding a place that made the image of AJ open her mouth wide in a silent cry of pleasure.

He noticed her eyes were closed.

Were Andrea Jane's closed too? Was she experiencing this…this *incredible* virtual sex? She had to be. He watched her face as a new rich pink texture overlaid the color of her cheeks, and her throat moved slightly.

His fingers forced themselves upwards against something soft and welcoming, the merest brush of what felt to him like flesh. There was no heat, no moisture, it wasn't like feeling a woman.

It was…it was *different*, but watching his actions cause reactions on the figure of AJ was the biggest erotic turn-on he could ever have imagined. Well, hell. He never *could* have imagined this!

AJ's hands were starting to move faster, much faster than the animation parameters should have allowed, and Josh knew if she kept it up, then both he *and* his image were going to come.

He bit the inside of his cheek, letting the small pain hold his climax back, working his own hand frantically and hanging on to a virtual buttock with the other.

His eyes were glued to the screen, watching as AJ began shuddering in Joshua's virtual arms. Holy hell—she was *coming*.

Josh could swear he felt the twitches of her cunt around his fingers and he pressed even deeper, his fingers bunched now as he forced two of them inside her body. The silence was unnerving—he wanted to hear the scream he knew was erupting from her gut.

The pressure on his cock had almost fallen away as his ghostly partner sought her own orgasm. It didn't matter though. Watching her come like this, even though she was nothing but an assemblage of pixels, was the most erotic thing he could ever remember.

Unreal fingers dug into his shoulders and he gasped as AJ's head fell backwards and her mouth opened on a silent cry of ecstasy. She fell apart on the screen.

Literally.

Pixels exploded everywhere, scattering like dust over the control screen and making every damn light on his units flash like a Christmas tree on crack.

Within microseconds, AJ disintegrated.

Noooo…

* * * * *

Andy disintegrated. She fell, shuddering, onto her insulated mat as her cry of pleasure echoed around her room. This was so much better, so much more incredibly real than the fantasies she'd woven around Joshua's virtual body.

The orgasm racked her from head to toe, rolling her eyes back in her head and sending a flood of moisture into her shorts and over her thighs. Cables crackled, lights flickered, and Andy rode out the earthquake inside her body, wondering if she could ever survive the experience.

It became apparent after a few minutes of gasping on the floor like a hooked fish, that her life was, in fact, destined to continue.

Although given the state of her shorts, it would be an uncomfortable one.

Groaning, she eased up off her knees, peeled her shins off the plastic mat, and winced as the wetness between her thighs met cool air. *Shit*, she was a wreck. But a really happy one. Which was more than could be said for AJ. With horror, Andy surveyed the wreckage on her monitor. AJ was gone. Poofed out into cyber-infinity.

Note to self: orgasms are not good for pixilated images.

But hot damn, they were good for her. She grinned as she unsnapped the VR equipment and took a long deep breath. She hadn't felt this great in years. She wanted a drink, a nap, a shower and a large pizza. Not necessarily in that order.

She glanced at Joshua affectionately.

Oh *hell*.

The *poor* guy! He was frozen in an attitude of extreme arousal. And *extreme* was an understatement. His cock, visible now that AJ had met her cyber-doom, was one long length of flesh, hard as a rock, the head swollen and deep red, and there was even a little drip oozing from the tip.

His eyes were wide, his mouth open, and his expression one of agony.

She tried to hit the "save as" command...this was one hellaciously fine image of a man in the throes of his own orgasm. Or, correct that, *almost*-orgasm. Trembling on the brink of coming, his muscles were knotted and bunched, his lungs obviously heaving, and his arms holding an imaginary woman to his body.

If she zoomed in, there would probably be sweat on his face too. Curious, she reached for her mouse.

Fucking goddamn. "Program Not Responding—End Now?"

Shit, shit and *double shit*. Frantically, Andy clicked around, hit every combination of keys she could think of and waited, hoping against hope that whatever had happened would un-happen, and she could at least save this shot.

Nope. The cyber-demons were against her. Or at least against Joshua 4.0.

Andy had created a man hung like a god.

And he had hung the system.

* * * * *

Josh stared death in the face.

On his knees, wired to a gazillion dollars worth of state-of-the-art technology, and here he was, about to die from a fucking hard-on that wouldn't quit. He spared a sympathetic thought for the janitor who would find his body in the morning.

Did cocks shrink after death? He hoped they did, since his mother would probably have to identify the body, and the sight of him fully clothed with a massive boner sticking out of his pants would probably unnerve her.

Or maybe not. She'd always had the weirdest sense of humor.

Pain swamped his tangled thoughts as the flooding arousal refused to go away. There was no help for it. He grimaced and reached for a box of Kleenex. He was gonna have to do what a man had to do.

Ripping off the sensors, Josh took matters into his own hands.

Closing his eyes, he let the vision of AJ/Andrea Jane fill his thoughts. It was so easy. He could see her still, the cords in her neck taut as he finger-fucked her into her own personal heaven.

God, if she was like that in *real life…*

He needed only one stroke. With a hoarse cry, he came. Flooding the tissues in his hand and spilling out onto the floor, great jets of come spurting from somewhere in the vicinity of his back teeth. He sobbed with joy, rolling through spasms of heat, and shivering violently as his cock finally eased.

His balls ached with the ferocity of it, his heart rate pounded out a rhythm that would have sent a drummer out for Valium, and he struggled for breath as the final throb signaled that he was spent.

Finished. Done. His pop-up thermometer had popped up and exploded.

He sagged weakly against his desk and swallowed roughly.

Dear Jesus God in heaven.

Josh let consciousness seep slowly back into his crumpled brain cells. He had a cramp in his left thigh, his foot had gone to sleep, and he was drooling.

Fucking A, what a mess.

The computer system hummed on, of course, oblivious to the scene of sexual decadence inches in front of its sensors.

Oh God. If anyone came in… Josh pulled himself together. So what if the waste paper bin was overflowing with wadded tissues? And that spot on the carpet would probably dry out overnight and match the rest of the coffee/soda/beer stains that spattered the damn thing.

Awkwardly Josh struggled to his feet and tugged the zip up on his fly. The VR sensors were in disarray and he carefully straightened them out, then glanced over at the monitor.

It was blank.

No Joshua, lying in spent ecstasy. No AJ. Nothing.

Fuck.

Suppressing a snarl, Josh grabbed his chair and resumed his seat, ready to reactivate Unit three and Ms Andrea Jane.

A few clicks brought up the monitoring program. And those few clicks were followed by a knock on the door.

"Josh? Are you in there?"

He closed his eyes and prayed for death. Within moments of the best orgasm he could remember, his worst nightmare was outside his door.

He thanked God for small mercies. Errol "The Squirrel" Prince *could* have knocked five minutes ago.

"Yeah." He kept his voice harsh, not difficult since his throat felt like it had gotten shot out of his cock and sucked back in again.

"Oh good." The door opened and a short man tiptoed in. "I need a few words."

No you don't. You have too many as it is.

"Ah. I see you're running the monitoring software. Not that it will do much good of course, but we must keep our techs happy, mustn't we?"

The Squirrel had earned his nickname. He had tufts of hair that stuck up at odd angles, small beady eyes, and what looked like half a pound of birdseed in each jowl. His voice was high, his brow low, and his sense of self-importance was off the scale. Josh didn't even want to think about his nuts. There'd been enough jokes along those lines already. Not in the Squirrel's presence, of course, since he *was* the CEO.

"What did you want, Sq...Errol?"

Errol Prince puffed out his chest and twitched his nose.

Lemme guess. You buried something someplace and can't find it.

"I really just wanted to stop by and see how the experiment was going, since this is our first night up and running. I probably don't need to tell you that I was not one hundred percent behind this…um…unlikely notion of yours…"

Ha. Try "I sabotaged it every chance I could get." "No, Errol, you don't need to tell me that."

Errol leaned forward over Josh's shoulder. Josh curled his lip. The man smelled like roses. That was wrong. On so many levels.

"Oh, well look at that. You are getting actual feedback readings, aren't you? My, my…"

You have NO idea. Josh swallowed. "Yes we are. Units one and two are functioning perfectly, Unit three is now offline, probably done for the night…" *Damn, if she's feeling what I'm feeling right now, she's waaay overdone.* "And Unit four has just logged in."

Errol shook his head slowly. "Well, I must confess to being slightly surprised. And pleased—of course. But we must give it some more time. No sense in rushing into production until we've had several months of beta results. After all, there's no knowing what might crop up with our users."

Or our staff. Things had 'cropped up' quite nicely, to say the least.

"Have you tried the VR connections yet?" He fingered the cables.

Josh leaned over and firmly removed them from Errol's pudgy little hands. "Not yet." His conscience snorted at him. He paid no attention to the little shit. "I thought it would be best to wait until the initial readings leveled off before attempting the VR interface."

Errol nodded sagely. "Most wise, Josh. Most wise. Of course, I have still to be convinced that this system is workable. In my opinion, the old ways are the best ways. To permit that artistic spirit free rein, you know…let the graphics paint the picture that's in one's mind…"

Errol launched into his spiel and Josh tuned him out. He'd heard it all before. "Creating art with digital brushes…" and "allowing the spirit free rein to invent the vision" yada, yada, yada.

Basically, it translated into "I want *my* name on this graphic arts software, not yours." With an additional helping of, "And some of your stuff might be better than mine, which is a threat to my miniscule rodent dick."

Josh hit a few buttons and reduced the screen to a glow. "Well, Errol, I won't keep you. I'm sure you're busy this evening, I'm pretty much done here for the night…" *and wasn't THAT the truth*, "…So we'll see what the readings look like in the morning."

"Oh…er…" Errol floundered, having been cut-off mid speech. "Yes. Well. All right then. I shall expect a report, let's say about four o'clock tomorrow."

He frowned at the screen again and turned away. "Have a pleasant evening, Josh."

Josh nodded.

Errol turned back, and wrinkled his furry eyebrows. "Um, Josh, I hate to mention this, but your…er…" He waved his hand towards Josh's body. "You really should take more care with your personal appearance, you know. We do have a professional reputation to maintain."

Josh glanced down. A piece of his shirt was caught in his fly, and was waving proudly like a flag in the breeze.

He sighed. When he thought of what else might have been caught in that zipper, a small piece of cotton was the least of his worries.

As the door closed behind the Squirrel, Josh reached for his files. He had plans for this evening. Plans that included a certain woman. One who was now offline, probably still shaking, and maybe staring in awe at Unit three. And *him*. Fuck the ethics of this situation.

It was time for Ms. Andrea Jane Thompson to meet the *real* Joshua 4.0.

Chapter 5

Andy wrapped a towel around her head and slipped on her robe as she left her steamy bathroom. The shower had invigorated her, she was as hungry as a bear, and now would be a damn good time to order that pizza.

The phone rang as she reached for it, making her jump. "Hello?"

"Hi, Ms. Thompson? This is the VRG Concepts' technical office."

Shit. She'd broken something. She just *knew* it. Well, screw 'em. The agreement she'd signed had said absolutely nothing about virtual orgasms. "Yes?"

"We've been monitoring your usage, and noticed a couple of external power spikes in your signal."

No shit. Although she'd describe them as *internal* rather than *external*. "Really?"

The voice on the other end of the line cleared its throat. It was rather a nice voice. "Yes. We were wondering if it would be possible to send over a technician, just to double-check the connections and the wiring? All in the interests of your safety, of course…"

Andy paused, thinking. If she ordered the pizza now, it would be here in ten minutes or so. That gave her time to wolf it down, throw on some jeans, and play Miss Innocent, I-Haven't-A-Clue-What-You're-Talking-About, to whichever dweeb showed up to fix the damn thing.

"Well, I suppose that's okay. Were you planning on having someone come over this evening?"

"Oh yeah," growled the voice.

Andy stared at the phone.

The sound of a cough came through the earpiece. "Sorry...soda went down the wrong way. Um...yes, if it's convenient. Mr. Miles, one of the primary architects, would like to stop by and check you out. Um..." The voice sounded a little strangled.

God save her from geeks.

"Check out your equipment." There was a pause followed by another choked cough.

Andy was starting to get a serious fit of the giggles. She envisioned some poor little hunch-shouldered guy, glasses like soda bottles, fiddling with his pocket protector and blushing bright red as he tangled himself up in his double entendres.

"I mean...er..."

Andy laughed. "No problem. I'm in for the evening. In about half an hour or so, maybe?"

"That would be great, Ms. Thompson. I'll see you then."

The dial tone hummed, and Andy narrowed her eyes. "*I'll* see you then?" Mr. Geek had slipped. He was coming over himself. To check her *equipment* out.

She snickered. *Right.* Like she needed checking out by a Bill-Gates-wannabe. After her experience with the 101X, the only person she needed to be checked out by was her gynecologist to make sure her orgasm hadn't driven her kidneys up into her tonsils.

She hit the speed-dial for her favorite pizza joint, and threw in an order for a couple of bottles of high-caf soda while she was at it. That was what geeks lived on, wasn't it? The least she could do was offer this poor guy a drink. And God forbid it should be alcoholic. Probably muddle his synapses or something.

She toweled off her hair and tugged her robe tight. It was good that she wasn't going anywhere, since the last thing she wanted to do right now was dress. The robe slipped over her skin like a kiss, and she sighed at the sensation.

Yeah, she had really needed that moment of bliss. Come to think of it, she could use a couple more. Perhaps Joshua 4.0 might be in the mood for some action after dinner. And she didn't even have to feed him. More pizza for her.

Another advantage to a virtual man.

The doorbell rang. Aha. Pizza time. Her mouth began to water.

She reached for her purse and moved to the door, taking a quick peek through her spyhole at the large box the man outside was holding. Damn, she could almost smell the pepperoni.

She opened the door with a flourish and a grin.

And froze.

Holding the pizza box and smiling at her was…*Joshua 4.0!*

* * * * *

Hooookay. The deer-in-the-headlights thing was throwing him for a loop. She was staring at him with a really strange expression in her eyes. Her incredible blue

42

eyes. He hadn't realized how lovely her eyes were. He'd been too busy staring at other things...like those breasts whose nipples were pebbling right this second under that wispy piece of silk she almost wore.

Fuck! She was incredible. She had a little beauty mark at the base of her throat. Josh wanted to nibble on it. It moved as she swallowed.

Josh felt his heart lurch into overdrive. She was all he'd seen, all he'd craved, and then some. It was like he'd walked into someone else's dream and found it was his own. And it was real.

"*You* work for Papa Marco's?"

What the fuck was she talking about? His hands burned as he fought the urge to reach out for those breasts and cradle them. Then he realized it wasn't the urges that were burning him—it was the frickin' pizza.

He looked down. "Papa Marco's Primo Pizzeria". *Duh.*

"Um, no. I met the delivery boy on the way in. I'm sorry..." *No I'm not.* "I didn't realize how close you lived to VRG. I'm Josh Miles, by the way. Your technical representative."

He juggled the pizza and held out one hand.

She put twenty dollars into it, never moving her eyes from his.

"Ms Thompson? You *are* Ms. Andrea Jane Thompson?"

"Pepperoni. Yes. Call me Andy."

"Pardon?"

Andrea Jane's throat moved again and she blinked. "Good God. You're *Joshua*. I can't believe it."

Josh was starting to have the same feeling. He was standing in her doorway, doing some serious mental lusting, with a pizza in one hand and a twenty in the other. And she was staring at him like he was a cross between Santa Claus and the Devil himself. So what to do next?

He did the only thing he could. He handed her the pizza and pocketed the twenty.

"*Hey.*"

He snickered to himself. That worked. "May I come in?"

"Of course." She pulled herself together as he watched, and tugged her robe across her body. *Sheeeeit.*

With a smile, he handed her back her money and stepped inside, closing the door behind him. "This pizza sure smells good. Um…were you expecting company? I can leave if…" He let his words taper off, hoping she'd take the hint.

She did. "No…no…just me. And…and the 101X of course." She managed a small laugh, and led him into her small kitchenette. "If you'd care to share? After you've checked me out, of course."

Her words fell into the room like bricks and she blushed bright red. "I mean after you've checked out the *101X* unit, that is."

Josh grinned. "I had that same problem. Tangled tongue."

His cock ached. Damn, he'd like to do some tongue-tangling right about now. With her. She was everything AJ had been and more. Living, breathing, hot, smelling-fresh-and-tasty-more. Or maybe it was the pizza. He couldn't tell.

But he sure would like to find out. "How about we have some pizza, you tell me how you like the unit so far, and then I'll run a few diagnostic tests…" *and get you out of that robe.*

"Oh sure. That'll be fine." She paused and looked around. "Did the delivery boy give you any sodas?"

Josh, who had nearly mugged the kid in his eagerness to play pizza-man, blinked. "I didn't see any." Well, that was the truth.

"Shoot. Stiffed again. Oh well. I don't suppose you drink beer, do you?"

Josh fell in love. For a man who had earned the nickname "Suds" in college, his response, however, was remarkably mild. "I have been known to indulge on occasion. A beer would be great right about now. It's been a long day."

"Oh, yeah, the units and stuff. How's it going?"

* * * * *

Like she cared.

She had to sit and watch him, Josh, *her Joshua*, eat pizza. Watch the little strings of cheese get hung up on his lips and *not* rush over and help him remove them. With her tongue.

He was shorter than she'd expected and his hair wasn't long enough. But the rest of him? *Hooo mama.* He was everything she'd dreamed of, created on her screen—and then some. Right down to those heavenly, to-die-for eyes.

Inside, Andy trembled. This man, or the virtual image of this man, had seen her *naked*. She tried to gauge his mood from his expression. She hoped that it was some kind of sexual heat she noticed now and again behind his gaze, but she was so frickin' rattled by him showing up like this, it was hard to be objective. Just because she was suffering a major case of the *I-gotta-have-you*'s, didn't mean he was, too.

There *was* something there, though. Some sort of…of…*connection* had been established in the second their eyes met over that pizza box. After all, she could have met him while waiting in line, right? They could have shared their food in the busy environment of a pizza restaurant, and one thing would have led to another and…

He was friendly, personable, and his virtual doppelganger had given her the orgasm of a lifetime not long before.

Doo-dee-doo-doo, doo-dee-doo-doo. She was in the Twilight Zone.

Her pussy started to moisten and she amended her previous thought. That would be the cable-TV X-rated version of the Twilight Zone.

He smiled at something she'd said—she had no clue what—and her heart turned over. Along with a sizeable portion of her spleen, her womb and several muscles around her clit. Fuck…she *wanted* him. Now. Right here. Push-the-damn-pizza-on-the-floor-and-get-naked type want.

It was as if they'd skipped all the preliminary stuff that went along with the first date. The "God, is he gonna kiss me?" bits, the "He probably prefers slim blondes" bits and the always-killer "He's not going to respect me if I let him come home with me and jump his bones too soon" bits. She'd bypassed the first weeks of a relationship with this man in one cosmic moment of bliss with his alter ego.

But did he know?

They chatted, laughed, shared a beer, and acted like normal people, when all she wanted to do was remove his clothes with her teeth and lick him from head to foot. Paying special attention to certain bits that were presently concealed by his jeans.

If the rest of him looked as good as the outside…*damn*.

She jerked her thoughts off of his crotch and realized he'd asked her a question. "I'm so sorry, my mind was miles away." *Right beneath your fly, actually.* "What did you say?"

"I asked if I might see your 101X unit?"

Andy sighed. It was too much to hope that he might have said, "I'd like to see your body." Or perhaps, "Strip me naked and fuck the daylights out of me, baby."

Hell. She'd have to settle for long distance lust. "Oh of course. It's through here."

She led Josh to her office-cum-living room, and showed him the clutter of cables, connectors and her desktop. She wondered if the pheromones she was probably shedding right about now were going to drown him.

He dropped to one knee and she admired the tight fit of his jeans around his ass. His really nice, firm, munchable ass. Her fingers twitched and her nipples beaded up. *Shhh, girls.*

"So how do you like it so far?" His voice came from beneath her desk.

"Oh I like it a lot," she growled.

So? It was the truth. She liked the view from her vantage point very much. His muscles moved as he slid back out, and she sighed. Some things should be bottled and sold to single women. The look of his ass in those jeans was one of them. Come to think of it, she knew a few married ones who'd probably grab a bottle or two as well.

"I wonder if I might ask a favor?"

Oooh…sure. Slide over here and unzip those jeans.

"Um, sure. What?"

"Could you slip the virtual system on for a moment so that I can run my checkup software?"

"Okay." So he didn't want *that* sort of favor. God, they'd just met. What was she thinking? That he might be getting a major input of "Lust Uncensored" from some vibes she was probably throwing out? She slapped her inner slut upside the head and sat in her chair, taking the cables and VR sensors from him and fitting them to her hands.

He moved behind her and delicately brushed her hair away from her ears as he slipped the headband into place.

She bit back a moan of pleasure as his hands caressed her cheek.

"How's that?" His voice was low and a little hoarse.

"Gooood." She breathed rapidly, fighting down the urge to tear off the equipment and do a variety of things to him, three of which were probably illegal in some states.

His hands dropped lightly onto her shoulders for a fleeting moment, burning her skin through the thin robe.

"Now call up your program…" His head was next to hers, his breath a whisper against her ear. Who knew ears were such a sexual turn on? Christ, she was getting wet.

She pressed her thighs together and did as she was told without thinking. She gasped when she realized what she'd done.

Before her on the screen, in all his glory, was *Joshua*.

Behind her, in all *his* glory, was *Josh*.

Oh *fuck*.

* * * * *

Josh fought to control his urges, but seeing himself, bald and naked on the screen, tipped him over the edge. He knelt down behind Andy and nuzzled her neck. She shivered.

"You know, I thought it was a joke when the techs used my photo for that model." He kept his voice low and casual, although it damn near gave him a hernia to do it.

"You…you did?"

"Uh huh. But now…now I'm rather glad."

"You are?"

He chuckled silently. *Oh yeah, Andy, your systems are up and running very nicely.* "I am. Do you know why?"

She gulped and shook her head, still staring at the body on the screen.

He leaned even closer. "Because…" He drew a breath as he glanced down. Her robe had loosened and the curves of her breasts were glowing at him, drawing his hands, his tongue and probably his wallet out of his back pocket.

He refocused with an effort. "Because, Andy, *you* get to see me naked."

She jumped a little.

"And you know what else I like about this system?"

"No?" It was a squeak.

He grinned. "It's interactive."

She swallowed. "I know."

"But do you know *how* interactive?" He raised one hand and stroked her softness, finding a spot between her neck and her shoulder that made her shudder.

"No?" The squeak came again.

"Well…" He drawled the word out, dragging his fingers in concert. "It's so interactive that if you were to load another figure, like perhaps one you'd created yourself…let's call it 'AJ'…"

Her gasp thrust her breasts forward, and Josh held his breath.

In one swift move she ripped the sensors off and swiveled her chair around in a sharp twist. She nearly knocked him over, but he regained his balance and found himself where he'd wanted to be since he first set eyes on her image.

Right between her thighs.

"It was *you!*" Her yell was piercing and he winced. "Somehow *you* interconnected with my program. *You* were controlling Joshua. It was *you* who…who…" *made me come like that.*

Her eyes widened and her voice dropped into a whisper. "Oh God. It was *you*…"

He slid his hands onto her thighs and leaned close.

"Yeah. It was me."

And he kissed her.

Chapter 6

The second his lips touched hers, Andy lost control. She forgot where she was, who she was and what she was doing.

All she could focus on was Josh. His mouth. His tongue. His heat as he pulled her from the chair and tumbled them both onto the floor. His hands were everywhere at once and she could think of at least a dozen more places she wanted them.

Without a thought she ripped his shirt open and ran her hands up and down his chest.

"You were on the other end of that…that…whatever it was," she muttered.

Josh tore his mouth away from her breast to answer her. "Damn, Andy, it's never been like that before. I thought I was going to die."

"Me too. I never…it hasn't…oh…yeah…right there…"

Josh's lips were nibbling beneath her nipple and his tongue was doing wild and crazy things to the aching bud. He sucked her deep into his mouth and she groaned.

Josh groaned too. She felt the bulge in his jeans as he pressed into her, and any thought of caution disappeared. She wanted that wonderful Louisville slugger up at bat. Right this minute.

She reached for his jeans and unsnapped them with unerring dexterity. Maybe years of video game playing were finally going to pay dividends. She slid the zipper down carefully, gasping a little as he fell free into her hands. Good God, no briefs.

"I...I don't wear..." His voice was hoarse as Andy caressed him. Warm skin slid over hard muscle, rippled and ridged and tipped with a head that she couldn't have improved on if she'd used every single morph available on the 'net.

"Yeah. That's good. I like this..."

She grasped his jeans and pulled them down as he toed off his shoes. They fought with their clothes, ripping fabric from flesh until they were both naked. And touching.

"Oh man..." Josh rubbed his body over hers.

"Yeah," she sighed. "So much better. Sooooo much better."

Their lips met, clashing, tongues looping and tangling within each other's mouths. Hungry for him, Andy's hands groped and clutched him, running from hip to shoulder and back down again with extreme pleasure.

He groaned as she dug her fingers into his buttocks, and he rolled them over, setting her astride him. "I need to be inside you."

She watched through a fog of heat as he scrabbled with protection and sheathed himself.

"I need you too." She placed her hands on his chest, over his nipples and moved her palms, feeling the small buds harden beneath her touch. She raised her eyes and stared into his.

Heat stared back at her. Heat, and desire, and something else. A sensual need was glowing from the teal blue depths, and a warmth spread through her that had nothing to do with the sex.

She wanted him inside her, but it wasn't just her cunt that needed his cock. It was her heart that needed his touch. He was her Josh, her *Joshua* come to life. The man she'd created fantasies around, dreamed of during her solo sessions with her vibrator, and fallen asleep thinking about.

She eased herself up and found his cock, positioning it within the swollen folds that were now slick with her own juices. Slowly, oh so slowly, she sank down.

And found heaven.

Josh was already there. His angel image was real. Hot, wet, and slipping down over his cock like they'd been designed from the same specifications. They *fit*. No squirming, no effort to find the right position, just a slide of pleasure that damn near blew his ears off.

Her eyes closed as she began to move on him. He watched, spellbound, as her breasts rose and fell and her lips parted. She tossed her head back in that little move he'd seen the image of AJ make on the "Model Man" control panel, and it drove him crazy.

His hips thrust up, deeper into her, all the way to her heart. He wanted her with every single fiber in him, and then some. He wanted her to come, he wanted to come with her and he wanted to do it again. And again. And never stop.

Ms. Andrea Jane Thompson was his perfect woman. There wasn't a teeny doubt in his mind. She was smart, attractive, sexy as all hell, and everything he'd ever wanted in a woman. In that moment, Josh admitted the truth to himself. In a matter of microseconds, he'd gone and lost his heart to an image on his monitor, and the reality was even better. This, in his mother's words, was the *one*. His match—his mate. The one who could stop his heart, rev up the speed of his microprocessor into the red zone, and overload his hard drive.

And she was coming on top of him. Little whimpers escaped from her lips and her muscles were tightening around him. He slid one hand to her belly and traced a line with his fingers down to her pussy. He spread the lips apart and searched for that spot...she cried out...yeah, *that* spot. *Hot damn.*

He pressed gently, and in spite of his delicate touch, Andy's response was explosive.

She came. In waves of spasms around his cock, shuddering wildly and screaming out his name.

"Josh..."

He gave her a few moments then rolled them once more, still deep inside her and still feeling the tremors of her orgasm around his cock. He moved back, pulling away and then letting her body draw him back into her fire.

"More," she moaned. "More, Josh...come with me."

He was only too ready to do just that. His hips hammered her thighs, his balls slapped her body, and sweat dripped off his nose. He'd never taken a woman with such eagerness, or such a longing to watch her as he came inside her.

He got his wish.

Josh's spine electrified and his buttocks clenched. "Andy...Andy..." His voice was hoarse as his balls tightened into knots and pulsed with the need to blast into her.

"Josh...*now!*"

Her scream tipped him over the edge and he exploded into the orgasm to end all orgasms. Long aching pulses swept over him and he could feel his cock spurting violently into Andy. Her body met his with more spasms of her own, and she came again, milking him dry with her cunt.

Their cries echoed together, and they grabbed each other tight, looking for something…*anything*…to hold on to as they traveled the incredible journey into their release.

Sighing, Josh unlocked his elbows and watched Andy, as she lay panting beneath him.

She gasped for air. "*Holy fucking shit.*"

A tired grin crossed his face. He *really* loved this woman. Not only was she his perfect match in all things, but she could swear worse than him. What more could a man ask for?

* * * * *

Josh and Andy snuggled together in Andy's office chair. Andy was sprawled comfortably in Josh's lap as he ran a finger lovingly over her damp skin. "Damn, woman, do you have any idea what you do to me?"

She grinned. "Pretty much what you do to me, I'd guess."

"Mmm." He was too contented to breathe. His muscles were limp from their loving, and his body was humming something soft and jazzy.

"I have to tell you something, though…" She leaned over and nibbled his earlobe.

"What, honey?"

"It's better in *real* reality."

Josh's lips curved into a grin. "It sure is." He glanced over at the screen and something caught his eye. "What the…"

Andy turned her head and looked too. "That's odd."

Josh clenched his teeth. "That little fucker."

"Who?"

"The Squirrel."

"Huh?"

Josh slid the chair closer to the monitor, holding Andy tight. He wasn't about to let her away from him under any circumstances, but he needed a good look at what that little shit was up to.

He filled Andy in on his boss. "So he's done everything but take a hammer to this project since the get-go. I'll bet you anything he's in my office right now, strapping on that virtual reality gear, and planning on fucking it all up."

Andy was silent for a moment, and then her eyes turned naughty. "Josh…" She moved her hand to her mouse. "I have an idea."

Josh paused. There was something in her expression that told him he was going to like whatever it was.

"Look." She opened a new graphic.

Josh goggled. A huge blue alien had appeared on the screen. It had to translate to something in the range of seven feet tall, and had a cock the size of an elephant. An aroused elephant. It also had breasts.

The Joshua 4.0 image was stumbling, turning one knee inside out, and generally contorting itself into a variety of uncomfortable positions. *Frickin' Squirrel.* As inept with the VR unit as he was with everything else.

"Um, Andy? What the hell is that thing?"

She giggled. "It's Ro'ath'Min Kaln. A sci-fi erotica group I do some graphics for wanted it. It's from a hermaphrodite species in a galaxy…"

"Let me guess…*far, far away*, right?"

"I sure hope so." She clicked again. "But the thing is, these aliens? They're only happy if they're having sex up the ass. With other aliens."

On the screen, poor Joshua 4.0 stumbled once again and landed on forearms and knees, buttocks in the air, nose down. He stared intently at the floor.

Christ above, Squirrel was useless.

Andy slipped the VR sensors onto Josh's hands and placed the headband around his ears. "Now, I'm thinking that perhaps your rodent-person might like to make a new friend."

Josh could feel his face crease into a huge smile. Damn, he loved this woman. "I love you, Andrea Jane Thompson."

"I know." She smirked. "I love you too, Josh Miles."

"Smile at me like that again and I'll have to show you how much."

"Ooooh…really?" She slid her legs around and straddled Josh, heedless of the cables coming from his hands. His cock, which was now signaling that it had recovered nicely from its rest, thank you, and would like some more, please, was very happy indeed.

Neither noticed the image of Ro'ath'Min Kaln moving around on the screen, taking up a position behind the recumbent figure of Joshua.

With gentle eagerness, Josh cupped Andy's buttocks and eased them apart, opening her for his cock. Her cunt was still wet and hot, and she sighed as he lowered her down, filling her with all that he had.

As Josh moved, so did the alien on the monitor. Ro'ath'Min Kaln's hands cupped Joshua's buttocks.

Josh felt Andy's body welcome his. *Oh sweet fucking Jesus*. He could do this for the rest of his days and die a happy man.

He thrust up with his hips, sinking deep into his woman, losing his mind and finding his soul. It was bliss. It was heaven. It was *virtually* priceless.

Josh smiled.

And on a flickering monitor in a quiet corner office of a corporate building a couple of miles away, the image of Ro'ath'Min Kaln mimicked the actions of his controller as he leaned in to the image of Joshua 4.0 and thrust with *his* hips.

The Squirrel's howling scream echoed through the silent and darkened hallways.

Ro'ath'Min Kaln was a happy alien.

And, as all happy aliens do, he smiled.

About the author:

Sahara Kelly was transplanted from old England to New England where she now lives with her husband and teenage son. Making the transition from her historical regency novels to Romantica™ has been surprisingly easy, and now Sahara can't imagine writing anything else. She is dedicated to the premise that everybody should have fantasies.

Sahara welcomes mail from readers. You can write to her c/o Ellora's Cave Publishing at P.O. Box 787, Hudson, Ohio 44236-0787.

Also by Sahara Kelly:

A Kink In Her Tails

The Glass Stripper

Guardian's Of Time 1: Alana's Magic Lamp

Guardians of Time 2: Finding The Zero-G Spot

Hansell and Gretty

The Knights Elemental

Madam Charlie

Magnus Ravynne and Mistress Swann

Mesmerized

Mystic Visions

Partners In Passion 1: Justin and Eleanor

Persephone's Wings

Peta And The Wolfe

Sizzle

The Sun God's Woman

Tales Of The Beau Monde 1: Lying With Louisa

Tales Of Beau Monde 2: Miss Beatrice's Bottom

Tales Of Beau Monde 3: Lying With Louisa

Tales Of Beau Monde 4: Pleasuring Miss Poppy

BARBARIAN

Kate Douglas

Chapter 1

"You gave drugs to young women, some of them barely out of childhood. Drugs that brought them to a sexual peak and left them there...screaming, begging for release. Then you sold those poor girls, profited off their innocence and pain. How does it feel, Barbarian? How does it feel to hang there, your body screaming? Do you enjoy the *ultimate* pleasure? Does this please *you*?"

He groaned, fighting the drug that had kept him hard for more hours than he could remember. Drugs alone that would have been bad enough, but she'd touched him, stroked his hard shaft, wrapped her small hands gently around his balls in a parody of lovemaking. Brought him to the edge of orgasm over and over again—to the edge but not beyond.

His balls had quit aching hours ago. Now completely numb, they merely pressed against his body in a futile attempt to escape the pain and pleasure of her touch. Goddess...he'd hated her just hours ago. Now he craved her. Craved her touch, her voice. Why?

Barbarian? She called him Barbarian. His name? An epithet? It didn't matter any more. All that mattered was release, the end of this sensual, tactile torture.

Release only she could give.

He opened his eyes, blinded by the light focused narrowly on his immobile body. His hair hung wet and matted against his shoulders and he could smell the stink of pain and fear on his own carcass. His arms ached, tied over his head with soft leather straps anchored to an iron ring in the ceiling. The bindings cut into his wrists, though he held tightly with both fists to relieve some of the pressure. His ankles burned from the shackles holding his feet apart.

His cock…hell, his cock had become his entire being. All sensation focused on that damned organ, swollen now well beyond a normal erection. Hard as stone, hot as a furnace, throbbing with each gentle caress his jailer bestowed.

He couldn't really see her, not the way she remained in the shadows, but he'd learned to beg for her touch, learned to thrust his hips forward each time she stroked him. Her lips had caressed him, once only and for much too brief a time, but the feel of that soft mouth encircling the tip of his cock had been fire added to an already burning pyre. If only she would give him release!

She stroked his hips, his belly, touching him gently as a lover might. His cock responded, damned traitor that it was. Suddenly she ran her fingers around his ass and penetrated him quickly, roughly. He jerked, clamping his lips together, fighting the need to beg. He would not beg. Never.

"My sister was a sex slave. Was she one of yours?" Something else entered his ass, something big and hard and cold. "She didn't survive. She died under the *gentle* tutelage of her first patron."

She thrust savagely but he welcomed the exquisite combination of pleasure and pain, his mind wrapping itself around her words. *Sex slave*. He knew about sex slaves. He let his mind go blank, unable to think beyond the rhythmic thrusts to his ass, the throbbing erection that had become an integral part of his existence.

"She was only eighteen."

Eighteen. So young. So many young women. He opened his eyes, squinting against the glaring light. "Sorry," he mumbled, wondering what part, if any, he had played in a young girl's death. He barely recognized his own voice. "So sorry."

Whatever his captor thrust inside him was suddenly withdrawn. She moved into his field of vision, stepped within the circle of light, and stared at him.

She was a tiny thing, barely over five feet tall, her hair a mass of honey brown curls spilling over her shoulders, her eyes wide and green as the sea. Her mouth was wide, her lips compressed in anger. Breasts small and round and so perfect. So very, very perfect.

She clasped a wooden baton in her hand, the same one she'd violated him with only moments ago. "Sorry won't cut it, you bastard! Not until you suffer like she did. Not until you pay."

She stepped closer, tossing the baton aside and grabbing his cock. He groaned as she stroked him, her fingers gentle now in a parody of lovemaking, teasing him closer and closer to climax. He moaned and thrust his hips forward, praying for the long awaited release, the release he knew she would deny him once again.

A door slammed. Her fingers tightened, squeezing down on the base of his cock, then turned him loose. He sagged against his restraints.

"Captain! What the hell are you doing?"

"Teaching this bastard a lesson." Her voice was ragged, harsh with unshed tears.

"Do you know who he is?"

"Yes, dammit! He's the Barbarian. The most notorious sex slaver in this quadrant. I've been after him for almost two years. I've got him now and he's mine."

"No, Captain. He's ours. He's one of our operatives. Good Goddess, woman. You've captured one of the World Federation's top agents. If you've harmed him, if you've blown his cover...shit. I can't believe this. Turn him loose. Now."

* * * * *

"And that's how I lost my commission. Not only did I blow the cover of our top field operative, I kept him shackled for over 15 hours while in a state of arousal."

"Good Goddess, Bry. The same man I told you about? He was one of ours?"

"You got it. I did everything right, just the way we planned." Bry stared at the ring of condensation spreading out around the bottom of her glass, ran her fingers through the moisture. What she'd done with those hands, the harm she'd caused...she blinked her eyes quickly then raised her head and looked directly at her friend. "Yep. Drugged his drink at a bar and hired a couple of thugs to carry him to my ship. Marty, looking back, I can't believe I did what I did. It was one thing to plan his capture over a couple of drinks in a bar, but I used drugs on him, I restrained him against his will, I touched him inappropriately..."

"Like there's an *appropriate* way to sexually torture a prisoner?" Marty shook her short cap of dark hair, rolled her eyes and snorted. "C'mon, Bry. You didn't know who he was."

"I should have, dammit. We both should have. You, at least, had the sense not to participate in my stupid scheme."

Bry McKenzie clutched her drink in both hands, unwilling to look at her companion. Taller, stronger, her self-assurance and sloe-eyed, dark-haired looks a polar opposite to Bry's, Marty had been the one to point the Barbarian out to her. They'd both believed him to be exactly what they thought—the leader of a sex slave cartel.

"It's illegal to treat a prisoner the way I treated this man…do you have any idea what the penalty is when you do it to your own field operative?"

"I heard you lost your commission—the Nautilus?"

"Yeah. Actually, I resigned. I didn't want to give them the chance to can me. Goddess, how I loved that ship, but I was lucky. I could have spent thirty years in the brig…" She bowed her head. "That's the worst of it. He refused to press charges. Said he understood."

"I heard about that." Marty spun her glass between her fingers, then glanced sideways at Bry. "Do you know why?"

"No. I have no idea." She hung her head, still sickened by the sense of shame she carried with her. "I can't get him out of my mind. His face haunts me. As much as I hated him, something happened between us while I held him captive. He was absolutely beautiful…dark hair, dark eyes. His body was gorgeous. Marty, I looked at this man and *wanted* him!"

Bry glanced at her hands, realized they were shaking and clasped them tightly together. "It's sick. I believed him to be evil incarnate, a man who sold young women from all over the galaxy as sexual slaves, the most depraved soul on the face of the earth, yet while I was hurting him I was aware of some dark sexual satisfaction of my own."

She wrapped her arms around her middle, felt the hard ridges of her ribs, realized her entire body trembled. She'd sweated clear through her skinsuit so that the fabric clung even tighter, and she shook all over like she had some sort of palsy. *Damn.* The memories still ruled her life, destroyed her dreams.

Aroused her.

She clenched the muscles between her legs, unable to ignore the lush sense of need. Her body shamed her, responding to images of torture and degradation. Grew wet and ready when she remembered. Bry forced herself to relax, placed her hands, palm down, on the table and willed them to be still. She took a deep breath, let it out.

"At one point, I actually forgot what I was doing. Marty, I went *down* on him! The minute I tasted his cock, a little bit of sanity returned, but I wanted him as much as I hated him. I kept thinking of the Barbarian as a fallen angel, that it was my duty to punish him. The more I hurt him, the more I wanted him...and the angrier I got at myself." She shook her head. It still seemed unreal. "I took it out on him...my own depravity. Goddess, Marty...he had to be lowered to the ground. His legs wouldn't support him. His cock was swollen and his balls were hard as rocks. When they tried to lay him on the stretcher, he screamed."

Marty nodded as if she understood and briefly covered Bry's hands with one of hers. "You've never struck me as a cruel person, Bry. Do you have any idea why you went to such extremes?"

Bry rested her head in the palms of her hand. "I must have snapped! When Janie died, I saw the coroner's report. I knew what they did to her. The Barbarian's cover was so good, so thorough, I thought he was part of the cartel that kidnapped my sister. I had no idea he was working against them. I blew his cover and put a good man through torture." She shook her head, the tears falling faster than she could wipe them away. "I'm sorry to dump on you like this, but I had to tell someone. I can't forgive myself. I tried to find him to apologize, but he'd disappeared again. They wouldn't give me his real name. I needed to tell him I was sorry, that I would do anything to make it up to him. Now I can't."

Bry choked back a sob. "I don't think I can get through this."

Marty put a comforting arm around her shoulders and squeezed. "You're tough. You're a survivor. You'll be okay."

"Not without his forgiveness." She turned to stare at her friend through tear-filled eyes. "I left my humanity behind when I did those things to him. I gave away a part of what makes me who I am. I want *me* back, Marty. He is the only one who can give me back that part of myself. That part I lost over two years ago."

"Then find him."

"It's too late. He's dead." She stared at the stains on the barroom table. "I blew his cover and they killed him."

Chapter 2

One week later...

Jacob Hart kept to the shadows, nursing his third brandy of the night. He watched the young woman with the mass of tawny curls, just as he'd watched her every night over the past week.

She was drunk—again. Sloppy drunk and a danger to herself, should she leave the bar alone. He could only protect her just so much without blowing his cover. Tonight would be tough. Two star cruisers had docked and the bar was filled with predators. Men too long alone with one another, searching for an easy piece of feminine ass.

Maybe, though, it was time. He'd waited now for two years. Two very long years. Marty'd said Captain McKenzie was in bad shape. Jake wondered if the captain knew her best friend not only worked for internal affairs, but that Marty was also assigned to her case? He hoped not. Bry's self-esteem was already shot.

She stood up, swayed a moment, then caught her balance. *Damn.* Frowning, Jake tossed his brandy down his throat, threw some credits on the table and followed her to the door.

Three other men appeared to have the same idea.

He gauged their size against his own, decided surprise and his skill would have to make up for the difference in weight, and quietly fell into step behind them.

The woman walked slowly, head down, feet stumbling. Jake drew his eyebrows together, watching her. She'd lost even more weight. She looked almost childlike, a skinny little wraith moving slowly away from the bar. The pattern of her footsteps altered and she cursed. The atmosphere on this mining outpost was thin but breathable, and sound carried oddly, magnified by the iron-rich ore that made up the bulk of the planet.

Jake paused, slipping into the shadows, keeping the figures ahead of him in sight. The three men waited until the woman was far enough from the bar that no one would hear anything, then grabbed her and dragged her behind an old shack.

She didn't scream. As far as Jake could tell, she didn't even try to fight them. He stepped around the corner, whipped out his high intensity light and flashed them. He knew they'd be momentarily blinded, surprised by his quiet approach.

She was already naked from the waist down, the top half of her filthy skinsuit ripped away exposing her thin body, her breasts marked with red welts from grasping fingers. There was no fear on her face. Merely a look of resignation, of despair.

It was the despair that tipped Jake over the edge. He kicked out with his left foot, catching one of her captors between the legs. The bastard went down, clutching his balls and screaming. The other two cursed, shoved the woman roughly to the ground, and charged. Jake grabbed one man by the throat and stopped him in his tracks. At the same time, he threw a punch with his right fist, catching the other assailant in the nose. That one dropped like a rock, without a sound.

Jake tightened the fingers of his left hand around the last man's throat and slowly forced him, gasping unsuccessfully for air, to his knees. He held on just a bit longer than necessary, then released his hold. The man fell to the hard-packed ground, gurgling and retching.

The one he'd kicked in the balls lay curled up in the fetal position, moaning and hugging his crotch. A dark stain spread along his inner thighs.

Shrugging off the adrenaline, Jake turned and grabbed Bry out of the dirt and threw her over his shoulder. He planted his hand firmly against her ass to hold her steady, sliding his palm over the slim-fitting skinsuit and slipping his fingers into the warm crease between her legs. He told himself he was merely trying to get a solid hold on her, but *damn,* she felt good.

He tightened his grasp, imagining her wet and needy, then bit back a growl. Like he didn't know needy? *Shit.* Gritting his teeth against the sudden ache in his balls, Jake took off at a slow trot for the docks, jamming his fingers tightly against her crotch as he headed back to his ship. She didn't react when he groped her, merely hung limply along his back, arms bouncing off his buttocks and her hair swinging behind him as he carried her back to his ship.

He knew there was nothing waiting for her at her room. Nothing but memories and hopelessness. He had his own memories to heal. Memories of her soft hands on his cock, her fingers teasing him, violating him, leaving him unsatisfied and unfulfilled.

He took a deep breath and readjusted her small weight on his shoulder. Marty said the captain wanted his forgiveness. Well, he wanted something from her, as well. The orgasm she'd denied him when she'd held him prisoner over two years ago. Two Goddess-be-damned years.

He hadn't been able to come in all that time.

Chapter 3

Bry awakened slowly, squinting against the morning light. Her mouth was dry, but the foul taste she usually associated with a hangover was missing. Her hair felt damp, as if she'd actually remembered to shower last night...

Last night? Men...three men, grabbing her, squeezing her breasts, their boozy breath in her face, one fumbling with his pants to...

Heart racing, adrenaline surging, she jerked herself fully awake. Entirely aware that...

...Someone had bathed her, washed her hair, brushed her teeth...and tied her naked body very securely to a bunk. Not her own bed. No. *What the hell...?* She jerked her head from side to side, arms and legs flailing against the restraints, panic rising like bile in her throat. Air whistled through her flared nostrils.

Gasping, fighting panic, Bry drew on her training, forced herself to observe, banked her spiraling hysteria to a manageable level. She swallowed, then swallowed again and took a deep breath.

*Okay. You can do this. Breathe in, breathe out, in...*blinking, willing a calm she didn't feel, she looked around her, shocked when she realized the familiar lines and angles of the room meant she was on a small space ship, a Class Three Falcon, similar to her own beloved Nautilus.

Her ears popped with a slight pressure change and she swallowed back a new level of fear. Whoever had imprisoned her must have just left the meager atmosphere of Argon 9. A klaxon sounded, the ship shuddered and steadied, and Bry's body tingled with the passage into hyperspace. The captain of the ship would most likely go to autopilot any minute. She stared at the closed door, eyes wide, blood pounding in her ears, waiting.

After what seemed like forever, footsteps sounded just outside the cabin, paused, and the door slowly opened. Air rushed into her lungs, her heart seemed to stop in mid-beat. Lips parted on a gasp, vision narrowed to a single shaft of impossible light, she stared into the eyes of a dead man.

The Barbarian...her fallen angel, alive.

She closed her mouth, opened it again, and tried unsuccessfully to swallow. *It can't be!*

She narrowed her eyes and willed her body to find its center, praying her heart would beat, her lungs continue to function, that he not discover what was in her mind...or her heart. She studied him, calming herself as she searched out the subtle differences from the memories she carried. He was still darkly beautiful, but there was no anger in him, no outrage. Instead, she sensed about him a deep and unrequited sadness, like a ghost trapped on the wrong astral plane.

"You're dead." Her heart skipped, then settled. Tugging lightly at her restraints, projecting a calm she didn't feel, Bry licked dry lips and frowned. "They told me you were dead."

He shook his head. When she'd seen him last, lying on the stretcher in agony after they'd cut him down, his hair had been black and matted, stringy with sweat, his face darkly shadowed with a day's growth of beard. Now his face was closely shaved and his hair hung smooth and shining to his shoulders, a deep chestnut brown that matched his dark eyes.

He took a step closer. She searched for the anger she fully expected. There was none. His expression was bland, almost disinterested. "I only wanted to die. You did that to me."

The room was small. His massive body made it even smaller. Bry felt vulnerable, but, for some reason, no longer afraid. The calm she'd searched for descended on her like a protective blanket.

"You owe me," he said. Again, there was no expression, no sense of what he felt. What he thought. His voice was deep, rumbling up out of his chest without threat. He merely stated a fact. "I've decided it's time to collect."

Bryony sighed, accepting the truth. He was right. She did owe him. Maybe, once her debt was paid, she could get her life back. She licked her lips and nodded. "I know. I was wrong. What I did was cruel and unforgivable." She swallowed again, forcing the memories away. "Why did they tell me you died?"

He seemed to relax with her question. "It was part of my cover. It allowed the Barbarian to return, to finish what he'd started. The slave cartel no longer exists. We rescued what girls we could. It was too late for many of them, but your capturing and torturing the Barbarian actually aided my cover."

She thought about that a moment. It explained even more why the WF hadn't put her in the brig for the rest of her life. She'd actually done them a favor. No matter. It didn't change the terrible things she'd put this man through.

She studied him, recalling his pride and arrogance. He'd been unbelievably handsome then. He was even better looking now. His face reminded her of pictures she'd seen of Native Americans from Earth — high brow, wide cheekbones, a strong, slightly hooked nose. A fairly new scar creased his chin, slashed across his jaw.

Desire for him coiled, hot and needy, deep inside her. *Not now. Dear Goddess, not now!* She squeezed her thighs, unable to press them as close as she wanted because of the restraints, well aware of the thick fluid warming her pussy, dampening the coverlet beneath her.

No. She didn't want this, couldn't want…this. Her question sounded breathy, hopeful even to her own ears when she asked him, "What are you going to do to me?"

She wouldn't fight him. She owed him compliance. She…

Oh, hell and Goddess be damned! You want him. Admit it. You've wanted him for the past two years.

"You'll find out when it happens." His voice, though deep and gravelly, remained soft and even, the words spoken with very little inflection. A slight tick in his left eye was the only sign of any emotion, any sense of feeling. "I've had over two years to think about revenge. Two years of remembering."

Remembering. Were they both so warped by their memories? Bry composed herself, meeting his eyes without expression. They might have been carrying on a conversation over tea. "I had two years, as well. Janie died two years before I captured you." Bry looked away. She kept seeing him, tied against the bulkhead, his huge cock outthrust, his face twisted in agony. Her composure crumbled. "I'm sorry. I had no idea you…"

"It doesn't matter. Not anymore. What matters is that I take back what is mine. What you stole from me."

Once more she noticed the tic in his eye. Nerves? Why would he be nervous? It didn't make sense. What he said didn't make sense. "I stole nothing. I didn't take anything of yours."

He knelt down next to the bunk, mere inches from her face and placed his hands on her, one at her shoulder, the other resting on her thigh so that his fingers barely touched the tawny curls on her mons. His dark eyes flashed and his strong jaw clenched tightly. She felt his breath lift the scattered tendrils of the hair at her nape and sensed the raw emotion he'd been hiding so well. His deep voice rasped in a very personal, harsh whisper, the words meant for Bry and no other.

"Oh yes you did, my dear Captain McKenzie. You stole something very important. You have taken my manhood, and I want it back."

Chapter 4

Stolen his manhood?

Bry fought her first reaction, to stare at his crotch and see if he meant what she thought he meant. Instead, she concentrated on his touch. As if of their own volition, his long fingers lightly moved over her sensitive flesh. Gentle strokes across her shoulder, the occasional foray to her inner thigh. He wasn't looking at her, though. He was staring off into the distance with a thoughtful gleam in his eye, as if he recalled the hours of torture she'd put him through.

"Do you have any idea what it is like for a man to remain aroused for hours on end?" He looked at her then, his coffee colored eyes narrowed with intensity, his harsh whisper tickling her senses. The tic in his left lid quickened. His fingers never slowed their rhythmic caress of her skin. She felt tiny prickles of pleasure following each stroke.

Pleasure heightened by a frisson of fear.

"Imagine, if you will, silently begging for the release that never comes? It starts as a pain in the groin, an ache in the testicles that increases with each moment. Your cock is hard, harder than it's ever been and you want to thrust it deep into a hot, wet welcoming place. You want to keep thrusting and screwing until you come, until that pain and ache and pressure explode in the most exquisite pain of all, a pleasure that encompasses all of you, your body. Your mind. Your soul."

Tears prickled behind her eyelids at the gentleness of his touch, the painful reality of his words. "Will you ever forgive me?" The harsh sound of his voice, the knowledge of what she had done, burned deeper with each lazy sweep of his fingers. Without conscious thought, she arched into his caress.

He pulled his hand away. Folded his fingers tightly into his palm and pressed it against his thigh. He stared at her, his eyes dark as obsidian.

"At some point during the fifteen hours you held me, I lost touch with myself. Where I should have hated you, I somehow bonded to you. The anger I felt was turned inward. I found myself questioning my own sanity, questioning my assignment. Had I hurt those young women or had I actually helped them? It was all wrapped up in you, in your touch that brought me so close, promising but never allowing completion."

He glanced at the silver watch on his left wrist. "I began timing when you regained consciousness exactly twenty-three minutes ago. You are mine, to do with as I please, for the next fourteen hours and thirty-seven minutes. I will not kill you. I will not do anything that will cause you injury, nor will I use drugs to enhance your sensations."

He looked at her, his dark eyes like empty pools beneath his thick lashes. "I will, however, use implements. Tools to heighten your experience, to magnify both your pleasure and your pain. To remind you of the fifteen hours I spent in your care."

He paused, then stood beside the bed, looming over her. "The one area where our experiences will differ is that, at some point during this time, I will find release within your body."

He turned away, but Bry was almost sure of his soft whisper, not meant for her ears.

"Maybe then, I'll find myself."

She watched, aware of a sense of almost total detachment, as he opened a closet and removed a soft leather bag. There were items inside, some things she recognized, others unfamiliar. He held a pair of clamps up in front of her. They were metallic, attached to each other by a light electrical wire and what appeared to be a battery pack.

Suddenly, unexpectedly, he leaned over and suckled her left nipple into his mouth, biting gently with sharp teeth against the turgid flesh until it rose into a taut peak. She arched her back and moaned, shocked by her body's immediate response to his touch. He carefully placed one of the clamps on her nipple. She felt a sharp pain that eased into a dull ache.

He repeated the process on her other nipple, clamping it firmly, checking the wires, then slowly turning a small dial. Bry gasped as a sharp jolt of electricity burned through her nipple and left it tingling. It was followed by a continuous series of shocks, alternating one breast, then the other. Her nipples tightened beneath the clamps. She felt the shocks all the way to her pussy. The man studied a monitor on the battery pack and adjusted the current lower.

She was still concentrating on the sensation, trying to decide if it actually hurt or merely stimulated, when she felt him touch between her legs.

She was already slick and wet. His fingers opened her, slipping in and out for a few exquisite strokes before inserting something large, cold and smooth inside her. She was still adjusting to the size when she felt another sharp jolt. She choked back a cry. Her hips arched off the bed. Without a word, he once again adjusted the current.

The shocks no longer hurt. They were so mild she barely felt them, but she narrowed her eyes and concentrated on the sensation. What in the name of the Goddess was he going to do next?

His fingers moved over her body. More wires, more current, the electrical shocks all occurring in a linear fashion, one after the other. Left breast, right breast, pussy. He fashioned the next clamp directly to her clitoris, and that bit of flesh joined the others, all connected by the cycle of tiny sparks of current.

His large fingers probed her ass, and she clenched her jaw, remembering the baton she'd raped him with. There was no other way to describe what she'd done. The shame she felt overwhelmed any fear she might have of him, of what he intended.

She deserved this. Deserved whatever he might do to her. Relaxing the muscles around her anus, she concentrated on the sense of fullness as something cold and smooth slipped inside her.

Another link joined the cycle of electrical shocks. She closed her eyes, concentrating on the sensation. Her body tingled, each nerve and fiber sensitized by the mild current.

He no longer touched her. Bry sensed that he had moved. She opened her eyes just in time to see him with his hand on the door. "I hope you enjoy your evening." He glanced to his right, at something mounted on the ceiling. It looked like a camera of some sort. "That's so I don't miss anything," he said. "I'll be back later."

He stared at her a moment, his brows knit in a thoughtful frown, then walked back across the room. He picked up a black silk scarf that was lying over a chair and quickly blindfolded Bry, locking her away from the light. She felt his lips on her, felt his tongue testing the seam she quickly parted for him. Hot and sleek, he plundered her mouth, tangled his tongue with hers, stroked the sensitive flesh at the roof of her mouth. He drew her tongue between his lips, suckling her hard and fast, filling her mind with his scent, his taste, his heat.

Then he was gone. Lips still parted, Bry felt suddenly, unexplainably bereft at the sound of the door closing, the sense of his absence. It felt as if he'd taken the very substance of the air with him, leaving Bry alone with her body, this body that felt so detached and foreign to her.

The current continued, unchanging, a steady rhythm of shocks coursing lightly along its chosen path. Her nipples remained taut and pointed, her vaginal muscles tightly clamped around the cylinder inside her as if they anticipated each tiny shock. She was just as aware of the fullness in her ass reminding her of the object inside. Her clitoris reacted with each tiny charge, barely responding to the current.

If this is torture…?

Her nose itched. She wanted to scratch it, but of course her hands were still bound. Unchanging, the current continued its rhythmic course. Time passed. Her skin began to tingle, the sensation subtle at first, but growing as the minutes slowly crawled by.

The tingling, crawling sensations grew stronger, the subtle tremors over her body more intense. Her womb contracted with each pulse of current, her breasts felt swollen, the warm gush of liquid from between her legs soaking the bed covering beneath her.

She tried to hold her body still, tried to ignore the rhythm of the current, but soon her hips writhed with each passing jolt, lifting in anticipation of the orgasm that hovered just beyond.

She tried not to think of the sensations coursing through her body, thought instead of the camera just over the bed and wondered if he watched her. She tried to picture him, sitting in his captain's chair on the bridge, staring at a small monitor, probably beating off as her naked body twisted and shuddered in his bed.

The image should have disgusted her. Instead, she imagined his big fist encircling his swollen cock, the long fingers wrapped tightly along its length, stroking slowly from base to plum-colored head as his passion built.

It was so wrong! Her fingers should be on him, her hands stroking his thick length, slipping over the satiny tip, bringing the first drops of fluid to her lips. She groaned, awash in his taste, his scent, his touch. The tiny shocks practically buzzed through her body and she arched her hips in a desperate plea for release. Goddess, but she needed him. Needed that cock buried deep inside, needed to feel him stretching her, filling her until she couldn't take anymore. She was ready, so damned ready for him.

Her pussy clenched tightly, almost frantically around the metal cylinder. Her nerves stretched taut as piano wire—the pressure of orgasm denied was a scream without sound, trapped in a body no longer her own.

He hadn't been kidding when he said he'd make her pay.

Practically sobbing in frustration, Bry pictured him as he'd been two years ago, then replaced that image with the beautiful man who held her now. Who was he? She'd known him as the Barbarian, a man who never existed. Still, he'd been part of her thoughts, her fantasies, her nightmares and daydreams for the past two years.

She moaned, forcing her thoughts into other patterns, trying to ignore the increasingly sexual sensations, the need for a climax that hovered beyond her reach. Moaning again, she twisted her hips, fully aware of the futility of begging, of pleading with him.

She had done this and more to the Barbarian. He had a score to settle, one she couldn't, in good faith, deny him. Did he want her to plead? Was he hoping she would beg?

He hadn't begged. He'd only said he was sorry. Sorry for what? For Janie? For those other girls? How long had he searched for her? Bry hadn't told him who she was, but still he'd found her.

Of course. Legal would have told him. They would have offered him the chance to press charges, let him know who the idiot was who had captured and tortured him.

Bry'd been out of the service now for almost two years. She wondered how he'd tracked her down to Argon 9. It was such a miserable little outpost, but it had been the perfect place to spend her time in Purgatory following her resignation from Fleet. She deserved nothing better than this Goddess forsaken planet.

Nothing more or less than whatever he planned for her.

Chapter 5

Jake watched his captive on the small monitor near his chair on the bridge, feeling each writhing twist and turn of her body, experiencing the same sexual need that must now be burning in her gut. It killed him to hurt her, but he knew, deep within his own tortured soul, she'd never be free without suffering for her mistake.

When had his need for revenge become a desire to heal, both Bryony and himself? He'd followed her for the past two years, sometimes literally following her in the shadows, more often relying on Marty's reports, as they both watched Bry's slow descent into hopelessness. Thank goodness for Marty's last, in-depth visit. It hadn't been purely an accident that his sister had been assigned to ex-captain Bryony McKenzie's case.

When Marty'd contacted him last week, though, he realized immediately he had to act on the fantasy that had sustained him for the past two years. He had no idea his captor had been snared by the same desire as he had, no idea her life had been destroyed every bit as much as his own by her torture of an innocent man.

What goes around, comes around.

He had suffered and paid. So had she, but neither of them had been able to fulfill the secret desires created on that lonely outpost two years ago. He must make her suffer again, this time with the knowledge she was paying her debt to him, personally, finding forgiveness for the unforgivable acts she'd committed against him.

Absentmindedly, Jake stroked his erect cock through the light fabric of his skinsuit. The bastard was hard more often than not, a fact not lost on the women he'd slept with shortly after his torture. It had taken a very talented whore to convince him what he'd already feared — he could get an erection and sustain it until exhaustion forced him to sleep or he wore his partner out, but he couldn't come. The beautiful young captain's torture had stolen his humanity and forever denied him the ultimate pleasure of climax.

The next few hours would prove whether or not his theory was correct. Bry McKenzie held the key. If he couldn't find release within her body, he would be forced to accept that nothing more could help him.

* * * * *

Lost in her darkness, consumed by a desperately overwhelming, seemingly endless need for sexual release, Bry knew the moment he entered the room. She'd given up hours ago. Her mind had become a dark world of fearful imaginings — she knew he would leave her here, let her writhe and twist in carnal agony well beyond the time he claimed she owed him. Could she expect sympathy? Should she? Over-sensitized, over-stimulated, her body reacted to his presence with a tangible shudder that rippled across her flesh.

He touched her breast with his fingers. She bit back a scream and arched her back. "Your fifteen hours are over." His deep voice washed over her. Suddenly, the tantalizing current stopped and she collapsed back on the mattress, gasping for each breath. She felt him removing the clamps and probes, leaving her body a throbbing, humming mass of sensation.

He untied her blindfold, then, surprisingly, the restraints holding her hands and feet. She hadn't expected him to release her, had in fact expected some even more devious torture. She lay there a moment, whimpering softly, caught in the final tremors and shuddering spasms that had wracked her body. Finally, still trembling and weak, she sat up and rubbed her ankles.

"You may use the facilities. I'll know if you touch yourself, if you try to find your own relief. Leave the door open."

Bry suddenly realized just how much she had to pee. Her full bladder protested every movement, overwhelmed even the powerful, all-consuming need for sexual release. The open door to the head couldn't stop her. She finished her business, washed her hands in the small lavatory, then walked cautiously back into the room.

His skinsuit was open to the waist. His boots sat beside the bed. He nodded at her, jerking his head in the direction of the bed. She sat on the edge, her skin almost rippling with the lasting sensations from the current passing through her body. She watched him as he slowly undressed.

His body was beautiful. Powerful and strong, the dark hair on his chest following a narrow pattern over taut abs to spread out at his groin. His cock was as erect and hard as it had been when she held him captive. She practically salivated, imagining that hard flesh in her mouth, following the length of him, drawing his balls between her lips and suckling each egg shaped organ into her mouth.

Licking her lips, she forced her gaze away from his cock and tilted her head to look into his dark eyes. "You said I'd stolen your manhood. If that's all that's left…" She bit back the nervous laughter that almost choked her.

He grasped her chin between his thumb and forefinger. "Oh, you've taken something very important from me. Something I fully intend to get back. Right now, though, I want you to suck it. I want you to take it in your mouth and make me come."

If this be torture...

Her thighs slick with fluid, pussy clenching in frustration, Bry went to her knees in front of him and slowly, carefully, pressed her lips around the huge, plum-colored tip. His size stretched her mouth wide. She slid her lips along his huge penis, taking as much of him as she could inside her mouth.

Swallowing all of his cock was impossible.

She sighed and lay her cheek against his hair-roughened thigh. Goddess, but she could almost come just from the taste of him!

She suckled for a moment, then nibbled the length of him, drawing first one, then the other testicle into her mouth. He spread his legs wider, allowing her more access, but it was awkward, kneeling here, wanting so much more.

Clasping her hand around his cock, she guided him to follow her as she lay back on the bunk. He crawled over her body and raised up on his hands and knees, his huge cock pressed against her cheek. Her pussy throbbed at the close proximity of his mouth, but he lay his head on her thigh and avoided touching her between the legs.

A soft sigh escaped her lips. She concentrated on his pleasure, suckling his cock, licking the hot length of him, nipping at his balls and drawing them completely into her mouth, one side at a time. All the while, her hips swayed, back and forth, silently pleading with him to touch her, to use his mouth, his hands, anything on her.

Anything to give her the release her body craved.

His cock grew harder still, but he seemed to have no problem at all controlling himself. Bry licked and suckled, finding his persistence more of a challenge than she'd expected. Her own frustration grew, knowing his mouth was right there, that his tongue was so close, his big hands grasping her thighs, his long fingers mere inches from her weeping pussy.

Suddenly she felt him, the lightest flick of his tongue against her clit. Arching her hips, she almost bit down on his cock, so intense was the sense of pleasure from that mere whisper of touch.

Silently begging for more, she increased the suction on his cock, kneading the taut muscles on his butt with both hands as she held him against her mouth.

His tongue flicked over her clit once more and she bucked her hips. Her low moan vibrated against the head of his cock. Frantic now, dying for his touch, she found the tight little puckered ring of his anus. She worked her fingertip back and forth, until she finally found entrance. The muscled ring clenched against her finger and he thrust his hips forward, almost gagging her with his cock.

She pushed her finger deeper. His hips jerked. She wrapped her fingers around his cock and tugged lightly at his balls with her lips. He had to be close to coming.

Bry knew she was ready to scream, her orgasm just out of reach, her pussy clenching and pulsing with frustration and need, her senses all twisted up in his taste and musky scent. She moved her finger, probing further in his tight passage, finding exactly the right spot to apply pressure.

He didn't come, not yet but...*dear Goddess*, he found her pussy with his mouth! Bry's world narrowed to two diverse points in her own, personal universe—the space where the Barbarian's lips now covered her clit and the huge cock filling her mouth.

So close! Her climax hovered just at the edge of darkness. His cock strained against her lips, his hips bucked against her intrusive finger but still he didn't come.

And somehow, somewhere deep inside, Bry knew she couldn't either. Not until she'd given her captor his release.

Sighing, silently admitting defeat—for now—Bry pressed a kiss against the crease where his thigh met his groin and moved his hips aside. He rolled over to his back, one arm flung over his eyes, his cock erect, glistening wet and slick from her mouth.

"This is what you meant...what I did to you. Right?" She crawled up to lay beside him on the narrow bunk. "When was the last time you climaxed?"

"The night before you captured me." Once more his voice was flat, without inflection or emotion of any kind. He turned and stared at her, his dark eyes shadowed, the scar across his chin and jaw more pronounced. "Since that time, I've been unable to find release with any woman...hell, even with my own hand." He laughed, a short, angry bark that cut through Bry like shards of glass.

"That's what you did to me. What you took from me."

"I know you hate me, and you've got every right, but I promise I'll do whatever I can to..."

His sad smile almost broke her heart. "I don't hate you. What you did was wrong, but...I lost a sister in the trades, too. She was about the same age as yours, disappeared a few years before Janie. Her body turned up right before I took the assignment. I do understand your anger, comprehend why you believed you were doing the right thing. Understanding, however, and getting my life back don't necessarily go hand in hand."

Chapter 6

Bry showered first, then the Barbarian took his turn. Dressed in light robes, they ate a small meal together, his revenge apparently forgotten. Her captor had grown more silent. His erection had finally subsided, but there'd been no release for either of them. For Bry, the residual effect of the electrical stimulation and the man's touch left her squirming in her chair. It was only her personal code of honor that kept her from touching herself between the loose folds of her robe and taking her own pleasure.

She didn't think the Barbarian cared enough to stop her. Bry realized she cared enough for both of them. She'd heard of it happening, of course. Heard of victims falling in love with their kidnappers, developing a strong emotional attachment to the one who intended them harm. She looked at this man and knew she felt love for him, or at least some deep emotion masquerading as love.

Did he somehow feel the same for her? Was that convoluted tangle of emotions holding him back?

"What's your name?" She held her fork in mid air and wondered if he'd answer.

He stared at her for a long moment without blinking. Then he sighed and lowered his own fork. "Jacob...my name is Jacob Hart. I'm 34 years old and a commander in the World Federation Special Ops division. Or I was. I'm not sure if I'll re-enlist or not."

He was beautiful, masculine and strong, and totally messed up. Bry sighed and set her fork down next to her plate. "Jacob, if you'll trust me, I think I can help."

He looked up from his plate and stared at her. "How?"

"We recreate what caused the problem. Let me restrain you, only this time, I'll make you come. It might be against your will, but it will happen. I promise you." She pushed her chair back and stood up. "One more thing. You'll have a safe word. Merely tell me to stop. I give you my word that I will."

* * * * *

Jake almost laughed aloud at the surrealistic sensation of finding himself tied flat on his back to his own bunk on his own ship. This certainly wasn't the scene he'd imagined when he finally decided to kidnap Bry.

He'd thought her beautiful the first time she caught him. Right now, knowing her intent was to help him, not hurt him, made her even lovelier in his eyes.

She shoved a pillow under his hips, giving her better access to him. He wondered if she'd play with his butt again. Hell, the feel of her finger up his ass had been unreal. He still couldn't believe he hadn't exploded in her mouth, but it hadn't happened.

Maybe it couldn't happen. Therapy certainly hadn't helped, and he'd been to some of the best shrinks the WF had to offer. They'd tried everything. They'd...

Her soft hands forcing his knees apart, then her fingers massaging his butt drew him back to his immediate world. He raised his head to watch her when he felt her fingers slipping up the crease in his ass, rimming the tight little ring of muscle. Hell, he'd never realized just how sensitive that spot could be.

She tilted her head and looked at him from between his raised knees. Her finger pressed his ass once more, stroking sensitive muscle, and he clenched his butt tightly against her hand. He expected her to put on some of the lubricant out of the tube she'd been using, but instead she raised up on her knees and swept her finger between her own legs, catching some of her juices and spreading the liquid around his ass.

His cock twitched. He groaned and pressed his head down into the pillow. The visual alone should have made him come. He'd fantasized about her since she'd captured him, stayed hard thinking of her slight frame, the tangle of golden hair flowing across her shoulders, the matching tuft between her legs. She was thinner now, almost gaunt, but no less perfect in his eyes.

He expected her to touch him with her fingers, but she grabbed the probe he'd used on her, slipped it in and out between her own legs like a big dildo until it was slick with her juices, then rubbed it along the crease in his ass. It was still warm, either from the hot water she'd washed it in or its brief visit inside her pussy. The friction against his backside heated it even more.

Suddenly she twisted it enough to slip easily into his ass. There was no pain, merely the sensation of fullness. She pushed the smooth probe in and out of him a couple times, stroking his cock in the same, slow rhythm.

Shit. He'd never felt anything like this. He spread his legs as wide as the restraints would allow and lifted his hips, silently asking for more. Bry complied, fucking him in the ass with the smooth metal probe, sliding her fist up and down his cock.

So close…she almost had him there. She kept if up for a few more strokes, smiling at him as if she knew exactly how it felt, then she leaned over and nipped at his chest, licking first his left nipple, then the right into tight beads.

"I want you inside me, you know." She crawled up over his thighs, straddled his abdomen and kissed him. Her fingers teased his left nipple. Her right hand still worked the probe, slowly in and out of him.

"I want you inside me, fucking me with that huge cock of yours." Her whisper tickled his chin. She leaned over and licked the spot, dragging her tongue across his rough day-old beard. He felt her pussy, hot and wet, against his belly. His cock was trapped in the crease of her ass. Her mouth tasted lush and warm, her tongue dancing with his and he was more than aware of her gently fucking his ass.

No electrical current. She said she wanted to make him come on his own, naturally, so that he'd be able to do it again. Right now she was all warm and willing woman, the same woman who had filled his nights with frustrating, fruitless hours of fantasy. Her lips were soft and sweet, and already he felt it, felt the coil of heat building in his gut, the tight clenching of his balls, the pure incandescent pleasure of climax building.

"So, you think this will help?" He had to talk, had to say something, anything, to diffuse the slow rise of pleasure, the unfamiliar sensations coursing through his body.

Bry didn't answer. Instead, she slowly removed the probe at the same time she raised up over him, so that the sensations seemed to melt, one into the other. His cock pressed against her soft nether lips, and slowly, so slowly, she eased him into her tight passage.

Hot and wet, her muscles clenching at him, rippling over his hard cock, every bit as perfect, as lush and sensual as he'd imagined. She arched her back, driving him even deeper inside, until he felt the hard knot of her cervix, the mouth of her womb up against the head of his cock.

"More," he whispered, begging her. "I need more."

Whimpering, shivering, she began to move, sliding slowly up and down his erection, her muscles fluttering and rippling over him, her thick fluids easing the way. She was beautiful, her mouth twisted in what might have been agony, but was most certainly pleasure. Her lips were parted, eyes closed, the soft pants of breath and the sucking wet sounds as she rode him a primitive music to his ears.

Her fingers dug into his pectoral muscles, her thighs gripped his sides and he knew she held her own orgasm at bay, sensed the control she exerted over her own fevered body. Suddenly she reached behind her, stretching her fingers down between his legs to grasp his balls firmly in her hand.

Oh Goddess…

Suddenly, all sensation, doubled, tripled, expanded beyond comprehension. He ripped at the shackles holding him to the bed, but the bindings held secure. He jerked his body, fighting Bry, fighting the restraints, fighting himself. "More!" he shouted, the words tearing his throat. "Harder, dammit. If you're gonna do me, fuck me harder!"

He growled his frustration—he had to touch her, anywhere, needed to hold her, to grasp her perfect breasts between his fingers, to stroke the soft cleft between her legs. Frantic, completely restrained, he snarled like a trapped beast, arched his hips, forcing her closer, filling her deeper.

She rode his twisting, writhing hips, her mouth contorted in a painful grimace, her breathless whimpers touching his soul. Gently, a surreal counterpoint to their frenzied coupling, her fingers massaged his balls, probing and stroking, rubbing all the right places, compressing and rolling them and it was too much. *Too much.* "Oh Goddess, oh…shit, oh shit…oh fuck."

"Come for me, dammit. Fuck me! Now!" Her sobbing demand lifted him up to the edge, held him there, balanced between pain and pleasure. Eyes closed, he let go, gave himself over to Bry—to her sweet feathered touch between his legs, the hot wet muscles rippling around his cock, the conflicting emotions of need and desire, anger and fear. Passion consumed him, the emotion, the frustration, all coalescing into that coiling fire, the almost forgotten sensation of pleasure, pain and expectation.

"I said now!"

Ripping at the restraints, he arched his hips, driving into her just as she penetrated his ass with her finger, spearing him deep and hard. He shouted, an unintelligible cry jerked from somewhere deep in his gut. Then suddenly…*coming.* Good Goddess, he was coming he was…*Fuck. Oh fuck…oh…fuck.*

He bucked his hips, caught solidly in the almost forgotten sensation of orgasm. His cock jerked deep within her as she slammed down against him, riding him hard and fierce, her cry a high, keening wail, an incoherent litany of sound and soul-deep emotion.

"Damn you. Damn you. Damn…" Trembling, cursing, crying, she collapsed against his chest. He pulsed hard and strong, his cock trapped in the tight, rhythmic contractions of her climax. His chest heaved with each strangled gasp as he struggled to draw enough air into his starved lungs.

Still trembling, each breath caught on a throaty cry, Bry reached over his head and undid the shackles, then, still impaled on his cock, turned and released the restraints on his ankles. Before she had time to turn back, he grabbed her and shoved her roughly to her knees.

His cock slipped free, still hard. He wrapped an arm around her waist and slammed back into her hot pussy. She arched her back and cried out, a shout of triumph, not fear. "Yes!"

He plucked at her nipples, pinching them hard between his huge fingers as he drove into her. She put her head down on the bed and raised her hips higher, giving him better access. His balls slapped against her crotch.

"Harder," she cried. "More!"

She was sobbing now, crying so hard her breath exploded in sharp gasps. There was anger here, anger and pain and years of desperation. His. Hers. It didn't matter. He twisted her nipples harder, ramming into her without any pretense of gentleness, but she welcomed him, begged him with every sob, every moan, every thrust of her hips to ease his way.

She twisted her neck to look back over her shoulder, saw once again her fallen angel, his dark hair hanging in sweaty tangles around his face, his dark eyes beneath darker lashes wild and angry, his lips slightly parted.

"Fuck you, Captain," he shouted. "Fuck you." He climaxed again, hard and fast, filling her pussy with hot seed, wringing yet another fierce orgasm out of her, out of himself. Weeping, shoulders shaking, Bry lowered her head and collapsed beneath his weight.

Slowly, he eased himself down on her, then rolled to one side, taking her with him. She wept, huge sobs tearing from her throat, shuddering with the final vestiges of her orgasm, her sweat-covered body curled tightly against his.

His own body trembled just as hard. Jake tucked her head under his chin, slowly stroking her back, easing her cries, kissing the tangled mass of curls. He held her until her shuddering eased, the tremors left her body and she fell into a deep, motionless sleep.

Sleep was the last thing on his mind. His shivering reaction eased, but his body still throbbed with the power of his release. His cock was blissfully flaccid—he felt replete for the first time in over two years. This was not the gentle lovemaking he had often dreamed of. No, this was possession and exorcism, pure and simple. Why, then, did his heart feel so full, his arms so right where they held her?

What next? Sighing, he kissed the tousled curls once more, felt his body relax, his muscles lose their tone. He held her close, kissed her again, then drifted into oblivion.

Chapter 7

The bed was empty when Bry awoke. She sensed a change in pressure, knew the ship had once again entered normal space, and figured Jacob must be at the helm.

Jacob. He'd been the Barbarian for so long in her mind, it was hard to think of him with an average name. *Jake. Jacob.* She rolled the two around on her tongue, finding each as pleasurable as the other.

She stretched, well aware of every kink and cramp, each small bruise where he'd clasped her a bit too tightly, held her a little too long. The small pains made her smile. He'd done his best to exorcise her ghosts. Had she managed the same for him?

The sticky wetness between her legs was proof she'd been successful. He'd found his release with her. That was obvious. Were his demons gone forever?

What about her own?

Rolling to one side, Bry slid off the bunk and headed for the small shower. She grabbed a skinsuit out of the overhead storage and found her boots tucked neatly beside the door. In a matter of minutes she managed to bathe and prepare herself to meet the day.

To meet Jacob? Sighing, she stared at herself in the small mirror. What a convoluted relationship! When she thought of him, she was immediately aroused. Her addiction had begun the night she captured him, had only increased over the ensuing years.

Now that they'd finally come together, she felt more confused than ever.

* * * * *

She found the bridge easily. After all, this ship was identical to the one she'd given up. Jacob leaned over the control panel, his hands flying across the screen as he brought the ship into orbit around a large space station.

A narrow band circled his head, holding the thick waves of chestnut hair out of his eyes. His muscles rippled and bunched beneath the shiny gray fabric of his uniform and he leaned over the control panel as if he was preparing to leap into space himself. Energy practically radiated off him, the air on the bridge crackled with an unseen power.

Bry slipped into the co-pilot's chair and fastened the harness. She glanced at Jake, but his attention was focused completely on the job at hand.

Much as he had previously focused on her.

She watched while his fingers flew over the controls, adjusting speed, angle, approach. He was an essential element—one with his ship.

As it should be.

Finally, he flipped a final switch and sat back in his chair. Bry studied his lean profile, the hawk-like nose, the full lips that had so recently tasted her in such an intimate manner. He watched their approach to the station, their tiny ship dwarfed by the huge wheel of metal floating in space.

"What now?" she asked. That wasn't what she'd meant to say at all. The words slipped past the knot in her throat, made themselves heard on their own.

He turned and stared at her, his eyes glinting with the multi-colored lights from the control panel. He looked like a stranger, a man who might have bumped into her on a street corner, apologized and moved on.

"How did you find me? How did you know who the Barbarian was?"

The question was so unexpected, Bry shook her head. "Everyone had heard of the Barbarian. His name was legend."

He swept a hand through his hair in a dismissive action. "No, that's not true. Someone convinced you of this, told you about the Barbarian."

Bry tried to remember the early days of her search. She'd been so lost after Janie's death. Angry, confused and filled with an overwhelming need for vengeance. She and Marty had met one night in a bar, running into each other accidentally after a long separation. They'd both lost sisters to the sex trades. Bry recalled the anger in Marty's voice, how they'd fantasized what they would do should they ever capture the leader of…

"It was Marty. My friend Martine Hartsdotter. She's a lieutenant with Fleet. Internal Affairs, I think. She told me about the Barbarian. As I recall, she'd accidentally seen a classified report. There was enough information in it to tell her he was the one responsible for Janie's death. She knew where I could find him, even helped me get the drugs I slipped into his drink." She dipped her head, ashamed. "Your drink."

Jake sighed. "That's what I was afraid of. We were set up. You as well as me." His jaw clenched. Bry noticed the small tic had reappeared in his eyelid. "I had three sisters. Glynna, Danae…and Martine. Glynna's a flight surgeon aboard the StarCruiser, Gull. Danae was a victim of the sex slavers...and Martine wanted vengeance. She felt my investigation was moving too slowly, my character—the Barbarian—not authentic enough in the eyes of the cartel."

"Marty? My friend Marty is your sister?" Blinking slowly, Bry tried to bring her world back into focus. *Marty?* Jake was still talking. She shook her head in denial. *No, not...*

"She's also an IA operative. How do you think I found you?"

Marty? A spy?

Bry suddenly recalled all the intimate conversations she'd had with her friend, the way Marty had drawn her out, finally gotten her to reveal the full scope of her torture of the Barbarian...of Jacob. She shuddered, her violation complete. "But why? You're her brother...she knew what I planned for you."

"Your torture of me authenticated the Barbarian. Once word got out that he had been held and brutalized by a rogue captain from the WF, no one questioned his authenticity. Before that, I was having trouble getting inside, but the cartel welcomed me once I *escaped* from you. I thought at first your treatment of me had been under orders of Fleet—maybe it was, through Marty, but I realize now it was totally without your knowledge. Until now, I couldn't make the link between you and his...my, capture."

A voice crackled over the intercom unit. Jake turned his attention back to his ship and the myriad details of docking.

Stunned, Bry turned the events of the past two years over in her mind. *Marty.* Her confidant, her best friend, her betrayer? Jake's betrayer? Thoughts spinning, Bry watched as he skillfully brought the ship into the docking bay.

She hadn't even asked him where they were.

As if he understood her unspoken question, Jake glanced in her direction. "We're at Fleet headquarters. I intend to get your commission back. You never should have resigned. I don't know if Marty acted alone or under orders from her commander, but you are a victim of this every bit as much as I was."

Bry clenched her jaw, fighting back tears. "I could have killed you. How could your own sister…?"

Jake covered her hand with his. "I imagine Martine underestimated your passion, your anger. She has a lot of explaining to do." He unbuckled the lap and shoulder harness and stood up. "You asked me, *what now*?" He held his hand out to her. "I don't know what will happen next, but I don't want to lose what I have so recently found."

She couldn't help flashing him a cheeky grin. "What? That missing manhood of yours?"

"No," he said, cupping her jaw in his big hand. "You."

Chapter 8

"Good Goddess. That has got to be the longest day I've ever spent in my life. I am so glad to be away from headquarters." Bry unfastened her harness, stood up and stretched as the ship steadied into hyperspace under control of the autopilot. "I can't believe Marty would do such a terrible thing, even if she was acting under orders. I thought she was my friend."

"She was. She is. You'll see the truth in that some day." Jacob stood as well and hauled Bry into his arms. "I can't believe you turned down your commission *and* a promotion."

"It would have meant leaving you." She snuggled against his broad chest, feeling the beat of his heart against her cheek. His fingers made lazy journeys up and down her spine.

"The whole thing was so convoluted and cruel. Marty's behavior is unforgivable."

Bry still felt violated by her friend's betrayal. Jacob, however, gave the entire episode a different slant.

"It worked. The end does not always justify the means, but in this case, it might have saved my life. We know it saved the lives of a lot of young women. If I'd continued with my original plan, the members of the cartel would have discovered I was with Fleet operations. As it turned out, they accepted me as one of their own. I have to forgive her. Marty's my sister and she was doing what she thought best, as well as following orders. You can't escape blood."

He nipped at Bry's lower lip, then soothed her with the very tip of his tongue. She parted her lips and took him on a sigh, suckling his tongue deep into her mouth. She felt his body harden, knew his arousal was every bit as strong as her own, but he ended the kiss with a tiny little bite at her full bottom lip, finishing it just as it had begun.

Resting his forehead against hers, he whispered, "You, though…you, Bryony, are my love."

Love? She'd not heard that word before from Jake. She looked up, gazing deeply into those dark, fathomless eyes of his. The tic was gone, replaced by long unused laugh lines at the corners of his eyes.

"Love? Are you sure?"

He surged against her, hard and ready, and grinned. "Or as close a facsimile as I can imagine."

"It's been a rather unusual courtship." She'd never seen him laugh. They'd never really made love. They'd only exorcised one another's demons.

He brushed the side of her face with the back of his hand. "A courtship that's beginning today. What happened between us before is over. You are not the same woman. I'm not the same man. The meetings we had today with Fleet command have vindicated both of us. I'm not going to lose you, Bry. I love you." He paused and lifted her chin with his finger. "At least I think I love you. I certainly would like to take the time and explore the concept." He laughed, a deep, sexy chuckle that tickled her senses.

She decided she really liked the sound.

As he spoke, he slowly stripped her out of her flight suit, slipping the sleeves over her shoulders, exposing her rounded breasts, her flat belly, the patch of honey colored curls between her legs.

His predatory gaze devoured her. The passion in his eyes brought a rush of moisture to her pussy, raised her nipples into tight peaks, sent a frisson of sensual awareness tingling across her flesh.

Jacob's desire enveloped Bry in a tangible surge of lust. He slipped her boots off her feet, helped her step out of her clothing, then stood back and blatantly admired her naked body.

She knew her breasts were too small, her hips too narrow, her hair a frazzled cascade of tangles and curls, but she felt beautiful, sensual—lush and truly sexual—under Jacob's gaze.

He rubbed his hand over his crotch, an absentminded touch that told her just how lost he was in thoughts of their lovemaking. Taking the first bold step, she crossed the short distance between them and slowly unfastened his flight suit.

He trembled beneath her fingers. His jaw was tightly clenched and his nostrils flared with each breath he took, but he let her undress him, allowed her to touch his chest, his lean hip, to trail her fingers along his groin as she slipped the stretchy fabric over his powerful body.

His cock surged forward when she tugged his suit down his legs. He lifted each foot in turn, balancing with one huge hand planted on her shoulder, so she could remove his deck boots and pull off his pants.

Naked, they stood and faced one another. Bry had never felt this deep awareness, this blatant self-knowledge, in her entire life. Her body tingled with a snapping, splintering charge of power, power she took directly from Jake. He touched her breast and she moaned, catching the back of a chair for balance.

His fingers traced circles around the areola, teasing her nipple to a taut, almost painful point, then he leaned over and drew the flesh into his mouth, nipping her gently with his teeth. She groaned and collapsed against him, but he caught her up in his arms and carried her to the navigation table. Shoving maps and readers aside, he laid her down on the table, her legs hanging loosely over the edge.

Kneeling before her, Jake buried his face between her legs. The musky scent of aroused woman filled his senses. He nipped the tender flesh of her inner thigh, then spread her legs wider with both hands. He cupped her bottom, lifted her up to his mouth and feasted on her, laving her streaming pussy with his tongue, lapping up the flow of moisture, then finding the hard bead of her clitoris and suckling it with his lips.

She bucked against him, but he held her firmly, his fingers grasping her full cheeks, kneading, massaging her closer to his mouth. He found her anus and slowly breached the opening with one blunt finger, sliding in and out in perfect sync with his tongue in her pussy.

She came hard and fast, arching her back with a long, keening cry. He nipped and licked her through her climax, then soothed her swollen tissues with long, slow strokes of his tongue. When her trembling had eased, he stood over her a moment, looking at the woman who had broken him, then made him whole.

Her eyes were closed, her lips parted in a satisfied smile. She whispered, very softly, "I think I'm going to like this, exploring the concept of love. I certainly think I love you, Jacob Hart." Her eyes opened and she giggled. "Make love to me. Fill me. Don't ever leave."

He growled, leaned closer and nuzzled against her ear. "I'll never leave you. You're mine." His voice dropped even lower. "Now. Forever." He slipped his rigid cock easily between her waiting folds, moving slowly to give her body time to adjust to his size. She raised her legs and wrapped them around his waist, her heels pressing firmly against the small of his back.

Jake found his rhythm, sliding his cock inside her, deep and hard, withdrawing at glacial speed, then filling her once again. The tight clasp of her hands about his neck, the even tighter clasp of her soft folds around his cock, her whispered sighs of pleasure, the tiny catch in her throat as she neared her climax—all of it. He wanted, needed, all of this.

Jake closed his eyes beneath the overwhelming sense of peace he felt, holding Bryony in his arms.

She pressed her lips against his throat, against the spot where his pulse beat strong and steady. He sighed as he loved her, his eyes half closed in pleasure, his soul, finally, complete within their love. He caught her lips with his, whispered against her mouth. "I do believe I love you. I know I will always need you. You complete me."

She answered him with her kiss, with tears streaming down her cheeks, with her bright, shivering cry as she came apart in his arms.

Holding her close, Jake finally gave up control. Thrusting deep within her rippling, clenching pussy, he filled her with his seed, crying out with the rightness of this joining. Body shuddering, gasping and dragging in great gulps of air, he rested his forehead against hers, marveling at such a twist of fate that had brought him this woman. In all his dreams, his fantasies, his hopes, Jake had never imagined his captor, his dear, sweet Bryony, a willing partner in his bed.

She was more than willing. She was his.

She touched the corner of his mouth with the tip of her finger, traced his smile. He brushed a tear from her cheek with the pad of his thumb and raised it to his lips.

He needed no restraints to hold her, no bonds, other than his love, to keep her by his side. Her sleek arms encircled his neck, her lips found his, marked him, forever willing…

Her captive.

About the author:

For over thirty years Kate Douglas has been lucky enough to call writing her profession. She has won three EPPIES, two for Best Contemporary Romance in 2001 and 2002, and a third for Best Romantic Suspense in 2001. Kate also creates cover art and is the winner of EPIC's Quasar Award for outstanding bookcover graphics.

She is multi-published in contemporary romance, both print and electronic formats, as well as her popular futuristic Romantica StarQuest. She and her husband of over thirty years live in the northern California wine country where they find more than enough subject material for their shared passion for photography, though their new grandson is most often in front of the lens. Kate is currently working on the screenplay adaptation for one of her contemporary romances.

Kate welcomes mail from readers. You can write to her c/o Ellora's Cave Publishing at P.O. Box 787, Hudson, Ohio 44236-0787.

Also by Kate Douglas:

Just A Little Magic
Luck of The Irish
More Than A Hunch
Star Quest 1: Lionheart
Star Quest 2: Night of The Cat
Star Quest 3: Pride of Imar
Threshold Volume 1

MANIMAL

Lani Aames

Chapter 1

"I can't believe my luck. The first snowfall of the year and I have to be out in the middle of it." Kelsey Locke grumbled loud enough for the phone to pick up what she was saying. She pushed a curly strand of dark brown hair out of her eyes and wished she'd remembered to pin it back before she left. "The wipers are on high and more snow is covering the windshield as soon as they clear it."

"You're almost there, Kels." Dee's voice was thin and tinny coming out of the speaker. "You passed the two crooked pines, didn't you?"

"Yeah, a ways back."

Both hands tightened on the steering wheel. She never drove on snow. Never. Two hours ago when Dee offered the use of her family's cabin at Lake Passion, there hadn't been a cloud in the sky. With a full moon, she had expected an easy trip. Now, the sky was shrouded in heavy dark clouds and the road was covered in a layer of white thick enough that not a bit of asphalt showed through.

"The lane to the cabin is just a few more miles. You'll be all right. Hold on a sec." There was a minute when all Kelsey could hear was the steady *swish swish* of the wipers and the low hum of the heater, then Dee's voice broke through again. "Charles Leland has been calling every five minutes and now he's text messaging."

Kelsey blew out a breath through tight lips. Charles was the reason she was in this situation. They had dated a few months, nothing serious, when Kelsey decided to stop seeing him. It wasn't fair to Charles that she was in lust with another man.

Dee's Delights, her friend's catering business, had provided the food for one of Charles' business dinners, and Kelsey agreed to help out because Dee was shorthanded that night. Charles had become infatuated immediately and lingered near her most of the evening to the point of ignoring the guests he wanted to impress. Exasperated by his persistence, Kelsey agreed to a date just to make him leave her alone the rest of the evening.

Later, it occurred to her she would have to follow through. Kelsey wished she had Dee's forthright manner, but she accepted she wasn't as outspoken as her friend. In her place, Dee would have told him to back off and get out of her face, but Kelsey tried to be accommodating to all, even at her own expense.

In other words, she was a wuss.

So she went out with Charles intending to try her best. Two of his men, who were always at his side, accompanied them at a discreet distance. The two men had been at the dinner, too, and initially Kelsey had been drawn to the tall, dark one. But he was all business that night and never indicated any interest in her at all. Oh, occasionally she'd feel his dark eyes on her, but when she turned to look at him, his bland expression never changed. Kelsey assumed Charles had ordered him to watch her.

Even after she started dating Charles regularly, he didn't act like he knew she existed as anything other than Charles' property. Time and time again, she found herself wishing she had piqued his interest rather than Charles'.

When Charles began pressuring her for sex, it finally dawned on her that she didn't really want Charles. She was consumed with desire for the tall, mysterious man who always stood to the side, watching her with his penetrating gaze.

Kelsey wouldn't sleep with Charles while lusting after another man. She couldn't even continue seeing him. She broke it off, then freely admitted to herself that she hoped the man would make a move if she was unattached.

Except Charles didn't think of them as detached. She'd told him it was over a couple of weeks ago, but his inflated ego rejected the possibility that any woman could say no to him. He was constantly calling her or sending flowers and gifts she promptly returned. The situation was so bad, she decided to go away for the weekend to get some work done. She even traded cell phones with Dee so she wouldn't be distracted with ignoring his calls and messages or left without a way to call for help in case of an emergency.

"Don't pay any attention to him. Maybe he'll finally figure it out." Kelsey squinted, tucking that annoying curl behind her ear, and tried to see through the white curtain of snow that surrounded her. She felt like she was caught in a snow globe and somebody had shaken it as hard as possible.

"Ooooh, I know. I can text him a message that'll put an end to his bullshit once and for all," Dee offered.

"No, no. I don't want to make him mad." Kelsey knew her outspoken friend would slice him and dice him if she said the word. But she was a little wary of Charles. While his landscaping business had made him rich and influential in the small town of Shadow Valley, Kelsey had a feeling there was something more...something not quite legit that accounted for most of his money and power. She didn't have any proof and had never witnessed anything underhanded, but the past few weeks had given her plenty of time to think. Why else would the CEO of a local landscaping company need two full-time bodyguards? Why would he need state of the art security to protect *manure*?

"Are you sure? I can tell him off and explain exactly where to stick those presents of his," Dee offered.

"Dee, just don't answer the messages or his calls. I'll deal with him when I get back. I think I'm coming up on the ess curve, so I'm going to hang up and concentrate on driving. In the snow. Which wasn't supposed to happen until tomorrow afternoon."

"Gee, Kels, I didn't know you believed in the weatherman. Do you still believe in Santa and the Tooth Fairy, too? How about the Easter Bunny?"

"All right. Point taken."

Dee snorted, an indelicate sound amplified by the speaker. "The lane to the cabin is less than a mile past the second curve, on the left. You can't miss it."

"I remember. I came up here with you and your family every summer for as long as we've been friends."

"Right, second grade. You were a crybaby in kindergarten and first. Be careful, Kels."

"I will."

Just as Kelsey reached over to push the disconnect button, a movement to the right of the road caught her eye. She had the sense that it was a four-legged animal, like a large dog. Seconds later, a man, not wearing a stitch of clothing, loomed in the path of her SUV. She screamed, a short, sharp sound, as he stumbled through the snow, one hand pressing what looked like a dark colored rag to his left side, his right arm thrown up in front of his face to ward off the headlights.

Instinctively, Kelsey swerved to the right and slammed on the brakes. The back of the SUV fishtailed, swinging around in a wide arc. She tried pumping the pedal lightly, but the effort was too late. By the time the SUV stopped, it had turned ninety degrees and sat crossways on the road, the front bumper less than a yard away from the naked man.

Kelsey's hands were locked around the steering wheel. Her heart pounded in her chest, and she shook as if she were the one standing naked in the snow. She caught a glimpse of her terror-stricken face in the rearview mirror. Her blue eyes were wide and fearful, and her mouth hung open as if to scream again but not a sound escaped.

When she looked through the windshield again, he had disappeared. At first, she thought he'd moved on to the other side of the road. But her gaze traveled downward and she realized he'd fallen.

What on earth should she do? Was this an act to lure her away from her vehicle so she could be hijacked, mugged, or worse? She waited a few moments, trying to decide if she should get out and help him or not. She couldn't believe any hijacker or rapist in his right mind would run around in this weather stark naked. There would have to be an easier way to do their dirty deeds.

The man needed help. As if suddenly released from some invisible force that had kept her hands bound to the wheel, Kelsey threw open the door and jumped out, slipping and sliding on the layer of fluff covering the icy asphalt. She approached the man slowly. If this was some kind of trick, he couldn't lie in the snow for very long.

There was something familiar about him, but she couldn't put her finger on it. By the length of his body and long legs, he was a tall man. He sprawled on his back, his face turned away from her. She watched his broad chest and sighed in relief when it rose and fell, but the movements were shallow and belabored. Her eyes traveled downward, following the trail of hair that narrowed as it neared his belly button and pointed straight to his genitals.

She was shocked to see that his penis was partially erect, its burgeoning length lying alongside one thigh. If she'd given it any thought at all, half a hard-on would be the last thing she'd expect in a man in his condition. She took a few steps closer and fell to her knees beside him.

Up close she could see that he hadn't been holding a dark rag to his side at all. His hand and the left side of his torso were smeared in the blood that seeped from a jagged tear at his waist, just above his hipbone. She reached out and brushed the snow away from his face, to see if he was still alive, when he groaned.

Kelsey gasped, shocked to find that she knew the man. "Durak?" she whispered.

Durak Voronin was one of Charles' bodyguards-slash-henchmen, and the man she had lusted after for the past few months. Sometimes Charles jokingly called Durak his enforcer. And sometimes, when she looked into Durak's hard brown eyes, she believed it...a shiver of danger would race through her body to merge with the physical longing.

What was he doing out here? Had Charles instructed Durak to follow her? Kelsey could see Charles giving the order and Durak complying. But as hard as she tried, she couldn't imagine why Durak would be naked, on foot, and injured.

He made another sound, interrupting her thoughts. A cross between a groan and a growl, it rumbled deep in his throat and chest. His legs jerked up as his face screwed in pain. Every muscle in his body grew taut and his arms twitched as his body curled into the fetal position.

"What are you doing here?" She brushed more snow away, startled by the coldness of his skin. She scrambled out of her coat, laid it over him, and leaned in close to his ear. "I've got a cell phone in the SUV, and I can call for help. I'll only be gone a few minutes, then I'll come back for you and we'll both get in out of the cold."

Before she could move, his hand shot out and closed around her wrist, snapping shut with the finality of a manacle. Kelsey cried out and tried to pry his fingers loose, but his grip was as unbreakable as iron.

"Durak, let me go. I'm trying to help you!" she shouted, hoping he would hear her and understand. His eyes opened and he pinned her with his relentless stare.

"*No!*"

The one word was short but powerful. Yet she didn't know what he was saying no to. Don't call 911? Or don't get him in out of the cold? Both? Neither?

"I don't know what's happening, but I do know one thing. I'm not going to sit out here freezing my ass off. Either let me go so I can get back in the SUV, or let me help you so we can both get warm."

She thought for a moment she'd lost him. He neither blinked nor lessened his grip, and it was almost as if he didn't breathe. Then he closed his eyes, his fingers relaxing around her wrist.

"Help me…to the SUV."

Kelsey breathed a sigh of relief and laid her hand over his. "All right. I'm not strong enough to pick you up. You're going to have to try to walk."

He nodded. Kelsey maneuvered around until she was holding onto his body, his arm slung across her shoulders. She moved her coat around so that it covered his backside. She didn't think it was doing him much good, but she couldn't expose that part of him to the snow and cold again.

He shuddered violently as she rose, forcing him to his feet. He slumped against her and she almost went down. And for a moment, she thought she felt fur, thick and warm, brush her cheek. As they uprighted again, she decided the cold had numbed her face and she was having sensory lapses. Or something. Disregarding the sensation, she took a step and Durak did the same.

Even though the SUV was only a few yards away, it became a long walk. When they reached the vehicle, Durak folded his tall body into the front passenger seat, Kelsey's coat covering part of him. He shivered, the chill racing through his full length.

She opened the glove compartment and brought out a flashlight. "There's a blanket in the back. I won't be but a minute."

She didn't know if he heard her or not because he didn't respond. She shut the door and walked around to the back.

Kelsey shone the beam on the ground, looking for his first set of prints. They had almost filled with fresh fallen snow, but she could still see where he had stepped. She remembered that just before Durak stumbled in front of the SUV, she'd had the impression of a large dog off to the right.

Had Durak been attacked by a vicious dog? Could his injury have been caused by canine teeth? But that didn't explain why he was as naked as the day he was born. A wild dog might have torn his clothing to shreds, but wouldn't have totally destroyed them. It wouldn't have ripped off his shoes and socks, too.

Kelsey walked away from the road and into the trees, shining the light on each print, occasional splotches of blood discoloring the snow. She went deeper than she meant to, until she could only see the faint glow of headlights among the trees behind her. Here the footprints stopped and…she didn't want to believe what she was looking at. After the last footprint was a pawprint. It was nearly as large as the footprints and twice as big as any dog's pawprint she had ever seen.

The strangest thing of all was there were no footprints mingled with the pawprints, and there were no pawprints interspersed with the footprints. The pawprints did not go off in another direction. And the footprints hadn't come from another way. It was as if the dog had disappeared into thin air and Durak had appeared out of nowhere. It was as if…

Kelsey didn't finish the thought. What she was thinking was preposterous. Impossible. Not only impossible, but improbable. Ridiculous. Mad.

With one last sweep of the flashlight that revealed nothing more, she ran back.

Chapter 2

Kelsey retrieved the blanket and got in behind the wheel. She spread the blanket over Durak and turned the heater vents toward him. He huddled beneath her coat and blanket, eyes closed.

He could be bleeding to death or suffering from hypothermia. Either way, he needed help. Kelsey eased the cell phone out of the speaker base. She squinted in the light of the dash and pressed the 9 button. Before she could reach the 1, Durak snatched the phone from her hands and slammed it against the dash.

The effort cost him. The phone fell from his hand and he slumped back in the seat.

"Why did you do that?" She looked at him and found him glowering at her, the glow from the dashboard giving his dark eyes an eerie cast.

"I told you not to call," he rasped.

"No, you didn't. But you do need help. You could be bleeding to death or have frostbite. In several places," she added thinking of one extremity in particular.

"I'm not. The bleeding has stopped."

"Well, something tore a chunk out of your side. You've lost a lot of blood and you've been exposed to the cold." Kelsey picked up the wrecked phone and stared at it, bewildered. Why would he destroy their only means to summon help? What was he hiding? The two sets of prints flashed through her mind, but she pushed them away. There was a logical explanation for them. There had to be!

Kelsey tried to get a dial tone, but the phone was dead. She dropped it in the space between their seats. "You'd better hope you don't need help now. The nearest hospital is back in Shadow Valley!"

"I don't need anything but time to rest."

"It's going to take more than rest to heal up that hole in your side. You need stitches," she snapped. Immediately, she regretted the harshness in her voice. He could be dying for all she knew, yet he didn't seem to be taking his condition seriously.

"I'll be fine," he murmured.

"You don't sound fine. You don't look fine, either!"

"It might be a good idea to get us out of the middle of the road before another vehicle comes along."

He was right. Although she hadn't seen another person crazy enough to be out in this weather for the past thirty minutes, it would be her luck for a car to come along and not be able to stop in time. With her foot on the brake, she shifted into drive and eased the vehicle around until it was on the road properly and headed in the right direction.

"It's less than two miles to the cabin."

"This cabin is where you were headed?"

Kelsey pressed the gas pedal lightly. The wheels spun a few seconds, then caught and the SUV jerked forward. "Yeah. It belongs to the family of a friend of mine. You remember Dee from Charles' dinner party. I used to come up here on vacations with them when we were kids."

She drove slowly around the ess curves and easily found the lane after the second one, just as she remembered.

"We're almost there."

At the end of the short lane, the headlights illuminated the rustic log cabin. Kelsey left them on to light their way. The snow wasn't falling as thickly now as it had been and the flakes were smaller. Luckily, they weren't the tiny icy bits that usually meant accumulation. So far there was less than a half-inch layer covering everything.

Kelsey got out and went around to help Durak out of the car. As she fit herself under his arm, she was immediately aware that his body temperature had changed drastically. Before, his skin had felt like ice, but now it was hot to the touch. She was afraid he was becoming ill and running a fever. If he grew worse, she would have to venture out and get help thanks to his temper tantrum with the phone.

His arm wrapped around her as if it belonged there, the other clutching the blanket to the injury at his side. As they trudged up the slight slope to the front porch, she was all too aware of his naked body pressed to hers. She tried to berate herself. After all, he was wounded and ill. But the pent-up lust she'd felt for him all these weeks was aching to break free.

Shoving her inappropriate feelings aside, she found the key in the flowerpot on the window ledge next to the door. It was just as cold inside the cabin as out. She switched on the lights, grateful the power was still on, and led Durak to the couch where he curled up, another groan escaping in a ragged rush of air. Kelsey grabbed the crocheted afghan off the back of the couch and spread it over him, too.

"I'll get a fire started. It'll be warm soon."

He didn't respond and Kelsey tried not to worry as she made a fire in the large stone fireplace. She tended it carefully until the kindling caught and the logs were burning. Warmth seeped into the room.

She went to Durak. His eyes were closed, and he looked as if he might be asleep. His hair was cut too short on the sides and at the nape for his angular face. A fringe of longer hair, thick and black, fell rakishly across his brow. She swept it back and laid her hand across his forehead. His skin felt hot, as if he were burning up with fever, but that could be because her hands were so cold. She could always do what her mother had done to check her temperature when she was young...kiss his temple.

Kelsey hesitated. He was asleep or unconscious. Either way he would never know. She leaned forward and watched him for a moment. His face was lean and hard with a not-quite-square jaw and prominent brow. His temples were slightly sunken, framed by cranium and sharp cheekbones. Only the soft lines of his lips relieved the starkness of his countenance and provided a hint of sensuality.

Kelsey pressed her mouth to his temple before she could give in to the impulse of kissing those lips. A secluded cabin was definitely the place, but this wasn't the time. He felt warmer than normal, but not dangerously so. With luck, his temperature wouldn't go any higher now that they were inside with a fire for warmth and he was wrapped protectively in blankets.

Brushing his hair back one more time, she started to stand when he grabbed her hand and pulled her back down close to him. His eyes were wide open and looking at her.

"This is developing into a bad habit," she said.

His grip was as solid as iron, and he didn't even flinch when she twisted her hand one way and then another, trying to break free. He was injured, cold, and possibly ill. It didn't make sense that she couldn't overpower him.

But none of this night made sense. Why was he out here in the first place? Why was he buck naked, sporting a hole the size of her fist in his side?

Why had the huge pawprints turned into his footprints?

"I need you," he whispered, his voice dry and shaky.

For a split second, a canine muzzle replaced his face. She blinked and had the feeling that he had turned from man to beast to man again, rather than the image of a large dog superimposed over him. She shook her head. She was letting her imagination run away with her.

"What do you need?" she asked softly. "I brought plenty of food if you'd like something to eat. Or do you want water?"

His head shook in the negative, one short sharp jerk to the side. "I want *you*."

Kelsey frowned. "You want me to what?"

He shook his head again. "I want you, Kelsey. No time to explain, but I need to discharge."

"You mean you want to…" Her voice trailed off.

"Fuck you."

Well, that was blunt. During her time with Charles she'd noticed Durak was a man of few words, and when he did speak he said exactly what he needed to say with no embellishment. His being delusional hadn't changed that.

"You don't know what you're saying. You've been injured and you're running a fever. When you get well, then we'll talk." She smiled and laid her hand over his to let him know that she was definitely interested.

He shook his head yet again and scowled. "You don't under*STAND*—" And his voice rose into a howl of distress. His face once again changed into a canine muzzle and his hand morphed into a huge paw with claws instead of fingers. Almost instantly, he changed back to human.

With strength born of panic, Kelsey jerked free of his grip. She scrambled away from him and *whatever* he was. It definitely wasn't her imagination. She rubbed her wrist where she'd felt thick fur and sharp claws against her skin. Her heart hammered in her chest as she once again recalled how the pawprints had suddenly become footprints in the snow.

"What is going on?" she shouted at him, fear making her voice quiver.

His body jackknifed and he groaned, a deep mournful sound, as fur briefly replaced smooth, taut skin. "Werewolf," he whispered.

"*What?*"

"I'm a werewolf. No time...no...time..." His hand-paw-hand reached for her. "Too much energy. Overload. Can't control. Need to discharge *now*—*need to fuck you now.*"

Kelsey drew back, beyond arm's length, and watched him. Werewolves weren't real! Yet, he was changing right before her eyes. And wasn't that the thought she'd refused to consider while looking at the two sets of prints in the snow? That he'd somehow transmogrified from a four-legged beast into a two-legged human.

What if the reverse occurred right now and he turned completely into a wolf? Legendary lycanthropes were ravening creatures that slaughtered anyone in their paths. Would he be any different?

Kelsey took a step toward the door, fully intending to run to the SUV and get the hell out of there. But his voice, crackling with the effort, stopped her in her tracks.

"I want you, Kelsey."

He needed her, but he also wanted her. She looked back and his hand was still stretched out toward her. He wanted her. Didn't that make all the difference in the world?

"I wish it could be different because I've wanted you a long time."

Kelsey took a step, then hesitated. "I want you, too, but I'm scared."

"No danger, I promise." He changed again, from man to wolf to man. "I won't hurt you."

With a deep breath, Kelsey made the decision to take a chance and trust him. She took his hand-paw-hand, fascinated by the way it morphed from one to the other. If having sex would release him from this flickering between wolf and human, what else could she do?

Durak threw back the blankets and coat and suddenly the cabin was much too warm for her. His cock was fully erect, long and thick, jutting at an angle from its nest of dark hair. Heat flushed through her, hot desire she hadn't felt in a long time curling in the pit of her belly. For months, she'd suppressed these feelings for him, thinking he was out of her reach. Now that she could allow them, they consumed her completely.

She undressed quickly, popping buttons in her haste to remove her sweater. She dropped her jeans and panties, already dampened with the juices of her desire, and pulled off boots and socks. She cast her leg over and straddled him. He must have reached critical because the change between human and wolf accelerated until she wasn't sure which she'd mount, the man or the animal.

His hands-paws-hands gripped her hips and drove her down onto his cock. Kelsey moaned with the pleasure of him inside her and trembled with her own need. She placed her palms on his chest and closed her eyes. Her back arched as she moved with him, her hips undulating with the rhythm of his as he thrust deep inside her.

Beneath her fingertips, skin changed to fur and back again in a continuous flow. She felt his cock change each time as well. Neither was better nor worse than the other, just different. Both heightened her pleasure, until her throbbing clit reached its own critical stage.

She came, hard, the eruption flashing through her body. Her fingers touched skin-fur-skin and her head fell back. Durak's thrusts quickened, his hands tightening on her hips, his groin grinding into her sex. As his body stiffened beneath hers, she felt skin against her hands…it was Durak the man releasing hot spurts inside her.

Breathing ragged, Kelsey leaned forward and watched his taut muscled chest rise and fall in deep breaths. Having sex must have worked because he hadn't morphed since his release. Looking down at him, as she had dreamed of so often in the past few weeks, the idea that he was a werewolf was preposterous.

Her hand trailed down to his side. Still covered in dried blood, the torn edges had closed and the injury was half the size it had been when she first found him.

Less than two hours ago.

No normal person healed that fast. It proved more than anything else that Durak Voronin was something other than human. He was a *werewolf*.

A breath hitched in her chest and she pulled away from him, removing her hands from him. She had to back away, emotionally as well as physically, from him and what he was. She had to take some time to think.

But Durak caught her hands and intertwined his fingers with hers.

"I'm sorry," he said, looking up at her through heavy lids.

Kelsey gasped and tears stung her eyes. Oh, wonderful. She had put her life and sanity on the line by having sex with him while he was in the throes of metamorphosis and now he was *sorry*. She reeled back, yanking her hands away.

"No," he said and reclaimed her hands, holding tightly even though she struggled to get away. "I'm not sorry we fucked. I wish it had been under different circumstances. It should have been because we want each other and no other reason."

Kelsey blinked back the unshed tears. He seemed sincere as he looked at her, his dark eyes intense. She took a deep breath and strengthened her resolve to trust him. And her own feelings.

"I'm not sorry either."

He released her and his fingers played lightly over her skin, sending little shivers through her.

She laid her hands on his chest again. "You don't feel feverish now."

"I'm all right. I'll tell you everything, but now I need...to sleep..." His voice trailed off and his hands stopped caressing her.

Kelsey raised up and looked at him. His eyes were closed and his breathing had evened. He was asleep. She eased out of his arms and stood over him, watching him as he turned on his side and settled in. She covered him with the blanket and afghan.

Man, animal, or manimal, males were all the same.

Chapter 3

Kelsey drummed her fingers on the kitchen table and stared at the screen of her laptop.

She wrote erotic romances under a pseudonym, carefully protecting her true identity, and only Dee knew what she really did for a living. The rest of her friends and family thought she mooched off her parents until she started telling them she had made some lucky investments on the internet.

It wasn't exactly a lie. Kelsey was electronically published online and considered it an investment in her writing career every time she connected to the net. She wasn't rich, but she was making a comfortable living wage off her writing at the ripe old age of 25.

But right now, she couldn't concentrate on finishing her latest erotic romance, *Deep Thrust*. And her deadline was Monday. The only deep thrust she could think about was Durak's…and the heat rose in her cheeks.

While it was fun to write about her heroines having such thoughts, it was an entirely different matter to have them herself.

She never dreamed she'd meet a man who measured up, in every way, to one of her fictional heroes. She had thought Charles should be it. After all, he had everything most fictional heroes possessed. He was handsome and charming, successful and powerful, but he just didn't quite cut it. He was controlling and too possessive, bordering on obsessive. To be brutally honest, something about Charles made her squeamish, but she wasn't sure what it was. He didn't seem…honest. He always acted as if he were hiding something.

She never should have gone out with him in the first place. And she never should have continued dating him because she wasn't being particularly honest with herself. The night of the dinner when she found she was instantly attracted to Durak, she should have said no to Charles and approached Durak instead.

Kelsey sighed and rested her chin in her cupped hands. It was always too easy to second-guess one's decisions in hindsight.

And it was easy to face the truth here in the kitchen in the dead of night, so she had to admit Charles' obsessive attention wasn't the only reason she had escaped this weekend. It had been her own obsession with Durak. She hadn't been able to keep her mind off of him long enough to finish the book. Whenever she tried to write, she spent most of the time daydreaming about him. A weekend away served double duty. It got her away from Charles and drove home the fact that she needed to get the book finished.

But here he was, dropped in her lap, so to speak. It was difficult to stop thinking about a man when he was in the next room, naked, and she had already had sex with him once. She had the opportunity she'd desired, and she'd certainly taken advantage of it.

In her daydreams, one time with Durak was enough to satisfy her lust. In reality, she knew she'd never get enough of him. Hell, he had surpassed anything in her wildest imagination. And they weren't really trying. She couldn't imagine what would happen when they did try.

And then there was that werewolf thing.

Weird, that's what it was. If she hadn't witnessed the shifting from man to beast with her own eyes, she wouldn't have believed it. And now that she'd had a couple of hours to get used to the idea, the only thing she was sure of was that she still wanted Durak. No matter what he was.

"Writing your next best-seller, Ms. L'Amour?"

Kelsey gasped and turned to find Durak standing in the doorway. He was no longer naked, unfortunately. After she hauled her supplies from the SUV, she had found some clothes that Dee's family kept stashed at the cabin and left them beside the couch for him. Dee's brother's jeans fit him well enough, although they were a little short. Durak wouldn't have fit into his shirts, and Kelsey had to raid Dee's father's closet to find a shirt to accommodate his broad shoulders. A pair of his boots fit well enough, too.

"I thought you were still asleep." Kelsey frowned. "And how do you know about Cherie L'Amour?"

Durak grinned and came to sit in a chair next to her.

"Charles Leland had me investigate you months ago."

Kelsey closed the file and snapped the laptop shut. She had added a final love scene to her novel that duplicated what she and Durak had done on the couch. Without the werewolf stuff, of course. Beyond that, she hadn't been able to write another word because her thoughts were consumed with Durak.

"Charles never said anything."

"Because I never told him."

"Why?"

"It wasn't any of his business."

Kelsey nodded. "Thank you. I've worked at keeping a low profile. Shadow Valley is such a small town, the news would spread like wildfire. I don't want the attention."

"I bought all your books and read a couple of them."

She waited. He would either like them or hate them. When he didn't say anything more, she stood and walked to the counter. "Would you like some coffee?"

"Yes, thank you."

She poured him a mug and handed it to him, then refilled hers, adding powdered creamer and sugar. She stirred it slowly, not at all ready to return to her seat and face him.

"I'm more of a visual person like most men," he finally said. "But I enjoyed them. You have a way with words. Your descriptive passages created nice pictures in my mind."

"Thank you." The awkward moment had passed and she sat down. "How's your side?"

"Almost healed." He raised the shirt to show her.

He had washed up before dressing as there was no trace of blood. A little puckering of skin was the only sign of the injury.

"That'll disappear in a few more hours," he added.

"Have you always been — you know…"

"A werewolf?"

Kelsey laughed a bit uncomfortably. "Yeah, a werewolf. It's still hard to believe."

"I was born a werewolf. My father is one, but my mother is fully human. So you see, I'm only half werewolf. I think that explains what happened earlier."

"No, actually it doesn't explain anything. How did you get that injury?"

Durak took a sip of coffee. "Leland ordered me to keep tabs on you. When I reported you were packing to leave, he suspected you were going off to meet another man for the weekend. I tried to tell him there had been no indication you were seeing another man, but he insisted I follow you."

Kelsey slammed down her mug. "You know I broke it off with him weeks ago. He has no right!"

Durak nodded. "I agree. I tried to tell him that, too, but he threatened my job if I didn't do as I was told."

"Why do you continue to work for him? You obviously have excellent skills if you dug up that I'm Cherie L'Amour. You could get another job anywhere."

Durak hesitated. "I'm sorry, I can't tell you why. Just know that I have to work for him for a while longer, and it is temporary."

That sounded fishy. But he had kept her secret and she could do no less than not pry into his. "All right."

"Because I'm only half werewolf, I need to shift regularly to keep everything in balance. It's been a while, so I thought I'd follow you as a wolf. There's a full moon tonight and that makes shifting easier. I knew you weren't going to meet a man, and I didn't think you were going far. And the run would do me good."

"How did you get hurt?"

"Someone was following me."

"Someone?"

"Sam Brady."

The other bodyguard-slash-henchman. "Oh, Durak, then he knows what you are."

He nodded grimly. "I was distracted by you and didn't notice anyone tracking me. When I realized you were on Old Stanfield Road and headed for Lake Passion, I took the more direct route through the forest. I had been waiting at a place about a mile back down the road for some time. That allowed Brady to catch up to me and he shot me."

"That was a bullet wound?" Kelsey cried out.

"It wasn't a silver bullet or I'd be dead now. Brady must not have known what I was until I shifted to follow you. He wasn't prepared."

"If he didn't suspect you of being a werewolf, then why was he following you?"

"I have an idea, but I can't talk about it." Durak sipped more coffee indicating that line of conversation was closed. "I ran but only about a mile. I was hurt too badly. Then all I could do was limp, and I thought I should be near the road again to watch for you. And then I shifted without conscious effort. I stumbled out of the trees, and that's when you came along."

"I thought I saw a large dog or something at the side of the road before you stepped in front of me."

"I was producing energy to fight the wound and heal it, but it was too much. That's a result of being only half werewolf. My system takes too much time to adjust to changes. By the time I adjusted, my body was on overload and had to release the excess energy."

"Like walking across a carpet will build up static electricity and touching something releases the charge?"

"Something like that. I had to discharge the excess and sex is one way to ground. I don't completely understand it myself. I just know it works." Durak stood and walked to the window. He pushed aside the curtain and peered out.

Kelsey thought he looked as if he was on alert, ready if something happened. "Brady's still out there, isn't he?"

"I'm sure he is. This is something he'd love to hand over to Leland, but he needs a wounded me as proof. Otherwise, it's my word against his and Leland will believe me, especially since I won't have a gunshot wound. Brady probably thinks he has time because he doesn't realize how fast I heal."

"Henchman rivalry," Kelsey murmured.

Durak dropped the curtain and turned toward her. "What?"

"I always thought of you two as Charles' henchmen. I could tell he favored you over Brady and Brady was jealous."

"Like you said, I'm good at what I do."

"But Brady's good enough to track you cross country in this weather."

"I never underestimated Brady. I was distracted by you."

"By me?"

"Yes. You. The night of the dinner. I haven't been able to think straight where you're concerned since then."

Kelsey stared at him. "You never gave any indication that you were interested."

"I couldn't. Charles Leland would have fired me on the spot, and I couldn't let that happen. As soon as I finished with Leland, you would have heard from me."

"Really?" Kelsey grinned and her heart jumped in her chest. He wanted her, too, and he would have come to her as soon as he finished his mysterious liaison with Charles. No longer out of her reach, all she could think of was how she wanted him...right now.

"Really." Durak set his mug on the table and reached for her, pulling her to her feet. "It was all I could do to keep my hands off you."

"You don't have to keep your hands off of me any longer," Kelsey said and wrapped her arms around his neck. "In fact, I insist you put your hands anywhere you want."

"Anywhere?"

"Everywhere," Kelsey amended.

Durak kissed her, his sensual lips soft against hers. Then he rested his forehead to hers. "You don't know how long I've waited to do this."

"Oh, yes, I do. Since that night of the dinner. I only said I'd go out with Charles so he'd stop bothering me the rest of the evening. It took me a while to realize it, but I kept seeing him to be close to you. I really wanted you."

"Is there a bedroom in this place? Does it have a bed?"

"Yes and yes. In the front room, the door by the fireplace. I built a fire in there earlier, so it should be nice and warm."

Durak scooped her off her feet and up into his arms. Following her directions, he kicked open the door and set her in the middle of the peeled log bed, the down comforter conforming to the shape of her body. He crawled over her, but Kelsey sat up and looked at him.

"I hope you're not expecting what I write in my books. That's fiction, you know. Just because I write it doesn't mean I can do it."

Durak tilted his head to one side. "We've already been together once. I wasn't out of it enough not to remember. And enjoy."

"Well, I don't want you to have expectations I can't fulfill." Kelsey lay down again. "It was good, wasn't it? We were good together even though the circumstances were crazy."

"It was good," he assured her.

His weight rested on his hands that were placed on each side of her. His dark gaze roamed over her, lingering at her lips, her breasts, and mound.

"What are you doing?" Kelsey squirmed beneath him, more than ready.

Durak's gaze swept over her again. "You said I could put my hands everywhere on you. I'm trying to decide where to touch first."

"Undress me and then decide."

He unbuttoned her blouse with care, working slowly, deliberately, skimming her exposed flesh with his fingertips. When her breasts were uncovered, he dipped into her bra and found a hardened nipple. She gasped as he caressed the peak, little shocks of pleasure trailing from the tip of the breast to between her thighs.

Deftly, he unfastened the front hooks of her bra and her breasts spilled free. He bent forward and took a nipple between his lips, suckling gently, while fingers pinched the other. The double sensations drove Kelsey wild and her back arched, pressing her breast harder against his mouth. She didn't know if she could stand for him to take the time to touch everywhere. She wanted him now.

Durak's tongue trailed across her skin to the other breast. This time he assaulted the tip, flicking his tongue across the sensitive bud, raking it with the edge of his teeth, and suckling greedily, pulling it to a fine point. At the same time, a swirling thumb massaged the wet peak of the one he'd just left. Kelsey burned deep inside, her writhing body aching for him.

The sweet torture subsided only when he lifted his head and his hands pushed aside her bra. He raised Kelsey enough to slide her clothing off her shoulders, raining hot kisses across her flushed skin as the garments slipped away. Kelsey moaned when his mouth took hers, plundering its depths with his seeking tongue. He laid her back on the bed, the comforter swathing her in feather softness.

"Durak," she whispered. "I don't think I can take much more of this. Make love to me now."

He raised up on his knees and pulled off his shirt, tossing it aside. "I haven't touched everywhere yet."

Chapter 4

Durak finished undressing until his magnificent body was completely revealed to Kelsey. Light from the lamp and fire played across tanned skin, his shoulders, arms, and legs corded with muscle and sinew. His thick cock, rigid in arousal, curved slightly upward and she felt the wetness gather between her thighs.

She had seen him naked and had made love to him only a few hours ago, but the sight of him again increased her excitement to new heights. He climbed into the bed again and knelt, removing her socks. He laid her legs together and crawled until his mouth was even with her breasts.

Durak placed his hands on her sides as his tongue flicked one nipple then the other, rekindling the sensations he'd created before. He then traced the undercurve of each breast in turn and planted a kiss between them.

His hands slid toward her hips as he moved further down, his lips tracking over her ribs and stomach, his hot breath fanning across her skin until he ran into the waistband of her jeans. One hand undid the button and zipper, pushing aside the material. The tip of his tongue circled her navel, plumbed its depth, and Kelsey nearly screamed.

He raised up once more and stripped the jeans from her, spread her legs wide, then fell back to where he had left off. Kelsey writhed and moaned as he blazed a path through the patch of curls on her mound. She anticipated where his lips and tongue would go next. She wanted it, needed it, prayed for it, but he prolonged the sweet agony instead.

He went lower, placing his arms underneath her thighs, his hands cupping her buttocks. His head dipped and he lapped her trickling juice, the tip of his tongue almost but not quite penetrating her. Her entire body ached with the anticipation. If he didn't touch her throbbing clit soon, Kelsey knew she was going to implode and collapse upon herself.

Kelsey wriggled against his mouth, trying to move so that he would touch her clit, but he avoided her maneuvers. Lavishly, he licked each soft fold of her tender, sensitive flesh. The tip of his tongue wove through each curve and turn, every dip and rise. Kelsey's fingers clenched in the down comforter, her hips undulating on their own as they moved in time with each caress.

Durak's tongue traveled up, through the wet creases, and circled her clit. When he finally touched the swollen nub, surrounding it with the wet heat of his mouth, Kelsey's body bucked, and the burst of pleasure spiraled outward. She cried out, her head thrashing to and fro. Before the sensations had completely dissipated, Durak bent her knees and plunged deep inside.

Each thrust rebuilt what he had just destroyed. He slammed into her clit again and again, his cock massaging her g-spot. When he came with a feral roar, she once again shattered, bursting into innumerable fragments, sending her farther beyond the edge than she'd ever gone before.

Kelsey breathed heavily and was barely aware when Durak lay down beside her. He fit his body to hers, his still warm cock snug against her backside, his arms around her protectively. Her last thought before drifting off to sleep was that she never wanted to be without his arms around her again.

* * * * *

When Kelsey awoke, it was still dark and for a moment she didn't know where she was. Then it all came back in a rush and she smiled. She rolled over, expecting to snuggle in Durak's arms, but the other side of the bed was empty. She sat up. The fire had died down, but from its faint glow she could see the dark shape of the wolf as it padded through the open door to the front room.

Durak had shifted and she wondered why. Had his system overloaded again? With thoughts of excess energy and mandatory discharging, Kelsey scooted out of bed. She found the robe she had laid out earlier, slipped it on, and tied the belt around her waist. Would he expect her to make love to his wolf form this time? She shivered, unsure whether she could do it or not. He might have to find another way to ground this time.

She walked through the door into the front room. The fire here had died down as well, but there was enough light to see that neither man nor wolf was in the room. Then she heard a crash and a threatening growl. The only place the sounds could have come from was the kitchen. She hurried down the short hallway.

In the doorway, she switched on the light just as the wolf bounded over the table, toward a man. The light startled both of them, throwing the wolf off-course. The man, whom she instantly recognized as Sam Brady, Charles' other bodyguard-slash-henchman, turned slightly and took a step backward. If the wolf's intent had been to hit him square in the chest, he missed the mark, but he did slam into Brady's shoulder. As his arms flailed against the assault, his hand released the gun he carried and the weapon skittered across the tile floor.

The wolf's weight drove Brady backward and slammed him against the wall. Brady kept enough of his wits about him to put his hands around the wolf's throat and squeeze. The wolf snarled, flecks of foam dripping from his sharp fangs. He lunged forward, his open mouth going for Brady's throat.

"Durak, no!" Kelsey shouted. Even though she knew Brady was a threat to Durak, she couldn't stand there and watch him murder a man.

The wolf stopped short of Brady's jugular, then threw back his head and howled. A terrified Brady released him, and the wolf landed lightly on his feet. Brady slumped against the wall.

The wolf looked at Kelsey and gave a short yip as if to tell her to go. She stood her ground and shook her head, refusing to leave. She was in no immediate danger, and she couldn't let him kill the man even though Brady had tried to kill him first.

The wolf turned toward Brady again. A steady growl, low and threatening, kept Brady in place. They couldn't remain like this forever. The gun had landed on the other side of the table, closer to Brady than her. But if she got the gun, she could give Durak a chance to shift. Kelsey took a couple of steps toward the table.

The wolf glanced back at her and yipped again. Brady, realizing the wolf wouldn't attack as long as she was in the room, straightened and also took a step toward the gun.

The wolf lunged, stopping Brady only for a second. Then he tried another step. The wolf snarled and snapped, catching Brady's insulated coverall pants and shredding the cloth leg. While Brady was busy trying to shake off the wolf, Kelsey moved a little closer. Now, both she and Brady were almost within arm's reach of the gun.

Kelsey made a grab for it at the same time Brady kicked free of the wolf and sprang forward. Instead of snatching at the gun, Brady seized her, jerking her back against him. Then he produced a knife and pressed the wicked serrated edge against her throat.

"Stay back, Voronin," he ordered. "Stay back or I'll slit her from ear to ear."

The wolf remained still but watchful, his dark golden eyes narrowed and lips curled back, revealing ferocious teeth.

"All I want to do is get the fuck out of this freak show," Brady said, his voice cracking.

Kelsey heard the fear in his voice and smelled it in his pungent sweat. She was afraid, too, but she knew Durak wouldn't let anything bad happen to her.

"If—you—" Kelsey began, but with each word her throat moved and the blade pressed closer. She tried again, speaking more softly. "If you want to get out of here alive, you'd better not hurt me."

The wolf growled as if in agreement.

"Fine. I just want the hell out of here. We'll move toward the front of the house. You hear that, Voronin," he said louder, almost shouting. "We're moving toward the front. You stay here, and when we get to the front door, I'll leave without hurting her. Do you understand?"

The key was to act more courageous than she felt. Although her heart was pounding in her ears and her palms were slick with nervous sweat, she said, "He's a wolf. He's not deaf."

Brady jerked her closer and pressed the blade tighter until Kelsey was afraid to swallow. "No more smartass comments or I'll leave a mark before I go."

Maybe false bravado wasn't such a good idea. The wolf snarled.

Keeping Kelsey between him and the animal, Brady edged around the table. Near the doorway, he stopped. "Stay in here, Voronin, and nothing'll happen to her. Got it?"

The wolf backed up a step, indicating he would comply with Brady's demands. Or that's what Kelsey thought. Brady, too, because he moved them sideways through the door and into the narrow hallway. As soon as they were completely within the hall, the wolf moved. And as he moved, he changed. Fur disappeared and smooth tanned skin appeared, paws morphed into hands and feet. He went seamlessly from four legs to two. Gaining momentum, he moved swiftly, almost a blur. Kelsey lost track of exactly where he was, but when she felt Brady's hand relax and the blade leave her throat, she dropped like a lead weight and rolled into the kitchen out of the way as the knife clattered to the floor.

Kelsey sat up and looked down the hallway, and all she saw was Durak's backside, steadily moving away from her. His arms and hands were a blur, but she heard the steady thuds as his fists smacked into Brady's flesh again and again. Brady cried out in pain each time. Then a bone snapped, the sound reverberating through the cabin, and Brady screamed.

Then Kelsey heard nothing but the sound of her own heavy breathing in the silence that followed.

She scrambled to her feet and raced down the hall into the front room. Brady sat on the floor, huddled against the far wall. He whimpered, cradling his left arm, broken bone protruding through skin and splattered with blood. Durak stood over him, daring him to move.

"That's enough!" Kelsey cried out.

Durak nodded. "I know." He squatted beside Brady and lifted a cell phone from where it was clipped to his belt.

"Kelsey, would you please get my clothes while I call some friends of mine to get this piece of shit out of here?"

In the bedroom, Kelsey dressed quickly in jeans, sweatshirt, and sneakers, then brought out Durak's borrowed clothing. Durak was looking out the front door, the phone to his ear.

"Yeah, there's enough room. I'll leave the SUV lights on so you can find it. That's right, the south side of the lake. Probably the only cabin occupied this time of year. Well, hell, Andy, half the time you can't find your ass with both hands." Durak laughed. "All right, see you in ten."

The clothes fell from Kelsey's suddenly nerveless fingers. She didn't recognize the name "Andy" as one of Charles' employees, but Durak was too familiar with the person on the other end of the line for it to be the police. Besides, he was a werewolf and Sam Brady knew it. How could he call the police without revealing his secret?

"You called Charles?" Panicking, her voice rose in pitch.

"No, of course not." Durak shut the door and came toward her.

"It didn't sound like you were talking to the police." She took a step backward, feeling betrayed. "I never wanted Charles to find out about this cabin."

"You never have to worry about Charles Leland again." Durak put his arms around her, and she let him. She desperately wanted to believe him.

"Then who did you call?"

"The people I really work for, the DEA."

"What?" Thoroughly confused, she looked up into his dark eyes. "The Drug Enforcement Agency?"

"Administration," he corrected. "I've been working undercover. I'll explain everything, but I have to turn on the SUV lights right now so they can find us."

Needing a few moments to take in this newest turn of events, Kelsey volunteered. "I'll do it since I'm already dressed."

Kelsey's mind whirled with what Durak had told her as she dashed out into the fine layer of snow. If Durak worked for the DEA, then he was one of the Good Guys, even if he was a werewolf. A weight she didn't even know she carried lifted from her shoulders. Werewolf didn't necessarily equate with evil as it did in folklore.

When she returned, Durak rose from where he'd been squatting beside Brady.

"I am so confused," she admitted. "Why have you been investigating Charles?"

Durak finished tucking in his shirttail. "I've been undercover for six months working for Charles Leland. He's been using his landscaping business as a cover for his real business, drugs. But you knew that, didn't you, Brady?"

Brady scowled, then winced in pain. Purple smudges were already forming on his face and arms where Durak's blows had landed.

Durak frowned. "Leland ships in drugs along with his landscaping supplies and distributes the drugs to the counties in this area. Brady knows all about it, and I'm sure he'll be happy to give the boys all the details. Because if he doesn't spill his guts and tell them all about Leland, then they'll have to assume Brady is behind it all."

Kelsey nodded then looked at Durak. "Do they know about...you know?"

Durak shook his head and drew her to the other side of the room.

"But Brady knows you're a werewolf." Kelsey whispered even though she didn't know why. Brady had seen Durak shift into a wolf, had followed him, shot him, and then had seen him shift back into human with a lethal wound that had miraculously healed within hours.

"Shhh." Durak glanced back at Brady, but he was nursing his arm and not paying any attention to them.

"Not that anybody would believe him, but it's a werewolf trick. A little like hypnosis and he doesn't remember a thing. Mostly it works because humans don't want to remember." Durak looked at her thoughtfully. "Most humans would rather not know about werewolves."

"You could do this to me?"

"I could. Do you want me to?"

Kelsey shook her head. "I've never known a werewolf before. I think it's neat."

Durak grinned. "Neat. I've never heard it called that before."

"Besides," Kelsey said and slipped her arms around his waist, "if I chose to have you wipe my memory, then I suspect we'd never see each other again. I can live with you being a werewolf better than I can live without you in my life."

"Can you?" Durak wrapped his arms around her.

"I want to see you, Durak, and be with you. I've fallen in love with you and that means I accept everything about you." Kelsey closed her eyes as he pressed a kiss to her forehead. "As long as you can accept that I write erotic romance."

His forehead wrinkled in confusion. "I don't have a problem with that. Why would I?"

Kelsey shrugged. "Some men might be scared off, thinking they couldn't live up to the prowess of my fictional heroes."

"Hmmm, I never thought about that. How do I measure up?"

Kelsey laughed. "Oh, no, I'm not going there. You'll either be insulted or get a big head. Either way, you might not feel the need to keep your technique up to standard."

Durak laughed with her and kissed her soundly, his tongue probing deep. She pressed closer to him, rubbing against the hard bulge in his jeans. She'd forgotten about Brady, the expected DEA team, and everything else except Durak and his cock and how she wanted him right then and there.

Her hands had slipped between their bodies, fumbling with his belt buckle, when a strange sound penetrated through the haze of her desire — the *whoop whoop whoop* of giant wings beating the air.

Durak's head snapped up. "Chopper. The boys are here."

Chapter 5

An hour later, as dawn turned the eastern sky to glorious shades of pink and gold, Kelsey stood with Durak on the snow-covered lawn in front of the cabin and watched the helicopter lift off the ground. Bits of snow and ice sifted over them as the rotors whipped the air, stripping the nearby trees of their winter frosting.

Durak waved a final time. They watched until the aircraft had gone above the tops of the trees and started moving laterally, disappearing in the distance.

"I was close to having enough evidence on Leland, but I expected to have to work for him another month," Durak said as they walked back into the cabin. "Now, with Brady's unexpected cooperation, I won't have to go back at all."

"That's good news." Kelsey stood in front of the dying embers in the fireplace, trying to get warm.

"It's been a long night, but I wouldn't trade it for anything." Durak knelt on the large shaggy rug in front of the fireplace and put on more kindling, waiting until the embers turned into flames before laying on larger logs.

Kelsey sat down beside him. "Wouldn't you trade it for a job where you wouldn't get shot?"

"I've been shot before, and it'll probably happen again." Durak prodded the logs a few times, then set the poker back in the stand with the other fireplace tools. "I have a dangerous job. And I'm a werewolf. Both are high risk. But I didn't mean the job. I meant spending the time with you."

Kelsey's heart thundered in her chest. To her, it sounded as if he considered what had happened between them as special as she did. She reached over and unfastened the top button of his shirt. She had found the man of her dreams, but did he feel the same? "Have you ever thought of going into another line of work?"

Durak sat back on his heels, his eyes riveted on her fingers undoing each button in turn. "I've thought about it, but I like my job."

"Even the risks?" Kelsey pushed aside the shirt and laid her hands on his chest. Her fingertips found the small, hard points of his nipples and rubbed them lightly.

Durak shrugged the shirt off his broad shoulders. "It's always been about the risk."

"Do you think you could live without that risk?" Kelsey sat up straighter and pulled the sweatshirt over her head.

She hadn't taken the time to put on a bra earlier, so her breasts were bare, the nipples tight and peaked. She gasped as Durak fondled them greedily, thumbs brushing the tips.

He lay back on the rug. "What would I do?"

"Security." Kelsey unfastened his belt buckle, then undid the button and zipper of his jeans. "It's what you were doing for Charles. I really didn't get to know Charles, but I do know you must be good or he wouldn't have kept you on. And he was grooming you to take Brady's place, wasn't he? That's why Brady was determined to find something on you, to show Charles you weren't as trustworthy as he thought."

"That's true." Durak pushed the jeans off his long legs while toeing off his boots.

Kelsey kicked off her shoes and shimmied out of her jeans. "You could develop and maintain security systems for businesses, couldn't you?"

"Yeah, but what are you getting at?"

Kelsey had him right where she wanted him, flat on his back and listening to what she had to say. She straddled him, preparing to settle down on his large, hot cock, her hands resting on his chest. Then she trailed a finger to the unblemished skin at his side. He was completely healed now with no trace of the gunshot wound.

"I want to spend the rest of my life with you, Durak," she whispered as she positioned herself so that the head of his cock was right at the opening of her sex. She rocked her hips back and forth, rubbing the engorged head.

Durak's hands tightened at her hips and pushed down, but she resisted.

"I know you enjoy the risk, but I don't think it's fair to ask me to take the risk, too. Or our children."

Durak stopped the pressure and looked at her. "Our children?"

"Of course. We're going to spend the rest of our lives together, aren't we? Don't you want children?"

"Some day, yes, but—" His hands left her hips and he raised up, propping his weight on his elbows. "Are you asking me to marry you?"

Kelsey nodded, suddenly frightened that she'd misread him. What if he didn't feel the incredible connection with her that she felt with him? What if he didn't want to spend the rest of his life with her? What if he didn't want to get married? What if he—? "You aren't already married, are you?"

"No, of course not. It's just that—this is a little sudden, isn't it?"

"Is it?" Kelsey once again rubbed against his cock. She wanted him inside of her, needed him like nothing she'd ever needed before, but she was determined to have her say. He moaned and put an arm around her, rolling them over until he was on top and kneeling between her legs.

"We've only really known each other for one night," he reminded her.

"Yeah, but it's been a very long night." Kelsey wrapped her legs around his waist and pushed her hips upward. Another moan sounded deep in his chest, but he didn't take the plunge. She quivered, ready for him. "And we know each other's secret. I know you're a werewolf. How many women would accept that about you?"

"There aren't many I've entrusted with the secret," he admitted. His hips surged forward, but he only teased her by going in partway. This time Kelsey made a sound, a whimper in the back of her throat. "It's not just my secret, but my family's, too."

"And…and you know my secret," Kelsey murmured. His cock beginning to fill the aching void of her sex distracted her. She had to make a conscious effort to actually remember her secret of being erotic romance author Cherie L'Amour. She pressed her legs against his hips, to let him know she wanted him fully inside. Suddenly, Durak's hips drove down, nudging her clit and sending a thrill along every nerve in her body. Kelsey closed her eyes and gave in to the rhythm of moving with him. "Will you?" she remembered to ask.

"Will...I...what?" he asked between hard, deep strokes.

"Will you marry me?" Kelsey gasped as she felt herself nearing the edge. And then she forgot she had asked a question as their hips pumped wildly together and they moved as one.

A low moan started in the back of her throat as her fingers and toes started to tingle. Her back arched and Durak drove deeper, sending her into the abyss of pleasure. As she cried out, she felt Durak's body stiffen, grinding hard into her. Her inner muscles spasmed with the last burst of pleasure just as his face distorted with his release. Then he collapsed across her, taking most of his weight with his hands.

As their bodies settled, Kelsey's fingers played along his sweat-slick skin, following the ridges and contours of taut muscles. She didn't want to move, and she never wanted to let go of this man. She hoped he felt the same about her.

He raised his head and smiled, then his cock slithered out of her as he lay beside her, taking her into his arms.

"You never told me," Durak said after his breathing returned to normal. "How do I measure up to your heroes?"

Kelsey looked up into his handsome face. Firelight played in his dark eyes and softened the hard planes of his countenance.

"I told you I don't think it would be good for your ego for you to know either way. But I think I'm the one who's always been afraid that I'd never find a man to measure up." Kelsey snuggled closer to him, placing a kiss on his jaw. "And now that I've found you, I don't ever want to lose you. Would you consider another kind of job? One not as dangerous."

"I'm still a werewolf, Kelsey. There are dangers connected to the circumstances of my birth that I can't run from. I stopped trying a long time ago."

He was quiet for a time, and Kelsey was sure she had frightened him off by pressuring him to get a new job and proposing marriage. Maybe he wasn't ready for the commitment, no matter what he felt for her. She opened her mouth to take it all back when he started speaking again.

"You know, I like my job, but I'm not in love with it." His hand roamed her body, caressing a breast, her belly, the curve of her hip. "I'm in love with you."

"You are?" She was surprised he felt the same way about her and was even more surprised that he admitted to it so quickly. Most men didn't readily admit to love. Because he was being so compliant, she felt a stab of guilt that she had asked so much of him. She didn't have the right to demand that he change his entire way of life just for her. "I love you, Durak, but you don't have to—"

He silenced her with a finger to her lips. "I learned a long time ago to grab what I want when I have the chance because the opportunity might not come around again. I've been feeling restless, so a career change will be good for me. And I think spending a lifetime with you is a fine idea. Yes, I'll marry you, Kelsey."

"You will?" she asked from behind his finger.

He laughed. "Weren't you serious?"

"Oh, yes, I was serious, but I didn't think you'd go for it."

"Why not?" Durak's hand slid up into her hair and brought her closer to him, her lips almost touching his. "I don't have anything else planned for the next fifty or sixty years."

Kelsey kissed him, igniting the fire of their passion once again, and murmured, "My hero."

About the author:

Lani welcomes mail from readers. You can write to her c/o Ellora's Cave Publishing at P.O. Box 787, Hudson, Ohio 44236-0787.

Also by Lani Aames:

Desperate Hearts

Lusty Charms: Invictus

Naughty or Nice

Things That Go Bump In the Night 2

A.D. 2203: ADAM & EVE

Ravyn Wilde

Chapter 1
Earth 2203

Eve strode restlessly out of the lab, walking quickly through the air shield and out into the night. She was tired but anxious, on the verge of completing a pet project. Glancing up, she swore, "Damn, it's a Lupine Moon!"

Her assistant, Charles, cocked one eyebrow at her and gestured in an offhanded manner, saying drolly, "Eve dear, I told you that three days ago. You grunted. But *noooo*...the greatest geneticist of our time was in the middle of bending over her microscope doing what she does ten hours a day."

"Shut up, Charles," Eve spat out.

Any minute she was going to start hyperventilating. This was not good. She was miles from home and the safety of her sealed lab, which wouldn't protect her now anyway. In order for it to work, you had to enter the damn airtight room three days prior to full moon. The three days were necessary in order for scent to dissipate.

"I hate full moons," she snarled. Quickly glancing around the compound she ran the options through her mind.

Nothing. Not a damn thing she could do about it now.

"Your stepfather is a werewolf, sweetie. How can you be so 'One Race' about this?"

Eve turned on the tall, elegantly effeminate male. "Charles," she said in a tight voice. "You and I have been working together for three months to create an inoculation that will give one group of Others a chance to have live, swimming sperm. In any way does this point to me being a member of the 'One Race'? No," she said before he could comment. "This puts me at the top of their Human Enemy Hit List. Yes, my stepfather is Were, my half-brother is Were, my sister is married to a Vampire—one of the leaders of the Others. I am *not* prejudiced, I just do not want to chance meeting up with one of the shaggy beasts tonight thinking I smell like wifey," she enunciated clearly.

Dragging her hands through her cropped, black as midnight hair, Eve nervously checked the compound again before stepping up to her glide. Her heart was racing. She smoothed sweaty palms over her softly curved body and regretted the fact that she hadn't taken the time for her morning runs in the last month. Like that would help if she were scented. Her amber eyes were narrowed, cautious. Her body poised for flight.

"Do you want me to follow you home?" Charles uncertainly offered.

Eve snorted. "Why? You know as well as I do if I'm scented and marked, I have no choices. The Lupine Act took care of that." She sighed, "Go home Charles. It was my fault I didn't realize Lupine Moon was tonight. I can only pray that there is no werewolf out there that is genetically tuned to my scent. I *do not* need a husband right now."

So saying, Eve settled into her glide and programmed it for home. She waved half-heartedly at Charles and leaned her head back, closing her eyes. The ride home from the lab would take exactly 15.6 minutes in the air glide. Its quiet imperceptible motion wouldn't disturb her thoughts.

Gee — what to think about? The fact that she had made a huge breakthrough in the development of a serum for Vampire males that would give them a window of opportunity to impregnate their warm-blooded mates? Or the fact that the development of that serum would probably get her killed by the One Racers? Nah, let's go with the fact that for the first time since her maturity at 18, almost 20 years ago, she'd not locked herself up safely in an airtight room three days before LM!

Eve winced. Lupine Moon. One night a month when lycanthropes everywhere were forced to change, and if they were "of age" they hunted for a mate. Only during LM from sundown to sunup did they have the ability to scent and trace their genetic mate. And her grandfather's work had helped to prove the fact that Weres did indeed have a true genetic companion. His work led to the Lupine Act, which meant that it didn't matter if you were a shape-shifter, human, or warm-blooded Other, if you were scented, found and cornered for marking before daylight — you were nuclear! Mated.

It didn't matter if you wanted a mate or not. The minute the furry beast found you and bit your shoulder — marking you for life — there was no legal, religious or physical way out. Mated pair.

And Were-folk mated for life.

What she'd told Charles was the truth. She wasn't prejudiced. The problem was she didn't want any male cluttering up her life. Trying to change her as her mother had changed. With a human or Other, you could JUST SAY NO. Saying no to a loupe-garou was against the law.

Please, dear Lord, do not let a werewolf catch onto my scent tonight…

171

Chapter 2

Adam stretched, trying to work a knot of tension from his muscular frame. As had happened well over 280 times in his life since his 18th birthday, it was a full Lupine Moon. Every month, throwing in a couple of blue moons over the years, he looked for her. It seemed as if he'd been searching forever. He was almost 40 and more than ever before he felt the essential lack of a mate to complete him. Energized, the predatory urge to track coursed through his moon-sensitized body. Some instinct whispered across his skin that this would be the time.

He knew he had come close to finding her the last couple of months. He'd caught the faint scent of her; enough to stir his mating instincts, but the hint always disappeared before he found her. Adam knew what that meant—a safe room. He could only hope that by following the trace he had of her to the same area, that this month she wouldn't make it in time…that she'd forget, or think herself secure.

Then she would be his. Muscles clenching in anticipation and hope, he moved resolutely into the night.

It was time. Adam could feel the energy of the moon calling to him. Changing him. Throwing his clothes off, he felt the first few tingling ripples under his skin. Opening himself, he welcomed the transformation, reveling in the sensation that would change him in a bright flash, from man—to wolf. His last thoughts in human form centered on how much he loved this life, but how he yearned for

someone special to share it with him. He could only hope
that the old stories were true, that you felt as if you
couldn't live without your mate one minute longer that
when it was you found them.

A large gray wolf moved out of the shadows shortly
after a brilliant burst of light. The early wars to grant
rights to all races, not just the dominant human race,
allowed him the freedom and relative safety to roam in his
second form. It had been more than a century since either
lycanthropic or the Others had to hide. The Lupine Act
two decades ago had given his kind the added benefit of
being legally allowed to hunt for their mate.

His mate had to be warm-blooded. She could be Were,
human, or one of the Others. In the sub species of Others
there were many that were warm-blooded, Faerie and
Sprites to name two. Vampires were cold-blooded. His
mate had to be genetically capable of having live young.
He knew of no Were that had ever mated with a
Vampire—the genetic codes never matched. Of course,
there were many additional sub species that were
compatible, and he wouldn't care what species his mate
was, just that she was his. He hadn't really kept up on the
science of Cryptozoology, the study, uncovering and
classification of hidden animals.

All Were-creatures and vamps had been among the
first studied in this field several hundred years ago. He
knew they were working on the classification of Big Foot
now. When it was proven that any man-like animals
existed, had the capacity of speech and the ability to
reason, verified that they could be good or inherently evil
just like their human counterparts, then they would be
given the rights and protections won during the early wars
as a sub species of man. So humans would be forced to

stop killing them for sport or putting them in cages. They would have to accept them. As neighbor, and mate.

Unfortunately that didn't stop the Ku Klux Klan mentality of groups like the 'One Racers', humans who felt that any sub species should be staked or kept in a zoo, and definitely not allowed to associate or procreate with one of pure human blood. Never mind that over the centuries it was difficult to find a family tree that hadn't intermingled their blood in one form or another with either Were or Vampire.

In human form, Adam had these thoughts. In wolf form, he concentrated on one thing—following the scent of his mate.

And this Lupine Moon that scent was strong.

Chapter 3

The glide's motion came to a gentle stop. Eve nervously stepped into her garage after the door shut behind the glide.

Doors wouldn't stop them.

She chastised herself again for not realizing three days ago that it was time to lock herself in her private lab. *Private airtight lab*, she reminded herself. Idiot!

The One Racers had discovered many years ago that it took three days for human pheromones to disperse enough that a genetic trace was impossible for the werewolves to follow. In their zeal to keep their bloodlines pure, they locked their sexually mature sons and daughters up tightly before each and every full moon. There was no law against locking yourself up, just one that if you were caught — you had to honor the mating.

While Eve disagreed with their politics to rid the world of all sub-humans, she heartily thanked their research. It had allowed her to maintain the ideal of strict independence. She did not need or want a mate in her life. Look what it had done to her mother.

After Eve's full-human father had died, Naomi had been a wonderful single mother to her sister, Jezi, and herself. She had also managed in three short years to become one of the world's leading Cryptozoologists. She had found, researched and documented the existence of several hidden species; the most notable was the Loch

Ness Monster. Nessie turned out to be a large, lovable, vegetarian serpent that was 50 feet in length at maturity.

Then "short and hairy" Maxwell, her stepfather, had marked her mother as his mate. In short order Maxwell had forbidden Naomi any outside work. They'd had Jonaa, her stepbrother, and her mother had given up the fight with Maxwell to retain her scientific position and had instead become Domestic Goddess extraordinaire. Ugh!!! That was definitely not for Eve.

Eve stripped the clothes off her tired body in the bathroom and opted for a quick air shower. Normally she enjoyed the ancient ritual of water bathing, but it would only irritate her tonight. She wanted to pace and watch the minutes until daylight.

Clean and feeling suitably armored in her old sweat suit, she downed energy pills instead of food. Another favored ritual she would forgo tonight. All Eve wanted was for the night to be over, and to be blissfully free from any man. Or wolf.

The windows and doors of her 100-year-old home were first rate, effective at keeping out the street noise. Everything was quiet. Normally she loved her little house; tonight she'd have felt safer in a compact. One of those high-rise apartment-slash-shopping-slash-entertainment complexes that were hives of activity…and smells.

Oh, hell. Eve's breath caught in her throat. Was that something scratching at her front door? She strained her ears and fought for some semblance of control. Surely she was imagining a sound?

This is stupid, she told herself. She forced her body to move towards the view panel. It was voice-activated and she could command a 360-degree view of the outside of her home. "House front," she managed to croak out.

At first she thought it was her mind playing tricks. A large, gray wolf was sitting patiently on her front step — looking directly into the monitor with flashing silver eyes. She ducked. Oh, my God! She needed to hide. Her mind desperately searched for an escape route.

"Oh, now that was just ridiculous." *It can't see me*, she thought. She could run. Where?

Closing her eyes, she frantically worked to calm her mind enough to review everything she knew about the Werewolf. She might be able to delay mating. Move out of town, out of state. But, if he'd truly scented her, and there was no doubt he had, he wouldn't be sitting on her doorstep...

No matter where she ran or how far, he'd find her. Wolves mated for life. And as dear old grandfather had proved beyond a shadow of a doubt, they had one genetic buddy. The law and God were on the wolf's side.

Eve had never been a coward. Well, not really. She didn't consider bolting herself into an airtight room 36 days a year, cowardice. It had been lifestyle survival, her own brand of manifest destiny...destiny that appeared to be shot to hell with the appearance of the large lupine on her front porch. She was royally pissed off about this. She didn't need or want some alpha male in her life. Her heart slammed in her chest and her nostrils flared in anger.

The only question now was did she let him sit there, wait to see if he'd break the gorgeous 22nd century antique steel door down in his hurry to make his claim? Or maybe he'd wait there for days until she needed to leave for supplies or her own sanity? Or did she open the door and begin to make his life miserable?

No way was she going to make this easy on him! Eve Longtree had no Domestic Goddess hidden within. The big bad wolf was going to have a fight on his hands. She was not her mother!

Okay, it was decided. Sniveling coward—not in this life. Take no prisoners, Red Riding Hood—yes. She just wished she had the man from the story with the ax.

Striding determinedly to the door, Eve unlocked it and swung it open. She swore the damned wolf grinned at her.

"My, what big teeth you have..." she muttered under her breath.

Chapter 4

Eve slammed the door behind the wolf. He turned to look at her with what appeared to be a patient gaze. She glared at him. She didn't want patience. She knew he could understand both her body language and anything she said to him. Living with her stepfather and brother had taught her that. He would remember everything she said to him tomorrow.

Well, she wouldn't waste time…

The wolf listened to his mate, watched her as she paced and ranted. She didn't want a husband, lupine or otherwise. He got that from the first few sentences. He also got the point that she thought he wanted nothing from her but a house slave and a warm, breeding body. Well, they'd get to that. He couldn't talk back in this form, reassure or fight her out of this mood. He would just have to be patient.

Hours later, she finally wound down enough to sit in one place for at least a moment. He had wandered around the comfortably decorated living area, wallowing in her scent while she raved. He had decided that he couldn't just jump her and clamp his teeth on her shoulder to mark her, as the wolf wanted him to do.

It could be gently done. The mark didn't have to be forced or brutal. He only needed to break the skin and mingle her blood with his saliva to ensure their joining and make it impossible for her to denounce him. But for his own sanity and territorial needs it would have to be done tonight. After waiting this long there was no way he could postpone the claiming. His eager body painfully tightened at the thought.

She settled on the white nuleather couch. Perfect. The sofa was situated with the back to the entrance hall, facing what had once been a fireplace. Years ago the office of Airquality had banned the use of the smog-causing instruments. Now, in his mate's home it served as a decorative display of candles and antique woven baskets.

Her shoulders were above the back of the couch. It would be easy to let her rest, then casually stroll behind, quickly moving up to graze his teeth across her shoulder. The shirt fabric wouldn't stop him. All that was required was her blood and his saliva mixed even minutely.

Eve was so tired. The adrenaline from the fear, anger and resentment that had fueled her ranting had passed. She just wanted to sit on the couch and doze off. She had been afraid he would pounce on her immediately, dragging her to the floor to sink his teeth in her shoulder. He hadn't. He watched her and moved around the room she was in, not letting her out of his sight to explore any other room, but he'd left her to her lecture. Now what? She just knew she wouldn't be able to keep her eyes open much longer. And it was still hours to sunrise.

She watched woodenly as the wolf moved around the room. Sniffing here, wallowing there. Yeah. She was well and truly scented. He walked around the couch and she turned to follow his movement over her left shoulder.

She had to admit he was a gorgeous specimen for a werewolf. His thick gray coat had black highlights with an almost white strip going from between his eyes, over his head and stopping about midway down his back. She idly wondered if that meant he had gray in his hair when he was in human shape.

He was huge. Almost twice the size of any werewolf she'd seen. He had to be a very large man. Well, she was about 5'8" herself. No shrinking violet here. Err...*what was he doing?*

Adam paused behind the couch, and then rose up to rest his front paws on the back. He did it slowly, carefully. He didn't want to scare her away. That would force him to wait, possibly, until she was asleep before he claimed her.

He wanted her awake so that she would experience the binding and there would be no question from her later that she was his.

Eve knew what the wolf was doing. Her mother hadn't raised an idiot. He had waited for her to sit, so that he didn't need to knock her to the ground. How chivalrous! She knew she could move, delay it for another hour or so until she fell into complete exhaustion, or he decided not to be patient. Why bother? She'd rather be awake for this, there was no way she'd let him put those teeth to her throat while she was sleeping.

"Might as well do it right the first time," she grumbled. She did not want her favorite comfort shirt ruined.

Turning her head forward, she raised her hands up to the sweatshirt's neck. She stretched it out and pulled it off her right shoulder, and then in seeming indifference she cocked her head to the left side. This exposed the area on her right side from neck to mid shoulder to his teeth.

As she did it, her mind flashed to the current lupine fashion craze and she wrinkled her nose. Shirts and dresses with cutouts to either show off mating marks or bare the area for marking. Some even came with fancy writing that said "bite me". She swore right then that she'd deck the first person that bought her one.

Adam could not believe after everything she'd said, that she was making this easy for him. Knowing that he would not understand this woman anytime soon, he internally shrugged and bent to take what was offered to him. The reason didn't matter.

Very carefully he opened his jaws and spread them over his mate's shoulder. A few inches away from her neck he rested his teeth on her sensitive flesh. He felt her shudder.

Gently he bit down, breaking the skin enough that she bled; he then drew his teeth in a scraping motion as he closed his mouth. His saliva mingled with her blood, and she was marked forever.

His. She was his, now and forever. The relief and overwhelming sense of rightness washed over him. It was such an incredible feeling to know he had found his mate. Those feelings immediately turned to lust.

Eve closed her eyes. She'd felt the hot breath of the wolf at her neck. Felt his teeth press together on her skin and the piercing sensation when he'd drawn blood. She'd been somewhat prepared for that. What she hadn't been prepared for was the way she'd felt. She was hot, sensitive, turned on, and her body was telling her it had craved this claiming her entire life. She felt as if a shimmering cord had been stretched between her body and the wolf's. The binding.

Well, she was more than just her body. Shaking herself out of the haze she'd fallen into, she stood up, pointedly ignoring the wolf that kept pace at her side, and went to the kitchen to run water over a clean rag.

It was done. Their genetic codes had been joined and Eve refused to give in to feeling sorry for her self or anger at the world in general. Nothing could be done about it now. She was tired and knew she would need to be rested for the morning. She had a few more things she wanted to say to him and she needed some rest if she was going to make any sense at all. Nothing more could happen while he was in wolf form and he wouldn't change until daylight. She was getting some sleep.

Eve wrung out the cool cloth and set it on her bleeding shoulder. She was going to ignore what would happen when he shape-shifted. She didn't even know what he looked like. Tomorrow was soon enough to worry about the rest.

Chapter 5

Adam had stretched out on the floor beside the couch and his sleeping mate sometime during the night. He woke as he changed. Every nerve ending screamed at him to posses her now; he glanced down at his naked body as he moved gracefully to his feet. He was certainly ready. He was anxious to view his mate through human eyes. The wolf saw things in black and white with strangely distorted vision. He knew she was tall, with short, wild hair that had appeared to be black. More than that he couldn't tell, but he would be able to find her in a room filled with hundreds of people, just from her unique fragrance.

He turned to glance down at her and quietly sighed. She was lovely. He'd been right about the hair, it was black. The silken gleam of polished black opals, it tempted him to bury his hands in it and never let go. Her facial structure was strong, yet feminine. Her eyes were closed of course. He wanted them to stay that way. Once she was awake, they would have to talk.

Her body structure was hard to distinguish in the oversized sweat suit she was wearing. But he would bet on soft curves. She didn't move like a muscled athlete and he remembered her saying something last night of refusing to give up her genetic research. She was a scientist. Developing the mind would come before developing the body. He could help her balance both. Right now it was her body he craved.

How to go about this? If she woke up before she was caught in passion, she would try and stop him. And he wouldn't be able to stop. His body burned and throbbed with insistence, he needed to possess her. His cock jumped with a life of its own, aching and straining to bring attention to its requirements. He wasn't about to disappoint it. If he carried her to bed, where he would prefer to love her, she would wake. So it had to be the couch or the floor once they'd started.

He knew that her body would be perfectly tuned to his; her arousal would come hard and fast this first time, in perfect concert with his own and heightened by the binding. The muscles in his neck corded with anticipation. Throwing his head back he closed his eyes for a second and clenched his jaw. He needed some control or it would be over the minute he slipped into her. His cock hardened even further at this thought. Dropping to his knees on the floor, he bent his mouth to the skin at her neck.

* * * * *

Eve sighed in her sleep. She was having the most wonderful dream. Never had she been touched like this, never could she remember being so hungry for a lover's touch. And her dream lover was fantastic. His lips and tongue seemed to taste every inch of her, his hands gently moving to caress her breasts, teasing them as he licked a path down her naked stomach. She felt as if she was burning inside. Moisture collected on her upper lip, she moaned and moved to provide better access to those hands, that mouth. She shuddered. Oh, God. How could a dream feel like this?

She swore she could feel wetness as the tongue laved her navel, she could feel the pressure so acutely on her nipples as the dream fingers plucked them, sending heat straight to her core. She moved again, her hips desperately shifting to allow her clothing to be stripped off her body and to entice her dream lover to pay attention where it was so urgently needed.

She was boldly picked up and laid out on a hard surface, one that didn't restrict her legs from being spread wide. Shocked with the movement, her eyes flew open. Only to see a man's head descend, flashing silver eyes meeting hers as his tongue flicked out to torment her clit. She moaned and shifted her knees even wider apart to give him unrestricted access to the pulsating nub that demanded her submission. Her mind was screaming at her to stop.

Her body told it to shut up.

She watched between lowered eyelids as the man put one hand under her hips and pulled her to him, while he used the other hand to separate her labia, exposing her swollen nubbin to the rasp of his tongue. He created his own rhythm, forcing her body to respond first to the long licks across her clitoris and then to the rigid tongue thrusting deep into her wet vagina.

She came quickly on a loud scream, and just as fast found that he would give her no mercy. He continued to suckle and probe, adding the torment of his fingers pushing deep within her.

He finally stopped when she was delirious with the pleasure. Setting her hips gently to the floor he moved over her, nudging her cunt with the hot, velvet tip of his erection. She opened her eyes and her body to a man she'd never seen before, a man she'd not spoken one word with. Moaning, she greedily took him in.

Eve's eager body welcomed his cock, as her mind vaguely noticed that the gorgeous dark haired, silver-eyed man did have a little gray mixed in his hair. It was the last coherent thought she managed.

She felt every unyielding inch of him as he pushed into her. And there seemed to be a lot of inches. God that felt good. He stopped. "No," she groaned. "Don't stop, please…"

"Look at me, my mate," he demanded.

Eve raised her eyes to his, looked at the intensity and the fire. Her inner muscles clamped tightly around him. He hissed, his face contorted in ecstasy. She could see him struggle for control. Well good. She didn't think she wanted him in control.

He rocked urgently inside her, then stilled again. "I am Adam. And I claim you for my own."

She couldn't suppress either the shudder that went through her at his movement, nor her giggle at his pronouncement. Adam. That was too much. She panted. "Well Adam, I'm Eve." Then she struggled to move under him, to entice him to finish what he'd started.

Adam shook his head, he didn't know if his mate was joking or not. But right now it didn't matter. Her frantic movements beneath him had destroyed all thought of drawing this out. Bad timing for introductions anyway, the only thing that was important right now was plunging his engorged cock deep and often into her hot cunt.

She scalded him with her juices. Tight. Damn, he wanted this to go on forever.

Eve's body contorted with the sensations. She was one raw nerve. One minute she was screaming at him not to stop, the next she was pleading for mercy. "I

187

can't...ohmygod. Don't stop," she whimpered. She knew he had erupted within her at least twice. She'd felt the explosions deep inside. He would pause, take a few deep breaths, and immediately grow rigid within her again. And it would start all over. She had lost track of her own orgasms. Lost any ability to think or count long ago. And it was starting again. "Noooo," she wailed.

He moved rhythmically within her, first grinding from side to side, never taking his hips from her, and then pulling back, almost leaving her. Clenching his jaw, he moaned low in his throat when she cried out in anguish at the loss. "I won't leave you, my pet. Never leave you," he gritted. He forced the words from deep within, it was almost beyond his ability to think.

Sweat was pouring from him; he felt his eyes roll back. "So good!" he cried. He was animalistic in his needs; he fought the urge of his beast to race to the end and started teasing her, rubbing the tip of his cock out and over the sensitive flesh of her clit until she was begging him to fuck her. Then he positioned his penis at her entrance, allowing it to slip in just an inch, and then back out, over and over again. At the same time he used his fingers to pull at her breasts. It wasn't enough.

Again she pleaded with him, crying and promising him anything if he would just finish it. "I can't take anymore, please...oh, please, no more!" Eve begged, beating her fists against his chest. She wanted him to *move*.

And then it was heaven. He slammed into her, pounding her with his body and his thick cock until her inner muscles repeatedly convulsed around him. She whimpered, "Yes!" and her soul exploded into a million scattered pieces that would never form the same pattern again.

Chapter 6

Eve slowly woke, her mind sluggishly processing her body's signals. She was warm—snuggly warm. Her body pleasantly ached in places she'd forgotten could have feeling. A hand was cupping her breast. Eve frowned.

She opened her eyes and glanced down at the hand that was cradling her left breast. Her first irreverent thought was that it would take more than her 36 C's to fill that hand.

The fingers were long and the palm large. The forearm attached to the hand was tanned, muscular and lightly covered with fine dark hair. Before her mind had a chance to wake enough to send off fight-or-flight signals, she had a sudden memory of the night before and that hand and the body it was attached to moving over her much lighter skin. The recollection caused her stomach to clench with arousal. Her nipples tightened at the remembered pleasure and her back bowed, the movement pushing the globes of her ass against the obviously aroused male body at her back.

The fingers at her breast slowly closed over her swollen nipple. When they pinched and pulled on her, a lightning bolt of sensation shot to her core. Eve moaned and tried to turn towards the man sharing her bed. Her mate. She had only a vague idea of what he looked like and she wanted to see his face, but it was obvious her body had no qualms repeating last night's performance with this stranger.

Adam knew the time of confrontation was coming. He also realized that with his body's current state no conversation would make any sense to him. He would never be able to convince her that he wanted her for more than a warm body. The scent of her arousal would keep his brain solidly between his legs.

With ease he kept her from turning towards him, and gently pushed her onto her stomach. His beast rumbled just under his skin. Yes! For a short moment he lay over her, reveling in the soft cradle her buttocks made for him.

But he wanted in. Shifting behind her, he sat up with his knees spread on either side of her legs. Quickly he moved her again, pulling her hips up and back until she was forced to brace her upper body on her forearms. He was focused on one thing, panting with need. There could be nothing but this for him now.

Eve sighed and tried unsuccessfully to look over her shoulder to see the man that had claimed her body. When she could find an active brain cell she would worry about the lack of control she seemed to have, but not now.

Now she was on her knees, her hips high in the air with her head cradled in her arms, her body begging for what she knew was coming. Breathlessly she waited as his warm palm skimmed down her back, gliding over her butt. She hissed as his fingers dipped into her wetness, moaning as he spread the slick moisture over her sex — preparing her.

"Please?" Eve cried.

Adam moved behind her, setting the weeping tip of his erection at her entrance. He nudged her, barely inserting the sensitized head into her opening. The feel of her was exquisite, all heat and slippery warmth. He placed one hand beside her head to brace his body, and moved the other hand to reach around and play with her nipple. Slowly he bent to nuzzle her neck, reaching out to lick the mark he'd created on her shoulder. His mark. The growl that forced its way from deep within was the call of wolf — to mate. And a warning to any that might hear. In that instant the full meaning of this incredible sex hit him. His body clenched in possession, his heart and mind cheered.

She was his. He was mated!

Eve's entire body wildly contracted as Adam ran his tongue over the mating marks and then let out a fearsome growl. She wasn't afraid; somehow she instinctively knew that this sound was linked to his possession of her. She had heard the gossip that said a werewolf could bring his mate to orgasm just by licking the symbols. She now knew it was a fact.

As her body convulsed, Adam drove into her. He had thought to keep the loving slow and maddening. But the emotion in this joining rushed through him and the unrestrained reaction of his mate unleashed the raving beast within.

"Mine," he growled as he moved forcefully, pushing back and forth into his mate. *Finally mine*, he thought with relief.

Eve had thought that the dream sex this early morning had been the best there could ever be. She'd been wrong. Her body shuddered and trembled beneath the Were-male. She climbed one extreme pinnacle after another, with little time between to make a distinction between the orgasms. The smallest sensation — the brush of the bed sheets against her overly responsive nipples, sent her body into ever increasing spasms. The hard thrusts of Adam's cock into her eager pussy sent her into madness.

"I can't," she panted, begging him to finish. "I *really* can't take this," she sobbed.

Adam's body had come to the same conclusion. Enough. With one thrust he came with a geyser of sperm, filling his mate with his seed. Gasping he collapsed next to her, reaching out to pull her to his side as they both struggled for breath.

Chapter 7

Eve fought to bring her thoughts into some semblance of order. She hadn't wanted a man in her life. But good lord the sex! What had she been doing without this all her life? No wonder her mother had caved. That thought quickly sobered her. No matter how awesome the sex, she reminded herself, she was *not* her mother.

Eve pulled out of Adam's embrace. Keeping her back to him she slid from the bed and walked to the closet. Frowning, she wondered how and when they'd made it to her room this morning; the last thing she remembered was being on the floor of the living room.

Mentally shrugging, she figured that was the least of her worries. Quickly she reached in the closet and snagged the least reveling of her robes, the antique blue terry cloth her sister had given her last Christmas. It had a large flamingo embroidered on the right shoulder.

Eve had a serious weakness for kitschy clothes and collectibles from the twenty and twenty-first century. Her absolute favorite was anything with pink flamingos. The birds were extinct now, and Eve loved the whimsical creatures. Or maybe she identified with them because she always felt as if she were balancing on one leg?

Nervously she smoothed the gaudy bird; she was procrastinating, putting off confronting the man who could make her life a living hell. She forcefully reminded herself that she had intended the reverse when she opened the door to the wolf last night.

Turning, she took her first clear-headed look at the man lying sprawled naked in her bed. Taking a deep breath she started her examination at the top.

He had dark, sable hair with a sprinkling of gray. It was thick and slightly curly, disheveled and unfashionably long, reaching halfway down his neck. His face was Roman perfect, with dark eyebrows and lashes, a regal nose and stubborn chin. His eyes flashed silver heat. That should be impossible. He was tall and muscular. His skin was tanned and dusted in soft dark hair that trailed down his broad chest, thinning out across his tight stomach and then dense again just below his navel. Nested in the dark curls was a thick, growing penis. Sucking in her breath, Eve whirled around.

"Cover yourself, please," she said with as much force as she could muster.

"I am not cold," he replied with a teasing lilt.

Eve shook her head. "You know that's not the point. Your manhood seems to have a life of its own. I refuse to have a conversation with you naked. And we *are* going to have a conversation." *A long one*, she thought to herself.

"Okay, my *manhood* is covered," he assured her with emphasis, turning his head to hide his amusement at her choice of words.

Eve refused to rise to his bait. Turning back to him, she moved to sit primly in the antique rattan chair that was several paces from the bottom of the bed. No way was she getting close to him. Even covered with a sheet and severe morning hair the man's sex appeal was overwhelming.

"We need to talk," she sputtered.

Adam winced. He was sure there weren't any other words in the world that would strike fear into a man of any species as quickly as those four. A man *never* said them. He had no choice but to go on the offensive.

"Is your name really Eve?"

She looked at him with a touch of humor. "Yes. Is your name really *Adam*?"

He groaned. "Yes. You know, of course, this means we will be the butt of many Biblical jokes?"

"Not in my family," she grumbled.

Adam cocked an eyebrow at her, the question obvious.

Eve sighed and shook her head; this was not what she wanted to talk about. But she supposed she could start with it. "My mother's name is Naomi, my natural father was Abel. They named me Eve, my sister Jezebel, Jezi for short. My stepfather is Matthew, my stepbrother Jonaa. Jonaa with two a's no h, but Jonaa just the same. My sister's husband's name is Luke." Pausing, she looked to make sure he was sufficiently awed. "To my family, it will make perfect sense that your name is Adam."

"Your parents actually named your sister Jezebel?" He was floored. What parent would do that to a child?

"No one has ever called her anything but Jezi. I will warn you not to make that mistake. She has a way of getting even." Eve grinned. Her sister took great satisfaction in making people pay who either slipped or unknowingly used her full name. They never made the same mistake twice. But they almost always made it once, thinking to tease the diminutive redhead and that her response couldn't be that drastic. Eve looked forward to

Adam testing her sister. She somehow knew her warning would be purposely ignored.

Inwardly she smiled — the last person to call her sister Jezebel, had gotten into his airglide, only to realize that it had somehow been programmed to go to Eastern Europe instead of his office. The glide had headed out to sea, without enough electrical power to see it over the ocean. Thankfully Jezi had also programmed a distress signal that kicked in as soon as it was over water. The man had been fished out of his glide, with full realization of what had happened. Jezi's programmed laugh at point of impact had insured he knew full well who was responsible. The fact that she'd later married him was secondary.

Pulling her thoughts back to the man on her bed, Eve looked at him questioningly. Tentatively she started, "I know your first name is Adam and that you are loupe-garou. But that is all I know about you. What is your last name and what do you do for a living?"

"My last name is Greyclan and I do whatever is needed for my people. What is your last name Eve?"

She frowned. What did "whatever is needed" mean? She hoped he actually did something to make credits. There was no way she would support him. She wanted to work, but not to be the full support for a family. That thought had all color leaching from her face. *No birth control...*

She jumped up, practically screaming at him. "Have you had your shots?"

Adam looked confused. "Calm down, what are you talking about, Eve?"

"Your shots...birth control...please say you didn't go out looking for a mate during Lupine Moon without taking some kind of precaution?" she stammered, looking anxiously at him.

Adam wanted to laugh. The look of panic on his new wife's face was priceless. He *had* taken a BC shot, not wanting to take the chance that if he found his mate she'd become pregnant the first time they mated. He needed time with her, without the hormonal hell that a lycanthropic pregnancy would put her through. But he wasn't willing to admit it to her immediately. "Don't you want children, Eve?"

"No! Yes! I mean no I don't want them right now before I even know who you are or if you'll make a good father, but yes... I suppose... someday..." she trailed off.

Adam took pity on her; she looked miserable as she considered the ramifications of the multiple orgasms they'd shared. His cock twitched. *No, better to stay away from thoughts of orgasms*, he told himself. "I have taken the shot, Eve," he reassured her.

Adam looked at her. Brows drawn together he asked, "Now, my turn for a moment to ask you questions. Thanks to your monologue last night, I know considerably more about you; however some of it is confusing and lacking sense." He paused for a moment.

Eve scowled, "What do you mean it lacked sense? I made perfect sense!"

Adam laughed and settled back on the bed with his arms crossed over his chest, "Eve, I know your stepfather is Were, and you resent him for keeping your mother from following her career. I also understand that you are a geneticist who is working on a special project and you seem to be under the misapprehension that I will force you to quit. Probably because you believe your mother suffered the same fate from her mate. Correct?"

Eve nodded, "Yes, you are right." She was a little bemused that he'd heard not only the words but also the feelings behind them.

He continued, "You have very strange decorative taste. I must have counted six of those bird things downstairs that you are wearing on your shoulder. One was a lamp, three were long stick things stuck in various plants, and several were small glass figures. You have two pieces of artwork that say 'Share a Coke and a smile'. Now for the questions…" Adam paused and looked at her with confusion clear on his face. "What is your last name, what project are you working on, what is the bird you seem to be so fond of, and what," he growled, "is a Coke?"

Eve blinked. He had not only listened, he had heard her. He said she suffered from the misapprehension that he would force her to quit. Misapprehension…meaning misunderstanding, false impression, and delusion…any way you looked at it he was promising her she wouldn't have to stop working. Wasn't he?

"Are you saying you wouldn't make me give up my career to stay home and take care of you? I want to make sure I understand what you just said, implicitly. No mistakes. This is very important to me." She held her breath.

Adam could see how important this was to her. She was holding her body completely motionless. Tense. Slowly he rose from the bed and moved to bend in front of her. He had wrapped the sheet around his middle as he moved. Not wanting to make this all-important declaration "buck nikid" as his great, great grandmother would say.

Kneeling before her, he pulled Eve's clenched hands into his own. "I promise you, Eve, I will never force you to give up your life's work," he pledged.

"Blood Oath?" she questioned, knowing that if a werewolf swore blood oath that it was a legal contract.

Adam shook his head. Sighing, he answered her. "If you had known me for any length of time, you would have known that Blood Oath was not necessary. My word is good. I will try not to be offended that you have asked this of me. But, I will give it."

Eve watched intently as Adam put the pad of his right thumb in his mouth, allowed the beast to rise within him just enough so that the canines formed, and used the razor sharp teeth to bite down and pierce the skin. When blood welled, he took the finger out of his mouth, banished the wolf and pressed the thumb into the palm of Eve's hand.

"I swear by Blood Oath not to force you to quit working as a geneticist nor will I interfere with your work in any way," he vowed, sealing the promise in blood.

Later, unbeknownst to him, he would regret this promise, but for now the reward was sweet. Questions temporarily forgotten, Adam allowed Eve to jump him, drive him to the floor and have her way with his body.

Chapter 8

Eve's relief at Adam's reassurance that she could continue her life's work without fighting him tooth and nail for it, and the gift of Blood Oath freely given, combined with the rampaging lust she'd been trying to control almost since she had risen from the bed. Chastising herself, she acknowledged that she had managed to command her body's reaction…for all of about half an hour.

She moved out of the chair in a rush, into Adam's arms, knocking him to the floor. When he tried to take over, she snarled at him. "My turn. Lay back and relax."

He did as he was told. Stretching his arms over his head and helpfully lifting his hips as Eve peeled the sheet from his body, he was anxious to allow her this, desperate in fact. He sucked in his breath as she knelt beside him, still dressed in that God-awful robe. He had been right about her softly rounded curves, and figured that he would get the chance to sample them soon; the scent of her arousal was strong. But for now, he would let her have the upper hand.

Eve couldn't wait to get her hands on all that lovely flesh. She had been a submissive participant in their lovemaking up to this point. Only capable of holding on for the ride, now she wanted to direct their play. She decided she would start at the top. Her fingers sifted through the wild mane of his hair, she let her fingernails scrape over his scalp.

Adam closed his eyes and purred. He moaned, "Ah, Eve, that feels wonderful."

She wickedly grinned and after a few minutes moved her hands down to his face, skimming each feature, mischievously tracing each and every detail. He moved into her touch. Eve bent over him to trace the line of his lips with her tongue, gently slipping into a deep kiss when he opened to her.

"Ummm…" Now it was her turn to moan. Eve's hands continued their journey, testing muscles here with a squeeze, teasing shudders from his body there with a feather-light caress. She frustrated his efforts to slip the thick robe from her body. Naked she would be lost. "Not yet," she murmured.

Moving away from the seductive pleasure of his mouth, she continued to explore the hard body before her. Smoothing her palms over his flat nipples, she tormented them into tight peaks. Other parts of his body came to attention as well.

Adam moaned and shifted his hips on the floor. His first instinct was to pick her up and impale her tight body on his wildly straining shaft. Her hands were driving him crazy. *Patience*, he ordered his body. His hips jumped when she lowered her mouth to his chest to further torment his nipples. Her hot, wet tongue circled one areola while her fingers plucked and pulled on the other. When she took him in her teeth and bit, the electric heat shot to his cock, his hand moved to hold her to him.

"Hands off or I stop," she demanded.

He hesitated. He could take over now, but he was enjoying it too much to give in to his beast. He lowered his hands. As she moved her head to trail her tongue in a wet glide to his navel, he clenched them into fists. His pelvis rolled in and out, the movement mimicked the fucking he wanted to give her. He pushed his fists into the floor. *He would not grab her. He could do this.*

Eve used her tongue and teeth to play with the crease where leg met body, alternately nipping, and then laving the area from hip to groin. She could become addicted to the smell and taste of his skin. She smiled as Adam groaned and moved uncontrollably. His sharply indrawn breath as she circled his jutting cock with her hand brought a wide grin of satisfaction. Sitting back to use both hands — he was so thick she couldn't get her fingers to touch with one — she concentrated solely on driving him to madness.

She was so intent on the feel of him in her hands, the velvet shaft with a glistening dark plum at the tip that oozed silk every time she got near its tip, that she didn't feel Adam part the robe she was wearing. She only felt the rasp of his fingers as he drew them across her. She was sitting cross-legged, so he had unrestricted access to her swollen wet clit. At his first touch she couldn't shift away. But paybacks were a bitch.

Eve sucked in her breath and bent to lick across the slit at the opening of Adam's cock. He went completely still. Humming, she set to distract him from his own play. She wanted the upper hand, but she didn't have the strength to move from his questing fingers, so she planned on diverting his attention. Opening her mouth over him, she took him in as far as she could. One hand stroked his staff in tune with her mouth, the other reached to squeeze his balls. She was rewarded by his deepening moans and frantic thrusts.

She was making him insane. Adam lost all reason with the first hot lick across the slit of his cock. The heated demand of Eve's mouth moving over him, taking him in and combined with the circling pressure of her hand sliding up and down forced every cell in his body to come to attention. When she added the pressure on the family jewels, he had to grit his teeth to keep from spewing like a teenager. Damn she felt good!

That thought brought him back to the wet heat drenching his fingers. If he concentrated on her, maybe he would have some control over his own body. Adam shifted slowly, careful not to dislodge Eve. He twisted his body to maneuver his head between her crossed legs. Having parted the robe and pushed it out of his way, he could just lean down and reach her inflamed clit. He moved his arm around her hips, pulling her up and into his mouth.

Eve groaned, vibrating the cock in her mouth, setting off Adam's growl, which in turn vibrated her to the core. Eve struggled to move her legs, wanting to allow Adam unobstructed access, and found herself flat on her back before she could blink.

"No more," he ground out as he used one hand to fit himself to her clenching channel, the other hand to move her right leg over his shoulder. He determinedly pressed into her, and moved her other leg into a similar position over his other shoulder. This position left her open and vulnerable to his assault. She couldn't control in any way the pace or depth of his strokes.

Eve waited for Adam to slam into her. She wanted this. Fast and hard. She needed it. *"Now."*

Her hoarse demand had a calming effect on Adam. Instead of pummeling her like she wanted, he moved slowly into her, and then drew back, almost leaving her.

She sobbed. "No!"

Adam's jaw clenched and he growled low in his throat. He then set about driving his new mate and himself to the edge of insanity. For long minutes he went in an inch, then out, moving fast but with no depth, keeping them both on the knife's edge of desire with no possible satisfaction. The constant sensation of barely breaching her, the tight pull over his pulsing crown, had him biting his lip to keep from giving in to the urge to bury his cock hilt-deep. One glance at Eve kept him at it.

She was sweating. Panting and thrashing her head from side to side, mumbling nonsense, "Yes, don't stop, don'tstopdon'tstopmore!" He was hitting all the nerves, except for the one that would release her from this frantic torture. She tried to force her hips up to meet his thrusts, praying for more than the scant inch he was giving her. She tried to move her hand up to rub her straining clit herself, but he wouldn't allow it.

"No. *Mine*," he growled.

He did allow her to cup her own breasts, pluck and pull and twist and pinch her nipples. That only added to her torment. She could feel her pussy trying to latch on to him, to pull him further into her, the frantic pulse increasing her frenzy. Wildly she reached out to him, her hands sliding down his sweat-slicked chest. Just by chance one of her fingernails managed to scrape one of his nipples. He faltered, sinking a little deeper.

The movement wasn't missed by Eve. "*Yesss*," she hissed. Both hands now went to his chest to find the nubs that might help end this torment. Finding them already hard and easy to latch on to, she rhythmically plucked one then the other.

Her fingers drove all restraint from him. He had reached the end of his control. Pulling her legs from his shoulders he spread them wide and maneuvered his body for additional leverage. Groaning, cursing, "Damn, you are so tight!" he ground his pubic bone hard against the swollen nubbin of her sex, touching her womb with his expanded cock, forcing her to splinter and contract around him. Her inner muscles milked him and he erupted, unable to do more than collapse on top of her.

Chapter 9

At some point during the night, Adam had moved them both to the bed. He lay there now, thinking of his family and the impact Eve would have on them. He smiled. They would love her. After all, she was his mate.

A communication link beeped somewhere downstairs. After glancing at his still sleeping wife, he moved carefully from the bed. They had been holed up in her home for almost two full days. They needed to eat, and it was possible someone in Eve's world needed her. It could be a family problem, or someone from work. Adam could at least screen the call for her and give her a chance for a little more rest. After he took the call he would see what he could make for her to eat.

Since Adam had come to Eve's home in Lupine form, he had no clothes. He would have to call someone to bring him something before they could leave the house. In the meantime, he had noted his mate's preference for baggy sweats. He found a cut-off pair and threw them on. On him they were tight and extremely ridiculous; he had to shift his nuts several times before he didn't feel like he was being emasculated. It wouldn't be a pretty picture if someone were to see him dressed like this. The only thing worse would be to be seen naked by one of Eve's relatives or friends. He wouldn't care, but he knew most humans or non Others had a thing about nudity.

He found the videolink just before the last ring. Not bothering to request audio only he snapped, "Answer." A male face looked at him in shock.

"Oh, holy hell! She is going to be impossible to live with after this." The man on the screen fluttered...there was no other word for it. "Do you have her chained to the bed, ummm, that thought is just too vile. I'd rather imagine you chained to the bed. Has she finished ranting and throwing things yet? The good news is that most of the stuff she can throw is that disgusting kitschy 1990's crap she collects. I mean, really, that stuff was called trailer trash back then. Whoever heard of collecting dashboard hula girls and one-legged plastic birds?" The man paused to catch his breath.

The advantage of this diatribe was that Adam had been able to figure out that whoever this was, he knew his mate well, he wasn't heterosexual, and that he also knew that Adam had been intimate with her. "Who are you and what do you want?" he asked grumpily. The man was getting on his one good nerve.

"Eve. I need to talk to Eve Longtree. I'm Charles, her assistant and it's important I speak with her immediately. Probably vital to her safety," he added before glaring at Adam. "I don't know you and I need to speak with Eve now."

The man had finally gotten some sense. He had been babbling information to a strange man in Eve's home. "Give me a minute," Adam mumbled as he turned to go fetch his mate. She never had answered him about her last name. Longtree. Of *The Longtree's* he was certain. Jacob Longtree (of course, biblical name) had been the genetic researcher that had saved his race and must have been Eve's grandfather; Naomi Longtree, her mother, had uncovered several hidden species for the world. Adam winced, but none in the last decade or so.

Eve, his mate, had already made her mark on the world. He should have put two and two together. Among other things she had discovered the cure, when she was still in college, for Were-parvo. A debilitating disease that struck only werewolves and one that most human scientists wouldn't have bothered researching. Interesting.

Eve was plucked out of bed, sheets and all, and carted down the stairs. "Adam, what are you doing?" Before her muddled brain could focus, jeez...around him her usually sharp mind seemed to be turning to mush...she was set down in front of her videolink. Charles watched her intently from the screen. "You could have let me get dressed first," she hissed at Adam.

"He said he had information that was vital to your safety. I didn't want to wait for you to dress to find out what he's yammering about."

Eve started to comment, but Charles interrupted, "It's serious Eve. Hunky and hairy was right to rip you out of bed. Nice look by the way, extremely well fuc—"

"Charles!" Eve spat. She could literally see Adam's hackles rise at her assistant's careless comments. He could be suicidal sometimes. "Get to the point."

"Are you sure you want me to tell you while your *friend* is listening?" Somehow he managed to mix sarcasm with a concerned question. One that Eve had no trouble reading after the hours they'd spent together the last three months.

"Charles, this is Adam and in answer to your questions, yes...he is werewolf, yes...he is my mate, and yes...he can hear what you have to say."

Charles sighed. "I hope he is as strong as he looks, Bella.... You are going to need a bodyguard."

"Why Charlie? What has happened?" she asked worriedly. But she was afraid she already had some idea.

Charles groaned and shook his head. "The worse possible scenario. Think money hungry boss, top scientist missing for two days and boss sneaking into scientist's lab and uncovering a smidgeon of information about the new project. Think idiot boss making a 'breakthrough' announcement to the governing counsel to generate excitement about the breakthrough and get their attention away from the investigation into his misuse of World funding."

Eve closed her eyes. She was dead. Without some public relations spin and time to prepare, the One Racers would kill her before her next meal. Her only hope was that her boss had no clue of what she'd almost developed. "Tell me the SI made something up and had no clue what we were really working on?" she pleaded.

Adam's eyebrows rose at the panicked tone in Eve's voice. Up to this time, he had listened but assumed the man was being high-strung. But Eve was worried. "SI?"

"Supreme Idiot," Eve and Charles said in tandem. Before Adam could ask about what the project entailed, Charles continued.

"No such luck, sugar. He pretty much nailed it. Except for the fact that you are not quite finished with it, he made it sound as if the serum was already developed." Charles grimaced. "In fact, I believe his exact words were that production of the serum was underway. You can catch his commentary on the next special newscast."

Eve looked at him, dumbfounded. Of course. Reporters. "Tell me he didn't mention my name or yours? Tell me he took credit for the discovery himself?" she pleaded.

"Actually he did both, mentioned your name but tried to take the credit. Mine was thrown in for flavor."

Trancelike, Eve stared at the videolink, her mind trying to process the horror of what her boss had done. Singled them all out for what would most likely be a violent and sudden death. The ridiculous part about this was that he probably had no idea what he had unleashed. Eve had joked with Charles about being on the One Racers' hit list, but she never doubted the resources she could pull, the public relations work that would help the final outcome, or the muscle she could hire until it all boiled over. Now that safety rug had been yanked out from under her. They would kill not only her, but also anyone associated with her. Eve closed her eyes to concentrate.

Adam made a move to go to his mate, he could feel her hurting and he wanted it to stop. But Charles stopped him. His whispered, "Don't! She is working out how to get through this, what needs to be done. Give her a minute." So Adam used his minute wisely. Keeping his eye on his mate, he reached for the earphones attached to the vid-screen and had Charles give him a quick rundown of the project Eve had been working on. What he heard took several years off his life. He started doing some plotting of his own.

Eve's house monitor beeped. The vid-screen spilt in two, with Charles on one screen and the front of Eve's house on the other. On her porch stood a man and a woman. Scratch that…a vampire and a woman. They didn't look happy.

Adam rose to answer the door, glancing first at Eve. She still hadn't moved.

The vampire's eyes showed no shock at seeing Adam answer the door, but the human woman went ballistic. "If you have so much as touched a hair on her head, I'll kill you!" she growled. And moved to go through him.

The vampire gently pulled her into his arms. "Jezi, dear, he has more than touched her, but I doubt he's harmed her in any way."

The small firebrand was Eve's sister. Jezebel. Their parents may have been full human, but this woman was trouble, you could see it in her. Adam could believe that she never forgave, she got even and then some. He made a mental note to always use her nickname. The vampire cradled her gently in his arms. Luke Skylord. If there was such a thing, he was king of all the Others. "Luke," Adam said in acknowledgement. They'd worked together for years.

"Adam. I am sure there is a fascinating story as to how you cornered Eve, knowing how she felt about Weremates, but right now we need to speak with her on an urgent matter," Luke said.

"I know why you are here, Luke. Her assistant just called with the news. Eve has gone into some sort of catatonic state that Charles has warned me not to interrupt."

"Of course not, she's thinking. Get out of my way. I need to see my sister."

Adam wisely moved from the doorway, letting the red-haired steamroller past him.

Luke sighed, "I have found that with all the women in the Longtree family, it is just easier to move out of their way unless it is vitally important. You might want to remember that, Adam."

Adam followed the odd couple back into Eve's family room. He wanted to laugh at the t-shirt the spitfire was wearing: "Vampires give the best hickies!", it proclaimed in dripping red letters across a black shirt. Cute. But he couldn't laugh; somehow he had to find a way out of this mess. If he hadn't sworn a Blood Oath...

"Why don't you just take her and hide her in Europe or Asia or something?" Luke questioned.

Adam shook his head, "Before I had any clue what I had gotten myself into I swore a Blood Oath not to interfere with her work. She seemed to have some sort of hang up about that. Foolishly, I wanted to reassure her."

"Understood. With Jezi you don't ever want to mention her appearance. God help you if you try to suggest how she dress, or say anything about what might be appropriate, or that you even like or dislike something she's wearing." Luke winced.

"Don't tell me. Matthew, the short and hairy werewolf stepfather, told their mother how to dress?"

"Oh, it was never so crass as to be an outright demand. Just subtle emotional warfare that was visible even to a child." Luke let out a pent up breath. "The good news is that he learned from his mistakes. Slowly, but he learned. He isn't nearly the Cro-Magnon, male chauvinist pig that he used to be. Or so Naomi tells me."

"Some day I hope to verify that for myself. What is Matthew's last name?"

Luke grinned evilly. "Nightclan."

Adam winced, his face showing his disgust. "Of course he is a member of a Neanderthal throwback clan. I should have guessed."

Adam moved to Eve's side. He couldn't bear to see her like this. "Eve, honey." Three people hissed at him to be quiet. Adam ignored them all. "Sweetheart," he said as he knelt in front of her. He watched intently as her eyelids fluttered, then opened and he met her warm amber-toned gaze. "You don't have to work through this on your own, Eve. I am in this with you," he reassured her.

"I can't come up with a plan, Adam. There are too many variables. My sister, Luke, my parents, my brother...Charles. I don't know how to protect all of them!" she cried.

"Sweetheart, let Luke and me worry about protecting all of you. Right now you need to concentrate on telling me how to gather up your research. Is it all at the lab? Is there more than one copy? We need to make sure you have it, so that when you have a chance you can finish it. And that someone else doesn't get a hold of it," he calmly stated.

Jezi loudly interrupted, *"How can you be concerned about her research at a time like this? What kind of a monster..."*

"Jezi, love, hush," Luke said firmly.

Eve blinked, and looked around the room to see her sister and Luke. "I didn't realize you two had come over."

Jezi rushed to her sister. "Luke heard about that jerk boss of yours making an announcement about some of your research and he felt you would be in danger. We came right over and *he* met us at the door." She pointed an accusing finger at Adam. "Now he is more concerned with your research than with your safety. Who is he, Eve? What is he doing here?"

Eve looked at her sister and sighed. "It's a long story, Jez. And one I don't have time to go into. You are going to have to be quiet and let me hit the highlights. Adam is my mate. He's a werewolf and he scented and marked me a few days ago."

In order to prove her point, Eve started to drop the sleeve of her shirt when she realized she wasn't wearing one. She was wrapped in a sheet. "Oh, for heavens sake! You can see the marks for yourself, sis," Eve continued, ignoring her sister's gasp. "The secret project I have been working on is a serum." At this she hesitated, looking first at Adam and then Luke. Both men nodded at her, giving their support. Heavily sighing, she turned back to her sister, her best friend. She was also the warm-blooded wife of a vampire and stoically acknowledged the fact that she'd never be able to have children, when she wanted them so badly. Vampire couples weren't allowed to adopt.

"I wanted to wait, Jezi. I didn't want to tell you about this until I was one hundred percent sure that it would work and I haven't finished my research. It hasn't even been tested. This serum will allow a Vampire male a small window of opportunity to produce viable sperm. If during this time, the Vampire mates with a warm-blooded female, he could produce offspring." Eve fell silent, waiting for her sister's reaction.

At first a look of happiness, so unbelievable in its intensity bloomed across Jezi's face. Then a look of abject horror. "Oh. My. God," she sputtered. "You're not just in danger like somebody hates your guts and might try and tamper with your glide. Eve, *they* will kill you for this! Painfully!" Sudden realization had her jumping to her feet. "And you did this for me. Well, Miss 'I can fix everyone's hurts'…take it back. I won't have you do this and end up dead. I refuse to have a child with your blood! With your blood on my hands….Oh…you know what I mean. I am furious with you, Eve!" Then she seemed to deflate before their eyes. "Evie, they'll kill you…"

Eve moved clumsily in her sheet to take her sister in her arms. "Look on the bright side, honey. I'm not the only one they'll try to kill."

Jezi closed her eyes for a moment, sighed and looked at her sister. Shaking her head she acknowledged the truth in Eve's words, "No, anyone and everyone in your family tree and even nodding acquaintances will be marked for death." Hugging her, she continued, "Good. Maybe they'll get rid of your idiot boss. We need to get you packed and out of here."

The Longtree's didn't waste time with worrying about things they couldn't change. This was a time for action.

Ravyn Wilde

Chapter 10

Much later that night Adam and Eve were getting ready for bed. For the moment Adam knew they were safe. The house was secure with a combined force of Were and Vamp protectors. A *recovery* team had successfully retrieved Eve's research and supplies from her work lab. Most of the equipment and necessary paraphernalia from her very impressive home laboratory/sealed room had been packed and would be moved to his place tomorrow. Eve had been shocked when she discovered he was not only a member of the largest and most powerful clan of werewolves in the world, but their leader.

She had looked at him blankly, muttered *whatever is needed indeed*, and then agreed that the best bet for her and her family — and Charles's safety — was to move them all to his home. At least for now.

His family had a large walled compound, almost a fortress. They had been the leaders of a strong werewolf clan through decades of war and unrest, but even in these 'enlightened' times it was necessary for them to have a stronghold to defend against the militant One Racers. His home had the best in latest technology and an army of werewolves to protect his new wife. It had only taken his agreement to provide her a separate room for her lab, and any normalcy he could provide for her family. She had actually seemed relieved to hand over all the details of their safety to him. And Luke and his reinforcements would provide backup and had promised any support

216

needed. After all, they had a vested interest in Eve's latest development.

Eve looked a little pensive as she came out of the bathroom. Adam quietly moved behind her to enfold her in his arms. "Now what are you worrying about?" he asked quietly.

"Ummm, nothing to do with our situation. Well, it has to do with the circumstances between you and me, not the safety issue," Eve stated. "I know that some human mates stay…well—human when bitten. My mother is one that didn't change. But some develop the ability to transform, become loupe-garou. I guess that since I found out you were a leader of your clan—a powerful clan—that you will be disappointed with me if I don't become lycanthropic." Eve turned in Adam's arms to look at him questioningly.

Adam looked at her seriously. "How do you feel about it? Do you hate the idea of transforming?"

Eve shrugged. "It won't bother me either way. I will still be me, whether I turn hairy once in awhile or not. It is you and your family I worry about. And the fact that we could have human, not Were, children."

Adam laughed. "You are worrying too far into the future, Eve. I can tell you that whether you *turn hairy* or not will not matter to me or my family. The same goes for any children we might have. Remember, Eve, you are my genetic match. More than that, I already know I love you."

Eve's eyes widened. "You do?"

"Yes, love. I do."

"Why?" she whispered.

"Your determination and love for your family that comes out in trying to make everything in their world right. Your dedication. And the weird fascination you have for anything with a pink stork on it."

Hugely grinning, Eve laughed. "They're flamingos! And you forgot to mention how my body drives you wild."

"Oh, I didn't forget that," Adam said as he slid the butt-ugly blue robe from her shoulders. Softly he added, "And someday, you will come to love me. I have decided to make it my life's work."

"Short work," she smiled as she lifted her arms to pull him to her. Just as his mouth was about to claim hers she moaned, "I already do."

About the author:

Ravyn Wilde was born in Oregon and has spent several years in New Guinea and Singapore. She is married, has three children, and is currently living in Utah. Ravyn is happiest when she has a book in one hand and a drink in the other—preferably sprawled on a beach! Readers may write to Ravyn at RavynWilde@msn.com.

Ravyn welcomes mail from readers. You can write to her c/o Ellora's Cave Publishing at P.O. Box 787, Hudson, Ohio 44236-0787.

Also by Ravyn Wilde:

AT HIS MERCY

Doreen DeSalvo

The man following the maitre'd to her table couldn't possibly be Jacob McIntyre. He looked too young. Too casual, in his sweater and trousers, a suit jacket slung over one shoulder. But he walked with a determined, confident stride, like a man used to getting his own way.

His gaze locked onto hers...and a burst of awareness filled her consciousness, so suddenly that it made her draw a sharp breath. The soft piano music faded, and a roar like the ocean filled her ears. The lights, already dim in this exclusive hotel restaurant, seemed to gray around the edges of her vision until nothing was illuminated but his staring, shining blue eyes.

She hadn't even tried to read him, but she knew this rush of feeling was coming from him.

He wants me.

Even if she hadn't felt it through a psychic connection, the appreciation in his eyes would have told her.

I like a soft, voluptuous woman.

What? Wow, she was hearing his thoughts. Hearing them without even trying. This never happened. She'd learned to control her abilities young. Learned to turn them on and off at will.

It must be nerves. This research grant meant a lot to her.

She looked away and took a slow, deep breath, consciously feeling the crisp linen tablecloth underneath her forefinger, the firm chair under her butt. She wriggled her toes in her tight high-heeled pumps. Concentrating on physical sensations always helped ground her. Yes, that was better.

He sat down across from her, and she met his gaze evenly. He couldn't be over thirty-five. Much younger than she'd expected for a university board member. And far more handsome, especially with that navy cashmere sweater lighting up his gorgeous blue eyes. His unruly dark brown hair was pushed back casually from a high forehead, but one lock slipped over his ear as though it was too fine to stay put for long. His nose was a bit too large, but it made him even more handsome. Without that tiny flaw, he'd look too pretty. He was a hell of a package, all right.

He gave her a brief nod. "I'm Jake McIntyre. You must be the psychic."

And you must be the tight-fisted skeptic. Too bad she couldn't say it. If she pissed him off, she wouldn't have a prayer of getting this grant. He was the only holdout on the review committee.

"I'm an intuitive," she corrected. "Faith Hartley."

His smile looked insincere. More like a sneer. "Is that the politically correct word? Does *psychic* sound too much like a charlatan?"

She'd heard that insult before. "It's simply the word I prefer."

A waiter appeared. "May I take your order?"

Even though it was late, she'd planned on getting dessert. But with the way this meeting was going, she didn't want to prolong it. "Just a cup of decaf for me, please."

"I'll have a mineral water. And the chocolate torte."

Damn him. Now she'd be drooling over his dessert. At least his arrogance made her less tempted to drool over *him.*

224

"No dessert?" he prompted. "The pastry chef here is legendary."

True. But she didn't want to give in to him, not even on something so trivial. "No, thanks."

"I've read your grant proposal," he said, after the waiter was gone. "Frankly, I'm concerned that any involvement from the university would be seen as a joke in the scientific community. The university's reputation is already on shaky ground after that marijuana study they financed last year."

That pot study *had* been a joke. "There's no comparison. My study doesn't involve an illegal substance."

"But it's still on the outer fringes of science. Metaphysics isn't really physics, after all."

As if that made it less valid. "There have been hundreds, if not thousands, of scientific studies on intuitive powers. Studies going back dozens of years."

"Not funded by a prestigious university. I hate to tell you this, but I'm planning to advise the university not to even give you the space to conduct the study, let alone fund it."

So why was he wasting her time with this meeting? She leaned forward, resting her elbows on the table, ready to argue with him.

His gaze dropped to her breasts. At least she wasn't reading his thoughts this time. But the expression in his eyes, the sexy tilt to his lips, made her breathing quicken.

And then she saw it—a picture from his head, from his imagination. His hands unbuttoning her shirt, pushing it off her shoulders, leaving it tangled around her wrists. He got her bra wrong—he envisioned it as beige, not white, and a lot flimsier than her ample breasts demanded. In the vision he yanked the straps off her shoulders without a word, pulling the cups down so his hands could cover her naked breasts.

A rush of heat flooded her face. Damn her pale skin—it showed every blush. Maybe he wouldn't notice; the flickering candle on their table didn't cast much light. At least he didn't know she'd read his mind. And how *had* she done that? She wasn't even trying to connect with him.

With trembling fingers, she reached for her water glass and took a gulp.

"Are you all right?" he asked.

"I'm fine." What had she wanted to say before she'd had that disturbing flash? Something about the grant…oh, right. About his reason for this meeting. "If you've already made up your mind, Mr. McIntyre, I'm surprised that you wanted to meet with me."

"Call me Jake."

After that heated fantasy of his, he probably thought they should be on a first-name basis. Maybe the informality would help them have an open discussion about her project. "Fine."

The waiter appeared with their drinks and his delicious-looking chocolate torte. Raspberry sauce was drizzled artistically over the plate in a crisscross pattern.

He took a bite and swallowed before answering her. "I just wanted an excuse to drive up to the city from Monterey. We don't have a restaurant equal to The Four Seasons down there."

Her mouth dropped open. Was that a joke?

He laughed—a husky, warm rumble that had her smiling back at him against her will. "I'm kidding.

226

Seriously, I thought it was only fair to give you a chance to try to convince me."

He didn't look like the type to be easily convinced. Too driven. Too self-assured. One of those infuriating, inflexible men who never changed his mind. But she had to try. "This study could make a huge difference in the lives of a lot of intuitive kids. They're isolated. They don't know anyone else like them. My study would give them a chance to bond with each other." *They don't have to grow up thinking they're crazy…like I did.*

He looked mildly interested, but said nothing.

"And since this is a long-term study, we'd learn if having a peer support group helps children develop and enhance their abilities over time."

"Sounds good in theory. There's just one problem. I don't believe that psychic abilities exist. Intuitive abilities, that is."

An all-too familiar attitude. She'd learned not to fight it. "If you're determined not to believe something exists, there's no way I can change your mind. You'll dismiss any evidence I give you."

His lips curved in a mocking little half smile. What a lush mouth. Too bad he used it for sneering. "If you can tell me something about myself that no one—and I mean no one—could know, I'll believe you. Something specific."

And he could easily dismiss that, too. Call it coincidence, or say it was too vague to be specific. She'd heard it all before. "You expect me to prove that I'm an intuitive?"

He nodded. "Why not? Let's do it now." He put his fork down and looked at her steadily. "Tell me what I'm thinking."

She opened her mouth to say she wasn't prepared, that she'd have to meditate for at least an hour, that he had to be *willing* to be read. Before she got a word out, another image burst into her vision. His hands tugging her bra down even further, the straps imprisoning her arms...his strong arm around her, bending her backwards...his mouth suckling on her breast, the hardened nipple straining against the roof of his mouth. She felt it all, the way he must be feeling it. Felt his hunger. His need.

God, he was getting to her. Knowing how much he wanted to suck and tease her breasts, how much he wanted to press his stiff cock against her stomach, made heat course through her body and settle right between her thighs. Her hips wriggled on the chair, pressing deep against the upholstery, trying to assuage the ache.

The image faded as she focused on the solid seat of the chair.

He looked condescending. "Not up to the challenge? Is psychic ability something I have to accept on faith?"

As if faith and science were incompatible. Typical skeptic. "Your ego won't permit you to have a little faith?"

"A little faith?" He smiled...a heated, sexy smile this time. Much better than the sneer. "I'd like to have a *lot* of you, Faith."

Her cheeks burned. And she saw that image again—herself in his arms, her shirt and bra pulled down, her breasts cupped in his hands. He liked seeing her arms trapped in the tangle of shirtsleeves and bra straps. He liked having her almost helpless. She could feel it.

"You're thinking about sex," she said, before she had a chance to stop herself. *And you like to dominate a woman in bed. Just a little.*

He raised an eyebrow. "That could be a lucky guess. I'm a man, after all. A man sitting across from a beautiful woman. And besides, I just told you I'd like to have a lot of you."

She wouldn't argue. Not yet. She let him think he'd won his point, let him eat more of his dessert. It tasted as good as it looked. She felt everything he felt, every sensation, in a way she'd never experienced before. And she had no desire to stop the connection between them. She'd never felt anything like it. So intimate. So exciting.

"It's white," she said at last.

"What?"

"My bra. It's white, not beige."

He coughed, nearly choking, and covered his mouth with his napkin. When his gaze finally met hers, he looked astonished. "How did you do that?"

She shrugged, determined to play it cool. "It's what we intuitives do."

He masked his shock with cynicism. Oh, he was easy to read. And he didn't even know it.

"Let's try again," he said. "I'll think of something different. Something more obscure."

She let her mind drift, her gaze unfocused, waiting…waiting…suddenly the image was there. She lay nearly naked on a bed, her breasts bare, her skirt pushed up around her waist…with his dark head between her thighs. She felt it all from his perspective, as if she somehow was inside his body. She felt her hips under his strong hands, holding her still…felt her soft thighs cushioning his head…felt her wet, hot skin under his mouth. She felt the deliberate way he moved his lips and tongue, sucking on the nub of her clit, then licking, then sucking again. He loved her taste. Loved her scent. And oh, how he wanted her to come against his mouth. Wanted it more than his own orgasm.

Oh, Lord. Could anything be more seductive than knowing a man loved going down on a woman? On *her*?

I could eat your sweet pussy for hours.

She heard herself moan in his fantasy, and her breath hitched. She blinked and gripped the arm of her chair, trying to ground herself. The image faded, and she saw him across the table again.

Another blush heated her face. "You're thinking about sex again."

He raised an eyebrow. "No, I wasn't. Guess again."

What a liar. She glanced around. The nearest customers were two tables away. No one would hear her over the tinkling piano music that filled the air. She leaned across the table until she felt the heat of the candle flame on her chin. "*Oral* sex," she whispered.

That rocked him, and she didn't have to be psychic to see it. He cleared his throat. "Okay. Let's assume you're right. How do you get the information? Is it as if someone's talking to you? Is it a picture? Or just a sense you have?"

She took a gulp of her coffee. "A picture." *And I feel what you feel. And your thoughts, God, I'm hearing your erotic thoughts.*

He still looked unconvinced. "So tell me, then…how accurate is my imagination?"

Now that was a loaded question. He didn't have to know that one of her breasts was bigger than the other, or that her hips were fuller. Her pubic hair was twice as soft and furry as he'd imagined, and several shades darker than the blonde hair on her head.

His blue eyes grew wide. "My God," he said. "How the hell did you do that?"

She frowned. "Do what?"

And then she saw it—his fantasy image of her had been changed, corrected, to look exactly like her. Somehow he'd picked up the image from her own head. "I don't know," she answered. "I thought it, and you…read it."

He shook his head. "Impossible."

"Then what's your explanation?"

"That I'm horny as hell," he growled, frowning. *For you*, she read in his thoughts, but he didn't say it. "And I have a vivid imagination."

Stubborn man. She still felt the connection to his thoughts, his fantasies. And unlike him, she knew how to use it.

She pictured him naked, pictured a strong, lightly haired chest, powerful legs. A thick, circumcised cock, fully erect, red and pulsing with heat. She wrapped a hand around it and pumped.

And then she sent the fantasy out into the void, knowing he'd see it.

His eyes widened.

"How close am I to reality?" she asked. Her voice shook, but she didn't care.

"I'm—"

"Don't tell me," she interrupted. "Show me."

"How?"

"Imagine it. Picture it in your head." She stared at him without blinking, concentrating.

He shook his head, looking dazed. But she saw it anyway.

His cock was longer. And he wanted her to pump him harder. Faster. Then he pulled her hand away and rolled her onto her back, holding her hands over her head in a bruising grip. He spread her legs with his powerful thighs and thrust inside her. She felt his savage pleasure.

Feeling what a man felt during sex…she'd never let herself experience it before. She'd always respected the boundaries of personal privacy, knowing that she wouldn't want someone reading her own thoughts in such an intimate situation. But the sensation was extraordinary.

Sticky moisture seeped from between her legs. And not just in this fantasy of his. Of theirs.

She drew a deep, shuddering breath. "Stop it," she whispered.

"You're the one invading my head," he said hoarsely. "*You* stop it."

"I can't." And she didn't really want to. She wanted to keep this image, this fantasy image of him fucking her…fucking her hard and fast with her hands held down tight. She'd never imagined being restrained, never wanted to give up control, but now…now she wanted to play along with his fantasy. She'd mold it. Shape it. Help convince him that this psychic bond was real.

And drive him wild at the same time.

She pictured herself struggling to pull her hands away from his grip. Pictured him growling. Resisting. Holding her tighter…fucking her harder. He bit her neck. *Don't fight it, baby. Come for me.*

Harder.

Yes. Take it. Take it all.

She moaned and pushed her hips up against him, struggling to climb higher...higher... His head dipped, and his teeth nipped her breast. She cried out at the stab of pleasure.

She hoped she hadn't cried out aloud.

Time to turn the tables. She rolled over, taking him with her, and pinned his hands to the bed. She looked down at him as she rode him, her breasts bouncing with each thrust.

He groaned. "You're killing me."

She blinked and saw him sitting across from her, candlelight flickering over the sharp planes of his face, reflecting in his intense blue eyes. His mouth was open, his chest moving with deep breaths. "I don't really care how you're doing this," he said. "I just want you to come upstairs with me. *Now.*"

"Upstairs?" she repeated, stupidly.

"I have a suite in this hotel," he said, his voice dark, urgent. "Spend the night with me, Faith."

Oh, she was tempted. But to jump into bed with a man she'd just met...

"I don't do things like this either," he said, as if he'd read her mind. Maybe he had. And she sensed the truth of his answer. "But I know you're not seeing anyone," he added. "I don't know how I know that, but I do."

No, she wasn't seeing anyone. And she could read that he wasn't attached, either. In fact, he felt rather...lonely. But still. "I'm not going to sleep with you just so you'll withdraw your objections to my grant."

"And I'm not going to withdraw my objections just because you sleep with me." He gave her that slow, sexy smile again. The smile that said, *let me take you.* "Well, I might if you're really good. As good as I've been imagining."

A bold streak took over her. "I'm better."

His eyes glittered. "Then come upstairs with me." His voice dropped to a deep, needy rumble. "Now. *Please.*"

This wasn't a man who begged for sex. She knew it intuitively.

He reached across the table and laid his hand over hers. His skin was hot, soft, and oh, so masculine. He stroked her fingers. "I wanted you from the first moment I saw you, Faith."

She knew that was the truth. He wanted her desperately, wanted to eat her until she came against his mouth, wanted to fuck her until she clawed his back and came again. She sensed it as clearly as if he'd said the words aloud.

And God, she wanted him, too.

"You don't have to sleep with me tonight," he went on. "But I warn you, I'm not giving up until you do."

But she barely knew him. Or did she? Hell, with this rampant connection between them, she probably knew him better than most of the men she'd slept with. She knew he wanted her. She knew he wasn't a psycho. She knew he didn't think she was an easy lay.

And she knew he was just kinky enough to guarantee that she'd have an outrageously good time.

She couldn't think of a single reason to say no. And oh, how she wanted to say yes.

Her gaze fell to his hand, covering hers with such warmth. Waiting so patiently. As desperately as he wanted her after all those feverish, shared visions, he'd let her make the decision. She knew it wasn't in his nature, this patient waiting game. He'd much rather toss her over his shoulder and carry her off. But he wanted the decision to be hers.

And once she'd decided, once he had her upstairs, he'd take charge. He'd eat her until she begged him to stop. He'd hold her down…he'd fuck her while she struggled.

And she'd love every second of it.

She turned her hand over and laced her fingers through his. "All right."

His fingers tightened on hers, but he said nothing. He reached behind his chair with his free hand, fumbled with the jacket of his suit, and came back with his wallet. He managed to get a bill out and toss it onto the table without releasing her hand. As if she'd change her mind if he let go.

He stood, came to her side, and tugged her gently to her feet. His arm slipped around her waist, pulling her closer. The warmth of his tall, strong body made her shiver.

"Cold?"

Before she could answer, he draped his suit jacket over her shoulders. The subtle scent of him, musky and masculine, made her mouth water just a little.

And then she saw a vision that froze her cold. Jake draping this same jacket over a small brunette woman's shoulders…Jake smiling down at the woman, all seductive heat and sexual promise.

God, no. She looked up at him and felt burning tears sting her eyes.

"Faith?" His voice sounded like it came from the end of a deep tunnel.

She couldn't form words. She could barely shake her head. Then she pushed the jacket off and ran.

* * * * *

She wanted out, just out.

Faith followed an exit sign and found herself stopped at the end of a long hallway. Escape was on the other side of a door marked with the words "Alarm Will Sound".

Great. The last thing she needed was to set off an alarm to match the psychic one already reverberating in her head.

She leaned against the cold glass of the door, watching her breath fog the surface. Her reflection stared back at her, so she closed her eyes. Hiding from herself. Giving herself some time to calm down. She took slow, deep breaths, a beginner's meditation trick to empty the mind. A worthless trick. She kept seeing Jake and that other woman, over and over again, like a movie on an endless loop.

Jake.

The man must have moved like a cat, soundless on the plush carpeting. But she sensed his presence an instant before his hands touched her shoulders. It took all her willpower not to jerk away from him. He didn't deserve that kind of rejection.

"What happened back there?" His voice was quiet, but she could feel the anger in him.

"Nothing."

"Don't be stupid."

She couldn't even get angry. He was right, she *was* being stupid.

The contrast between the heat of his body behind her and the coldness of the door against her front made her shiver. His hands left her arms, and she felt that dreaded suit jacket settle over her shoulders again.

She flinched, but no visions came. Just a wave of quiet concern from him, overlaid with anger and desire. He still wanted her...and he wasn't giving up without a fight.

He turned her to face him. She complied, but couldn't look him in the eye. She kept her gaze on his chin instead.

"Why did you run?" Still in that calm, quiet voice.

She couldn't put her fear into words. With him so close, radiating warmth and compassion, she just wanted to weep against his solid chest. She said nothing.

He touched her chin gently, and she looked up. His expression was serious. "Talk to me, Faith." A sliver of a smile touched his lips. "I can't read your mind, you know."

But she could read his. And she'd hear every callous thought, every lie, every cutting remark, even if he never spoke the words aloud. It was bad enough with other men. Considering her lack of control with Jake, she'd never be able to protect herself from his thoughts.

How could she tell him she was frightened of a future that might never happen? That she was jealous of every woman she'd see in his past? But she owed him an explanation. Faith Hartley was no cock tease.

She took a deep breath and looked at his chin again. "Sometimes I just know things. Things I don't really want to know." Her gaze met his then. "Things the men I'm dating wish I didn't know."

He didn't answer for a long moment. "What did you see about me?"

The vision replayed itself in her memory. God, that woman was beautiful. Petite, thin, young. Nothing like Faith. She couldn't speak, so she shook her head.

"Faith." He sounded annoyed now. "I'm a man like any other. You can't hold my past against me. I'm sure you have a past, too."

"Yes, but you won't know when I'm thinking about it."

He touched her mouth gently with his forefinger. "I might. I've been picking up on things from you, too."

Did he know what she'd seen? She looked up and saw the knowledge in his eyes. And she felt his feelings on the subject. *It's over. Long over.* She knew he wasn't lying.

"I don't lie," he said, no doubt because he'd sensed her thoughts. "Faith, I don't know where this…this thing between us is going. I can't promise we'll be together in a year, or even in a week." His hands tightened on her arms. "But I can promise you that I want to find out. I don't lie. And I don't cheat."

She could tell that was true, too. Maybe he was worth the risk. He could hurt her intensely…but the flip side was that he could make her intensely happy, too.

"And for every time you get jealous," he went on, "I'm sure I'll be twice as bad."

Oh, she could well believe it, as domineering as he seemed. She almost smiled. "You? Jealous?" She tried to feign surprise.

He gathered her against him, and she willingly snuggled against his warmth. "Yes, I'm horribly jealous. Jealous, possessive, territorial. Probably overbearing and arrogant as well." He kissed the top of her head. "There, now you know all my faults."

She leaned back and smiled at him. "Those don't sound like faults to me."

He gave her a cocky grin. "You won't find any faults if you come upstairs with me, either."

He'd see plenty of faults with her, though. She started to pull away, but he caught her close.

His eyes were angry. "Don't," he ordered. "Don't even think it."

He took her hand and pressed it against his cock, hard and hot even through the fabric of his pants. "Feel how much I want you," he demanded. "The only way you could disappoint me, Faith, is if you walk away from me."

She stared into his eyes and saw another vision — saw him naked, eyes closed in ecstasy while she knelt in front of him, sucking his hard, needy cock.

He gave a startled, embarrassed laugh, more of an exhalation than anything else. He pulled her hand away, brought it to his lips, and gave her palm a kiss. "Sorry," he muttered. "I know you saw that one."

"Don't be sorry." She met his gaze bravely. "Let's go upstairs."

His brilliant smile made her breath catch. He wrapped an arm around her waist, holding her tightly. "You're not getting away again," he growled.

Despite his smile, she knew he meant the words. He'd track her down no matter where she tried to run. She took a deep breath and blew it out.

"No," she agreed. "I'm not."

* * * * *

When they left the long hallway, he guided her away from the elevators, toward the lobby.

Where was he going? She gave a breathless laugh. "Your room isn't off the lobby, is it?"

He stopped and smiled down at her. Up close, his eyes were vividly blue. "You're not reading my mind anymore?"

He said it with a smile, but something in his tone, his expression, held a challenge. This was a test. "Give me a minute."

She stared into his eyes, let her concentration drift...and saw his hand roll a condom over his beautiful, erect penis.

"Protection," she said.

Another lucky guess, she heard, as if he'd spoken.

She pulled back a bit. "I'm not guessing."

He gave a start, then smiled. "Very good. You impress me, Faith. And you scare me a little, too."

"Ditto," she admitted.

He looked relieved. His head bent. "I'd kiss you right here," he whispered, his breath hot in her ear, "but once I start, I won't be able to stop."

She saw a different scenario in his mind—his hands ripping open her shirt, buttons flying. It only took a slight movement of her head to bring her lips against his ear. "That's not exactly what you're thinking."

"No?"

"No. You're thinking that once you kiss me, you'll start tearing my clothes off."

"Right again." His hand curled around the nape of her neck. "But first I'll take your hair down from this ridiculous bun."

She'd wanted to look professional. To convince him that her research was worthwhile. Vaguely hurt, she pulled back until she could see his face. "You don't like it?"

He gave a frustrated, thoroughly masculine groan. "You're beautiful, Faith. But the bun makes you look…"

"Serious? Respectable?"

He shrugged. "Yes. Maybe even a little…prudish." His hand slid around her neck; his thumb stroked over her lower lip in a slow, sensual glide. She had to lock her knees to keep from tilting into him. "And I know you're not a prude."

He drew her toward the lobby again. "Now come on, before I change my mind and drag you behind those palm trees in the corner."

In the small lobby drug store, he grabbed a box of condoms—a huge box. If he went through a dozen tonight, she wouldn't be able to walk in the morning.

She wouldn't be walking, but she'd be smiling.

He glanced around, headed for a shelf in the back, and picked up a toothbrush. "Do you need anything else for the morning?"

Thoughtful of him, considering he wasn't familiar with the etiquette of one-night stands. During one of their connections, she'd had a vague impression that this was rather new to him—almost as new as it was to her. When he had a woman, he kept her long-term…he didn't let her stray. And he didn't stray, either. Comforting thought.

She stretched up on her toes to whisper in his ear. No reason to entertain the clerk. "The only thing I'll need in the morning is breakfast in bed…naked."

When she lowered herself again, she caught sight of his wolfish grin. "I can handle that."

He paid the clerk and led her back to the elevators, keeping her close the whole way. A small group of men were entering the elevator, and one held the door for them.

Jake pulled her closer in the elevator, despite their audience. Maybe he wanted to hide the erection she felt pressing against her belly. But her head fit perfectly under his chin, and his sweater was soft and warm under her cheek, so she stayed in his embrace. As they rode silently upward, she saw two of the strangers exchange a smirk. With Jake's arm wrapped around her waist and his suit jacket over her shoulders, no doubt everyone knew how they planned to spend the night. She felt too excited to even blush.

Jake's arm tightened, forcing her to step closer. *Get your own woman*, she heard from his mind. His possessiveness made her smile. She probably weighed as much as he did, but he made her feel delicate. Womanly. It helped that he was so much taller…and solid muscle. The broad chest underneath this sweater was rock hard.

Their audience left on the 20th floor. Jake's suite was all the way at the top. He said nothing as they rode the rest of the way, just held her quietly. She could tell he was keeping himself reined in.

The elevator stopped, and she heard the door open behind her. When she moved away from him, a few strands of her hair caught on the faint stubble on his jaw. He tenderly brushed them behind her ear. *Soon*, he thought.

The walk down the hallway seemed to take forever. She only vaguely noticed the dimmed wall sconces, the delicately flocked wallpaper, and the soft, plush carpeting. All so elegant and refined.

He opened a door and stepped back so she could walk in. More elegance — a table and chairs, a sectional sofa in a light earth tone, a tall dark wood cabinet that no doubt hid the television. An open doorway probably led to an equally tasteful bedroom.

He pulled her gently into his arms. The jacket slipped from her shoulders as she tilted her face up to his. Her purse fell to the floor, hitting the carpet with a dull thud. She barely heard it, with his lips so close to hers. His fingers reached behind her head, tugging at her bun, until he had the pins out and her hair fell in a sweep over her shoulders. "Much better," he murmured.

His big, warm hands framed her face as he bent his head and kissed her. Slowly. Carefully. Too carefully. She could sense his reluctance…his fear of intimidating her.

"Don't hold back," she said. Then she touched his lips with the tip of her tongue.

And he went wild, thrusting his tongue into her mouth, backing her up against the wall, grinding his hips against hers. She moaned and pressed into him.

His hands dropped to her chest, cupping and kneading her breasts. Her nipples immediately peaked into hard, aching points under his tormenting fingers. A flash of an image burst into her consciousness—his hands ripping her shirt off.

She grabbed his wrists and turned her head away from his rampaging mouth. "No."

He groaned. "No?"

He thought she was stopping him. And his anger was so fierce, so primal, that she had to retreat from his mind. It took her a moment to focus and ground herself…and even then, passion made her a little unsteady. "Don't tear my shirt," she said. "It's one of my favorites."

He pulled back and gazed down at her with a speculative look on his face. "You have an unfair advantage over me, Faith."

She blinked. How could he sound so rational after that heated kiss? "I do?"

He nodded. "You can see everything I want to do to you…and stop me before I do it."

"I can't help it," she said. "What you're thinking—it just comes to me." She didn't bother explaining that it had only happened with him. With everyone else, she had to consciously work at connecting.

"Hmm. Maybe we can level the playing field."

That speculative look in his eyes made her wonder. "How?"

His smile looked positively sinful. "If you don't know what I'm thinking, you'll just have to be surprised."

She saw it then — saw herself tied down. Naked. Spread-eagled.

Sweet Lord.

He took her hand and led her into the bedroom. Yes, it was as classy and tasteful as she'd imagined. And soon she'd be naked and sweating on that tasteful bed.

With this sexy, handsome man.

She shivered.

He put his hands on her shoulders, his touch gentle and hesitant. She loved this gentleness, the way he tempered his natural dominance. He wanted to rip her clothes off with these big hands, to wrap his long fingers around her wrists and pull her arms behind her back, but he didn't want to hurt her. He didn't want her to fear him.

Not much.

She tilted her head and brushed her cheek against the back of his hand. "Do whatever you want."

He squeezed her shoulders gently. "You're saying that because you think you know what I want."

No, she didn't. Not exactly. But she knew what he wanted her to say. She had to close her eyes, hiding from him, before she could say it. "I'm all yours tonight, Jake. I only want to please you."

He said nothing, but his fingers moved down her blouse, unbuttoning. He slipped the fabric off her shoulders and left it hanging over her arms, the buttoned cuffs caught on her wrists. Just like the first vision she'd seen in the restaurant.

His forefinger drew a path down her front, and his gaze followed. "This still feels safe, doesn't it? You saw me thinking about this earlier."

She nodded.

"And you'd stop me if you guessed…if you somehow sensed that I was about to go beyond your comfort zone."

"Maybe. I don't know."

His hands cupped her breasts, then skimmed around her back. She felt him fumbling with the hooks on her bra. "You're used to being in control," he said.

I'm not in control with you.

"You know exactly what a man wants to do to you," he went on. "You stop him before he tests your limits."

She couldn't remember any men but him: his hard chest under this soft cashmere sweater, his hands peeling off her bra. Her breasts spilled out as the straps caught on her shirt sleeves, still hanging by the cuffs.

"That's why you want me," he went on. "Because I won't let you stop me."

She'd already forgotten what he'd been saying; the heated look in his eyes as he stared down at her naked breasts drove all thought from her mind.

"I want control, Faith."

Yes. "I'll give you control."

He smiled wickedly. "Control isn't something you give. It's something I take."

He dipped his head and caught one nipple in his mouth, sucking hard, using his tongue to press her breast against the roof of his mouth. His arms wrapped around her, holding her tight against his solid chest. She couldn't move her hands to hold him—they were trapped in the tangle of her shirt and bra.

He pulled his head away and gasped for breath against the sensitive skin between her breasts. "I'm going to take control. Total control."

"I won't stop you."

He chuckled. "I'm going to make sure you can't stop me."

Her breath caught at the sexy edge in his voice. It sounded like a promise.

Or a threat.

"Yes, that's a promise," he said.

He'd read her mind. She was already out of control—completely out of control, her intuition running wild, like a live current between their minds.

He moved behind her, and she felt his fingers against the small of her back, unhooking her skirt. The zipper sounded like a long, slow tear in the quiet room. He pulled everything down at once—her skirt, her nylons, her panties, all bunched around her knees. Being half naked like this, her clothes pulled helter-skelter to expose the parts he wanted to see—she loved it. She'd never felt so…nasty. So desired.

"Turn around," he ordered.

Did he expect her to balk? He'd already seen her nude—she'd given him an accurate picture. And she knew he found her sexy.

She'd face him naked. She stepped out of her shoes and bent to tug off the rest of her clothes.

"Did I tell you to get undressed?" His tone was low. Almost menacing.

She froze. "No."

His hand stroked over her bare ass, a heated, silky caress. "Naughty Faith," he murmured. "Already disobeying me." He wrapped his free arm around her midriff and pulled her back against his chest. His fingers found the crease of her ass and inched lower...lower... "I'll have to punish you."

Maybe I'll spank your luscious ass.

Her fingers tightened on his forearms. Would he really—

He slapped her ass, and the sharp sting made her jump.

"Surprised?" he murmured, his deep voice sending vibrations along the sensitive skin of her neck. "I'm getting little flashes from you. I thought this psychic stuff went both ways."

With his fingers moving lower, creeping toward her aching clit, she couldn't even think, let alone speak. "It's...sporadic. I don't see everything. It's like you said...little flashes."

He dipped into her with just a teasing fingertip. "You saw that little fantasy I had of going down on you, didn't you?"

She nodded.

"You saw me lapping up all this juice?"

Her breath caught. She nodded again.

"Do you mind if I talk dirty to you, Faith?"

Mind? She loved it. "No."

"That's too bad. Because I'd do it anyway."

His finger, wet from her silky fluid, slid easily back up her ass. He pressed against her asshole for a second.

She gasped, and her body went tight.

"You didn't see that one? Didn't see me thinking about fucking this sexy ass of yours?"

Oh, God. She shook her head.

"I guess I'll have to tell you about it, then." He bent low, his breath hot in her ear. "I imagined you on your hands and knees. I knelt behind you, and I touched you just like this. And you begged me for it."

I might. Even though I've never done it before.

Neither have I, she heard his thoughts answer.

His finger teased her again, pressing gently against her tight hole. "Would you let me in here, Faith?"

"I…I don't know."

He growled against her neck, making her shudder with the threatening vibrations. "You said you wanted to please me. That I could do whatever I want."

Yes, she had. And she trusted him. Trusted him intuitively. She'd been in his head, in his heart. She knew he was a good man at heart. A good *dominant* man. He'd take control…and he'd make it good for her. "Yes," she said recklessly. "I'll let you." *I'll even let you pretend you're forcing me.*

He groaned. His fingers moved lower again, back to the sensitive spot right behind her vagina. "You have no clue how tempting you are. But not tonight," he murmured.

"Why not?" Her voice came out like a croak.

"No lubricant. And I'm not leaving you to go get some."

His finger dipped into her vagina again. "Besides, I want in here just as much."

Oh, *yes.*

He set her free, backing away from her slowly. "Now get undressed," he said. More like a command.

She'd never let a man give her orders before. He'd been right—she was used to being in control. She'd never trusted a man enough to give herself up to him completely.

Until now.

She awkwardly pulled at one shirt cuff, tugging it over her wrist. Then the other. Her bra came off with the shirt in one tangled mess.

Jake's gaze never left her. As she bent to peel off her skirt and hose, their gazes met...and she saw his mental visions again. Saw him push her up against the bed, turn her back to him, and bend her over. Then he knelt and pressed his face between her legs from behind. Her hips wriggled, so he grabbed them and held her tight, forcing her back against his mouth. God, how he wanted to eat her.

She staggered a little, reaching out for something solid. One of her hands hit the wall, and she leaned against it. There. Stability. She grounded a little, but not enough to lose the connection with Jake. Then she peeled off her clothes in a rush, eager to get onto that bed with him.

When she finished undressing she walked to him boldly, slipping her hands under the bottom of his sweater. His skin felt hot and smooth over firm muscles. He didn't lift his hands, didn't touch her at all. And she couldn't quite read what was in his mind. Maybe she was too excited. She felt gloriously wicked, rubbing her naked body against his fully-clothed one.

"Don't you want to touch me?" she asked.

He moved then, taking her wrists in his hands and pulling them away…wrapping her arms behind her back. "You're still in control, Faith."

He pushed her back against the wall, so quickly that she almost stumbled. The solid heat of him pressed against her front. The silkiness of his sweater against her naked breasts startled a moan out of her.

His mouth swooped down onto hers, licking, nipping at her lips, teasing her. She tried to put her arms around him, to touch him, but his hands still held her wrists.

His thigh urged her legs apart, pressing against her cunt. "Spread your legs," he muttered.

She did.

Suddenly her hands were free. His thigh retreated, and his wicked, clever fingers were between her legs, sliding, stroking, probing. His hand made her crazy. And the connection between them grew stronger, until she could feel what he felt, could feel her wet heat against his fingers, her nipples grazing his chest. She moaned and leaned against the wall, clutching at his shoulders.

"I can't wait any longer," he murmured against her neck. He dropped to his knees and pressed his mouth between her legs, licking and suckling and moaning against her. She reached out blindly and found his silky hair, tangling her fingers in it as his lips and tongue devoured her. She could sense his hunger as he sucked greedily. God, she could almost taste herself.

Tell me what you need, Faith.

Up. Oh, there. There!

Mmm.

Yes, yes.

He knew exactly what to do, as if he felt what she felt. Maybe he did. The same way she felt his pleasure, his joy in eating her. She knew the moment he started rubbing his cock through his pants. She could feel his need as well as her own. And his passion magnified hers, brought her to an urgent height she'd never known, until she cried out and crashed into a resounding, trembling orgasm that left her drained and shaky.

His arms wrapped around her waist, and he panted against her stomach. He sounded as winded as she felt. And he hadn't even climaxed. He rubbed his wet mouth back and forth on her abdomen.

I love a lush woman.

I've got plenty of lush.

He chuckled, as if he'd heard her thoughts. He must have.

After one last caress on her belly, he stood and gave her a deep kiss, a kiss scented with her sex. She knew he wanted to fuck her. And she was more than ready. He pulled away, took her hand, and led her to the bed. "Lie down."

Another order. She obeyed meekly, lying on her side and propping her head up on one hand. He went to the dresser, pulled open a drawer, and came back with something cloth-like in his hand.

A necktie. *Two* neckties.

Her breathing hitched.

He sat on the bed and ran a hand down her neck, over her breasts, in one long, slow caress. His fingers teased the hard peak of her nipple. With his free hand, he pushed her shoulder so she fell onto her back. Then he brought her hands up over her head. One of the ties went around her wrists, binding her hands together in a silky prison.

He stood and looked down at her, holding the second tie in his hand. Suddenly he grinned. "I should have brought more ties."

He leaned over her, his sweater inches from her face, and fumbled with her hands again.

She tried to bring her hands down, but couldn't move. He must have tied her to one of the slats in the headboard. "Now I can't touch you," she said.

He licked down her forearm…a wet, hot slide that made her tremble. "That's the idea. I'll do the touching for both of us."

When he left the bed, she turned to watch him undress. His chest was beautiful—strong, broad and lightly furred. He tugged open his trousers, then pulled them off along with his briefs.

She had to strain her neck to see, but the view was worth it. God, he was sexy. Tall and muscular, but not too bulky. His cock, hard and red, stood upright against his stomach.

She reached for him and the ties pulled tight. Ah. For a second she'd forgotten that she was tied up.

At his mercy.

He knelt on the bed and ran a hand over her shoulder, up her arm, to where her wrists were tied. *You're mine*, he thought.

Yes.

He knelt over her and pulled at the tie. "Nice and tight," he commented. "How does it feel, being tied up? Out of control?"

He wanted her to fear it. Just a little. "Scary."

He froze. "Too scary?" He'd untie her if she asked him to. Couldn't he tell that was the last thing she wanted?

"No," she whispered.

"Good. But just in case, we need a safe word," he said.

"A what?"

"A safe word. A word you can say if you want me to stop."

"Can't I just say stop?"

A ghost of a smile touched his lips. *Naïve little Faith.* "You might say stop and not mean it. To pretend you're struggling." He bent close, until she felt his hot, teasing breath in her ear. "I might like that," he whispered.

She shivered. "But if I can stop you, you're not really..."

"Not really in control?"

She nodded.

He gave her a gentle kiss. "I don't want to do anything against your will, Faith. I want you to be able to stop me if you really do get frightened. But we need a word you're not likely to say in fun."

She couldn't think of a thing. Nothing but the incredible heat of his chest pressing against hers, the teasing strokes of his fine, soft hair against her cheek.

His tongue slid along the rim of her ear. "Violin," he whispered.

"What?"

"If you want me to stop, say *violin.*"

He played the violin. She could sense it. But he didn't think he played well. No doubt he was a perfectionist even when it came to his hobbies.

He kissed her, his mouth brushing against hers lightly, teasingly. When she tried to lift her head, to deepen the kiss, he pulled away. His gaze swept from her bound hands down to her legs. "Do you know what it does to me, seeing you like this? Knowing I can do anything I want to you?"

Oh, she knew all right. Pure lust filled his psyche. "I…I have some idea."

"I'll make you like it, too," he said.

"I already do," she admitted.

His mouth moved to her neck, his tongue trailing fire along her skin. "Mmm. I'm going to lick every inch of your body."

Oh, yes. "All right."

He chuckled, a husky sound that rumbled against her neck. "You couldn't stop me if you wanted to."

She wouldn't want to.

"Maybe I'll do something you don't want," he murmured.

A sharp bite made her gasp. Heat radiated out from the spot he'd bitten on her neck. "You'll bruise me."

"So?" He nipped her neck again, more lightly this time, but probably hard enough to leave a bruise. "I want to leave my mark all over you."

"You already have."

She felt a rush of tenderness from him, as though she'd given him more than a compliment. "You're good for my ego, Faith."

He certainly didn't seem to have problems with his ego. Or maybe he hid his vulnerability behind that veneer of arrogance.

He bit her neck again, higher, in the sensitive spot below her ear. She squirmed on the bed, pressing her thighs together, wishing he'd touch her there...wishing he'd go down on her...hell, wishing he'd fuck her. That first climax had left her primed. Empty and aching for more.

"Patience," he whispered. "First I'm going to brand you. *Everywhere.*"

His mouth moved to her collarbone, his hair brushing lightly on her chin. He licked, then bit. His tongue traced along her collarbone, then down, down to her breast. He grazed her nipple with the sharp edge of his teeth. Surely he wouldn't bite her there.

He took her breast in his mouth and held it in his teeth gently, threateningly. Then his tongue lashed her nipple back and forth. Her arms strained against the ties. If only she could hold his head there.

He pulled away, sliding his mouth to the side of her breast. He nipped, and she cried out.

He lifted his head and reached up to cup her face in one hand. *Hurt?* She heard his thoughts before he spoke. "Did I hurt you?"

She shook her head. "No. You just startled me."

He suckled her breasts for long moments, laving her with his tongue, letting her feel his hot breath on her moist flesh. When he lifted his head, he cupped her breasts in his hands. "So beautiful," he murmured. He rose above her, angling his chest over hers and swooping in for a deep kiss. He couldn't decide what to do with her next.

Eat me.

He chuckled.

Oh, now he was going to tease her. Damn.

He drifted back down her body, passing lightly over her breasts, and suckled hard on her stomach. When he pulled back, she sensed how pleased he was to see a little red mark, a bruise forming.

Her bellybutton filled with hot wetness—his tongue. He licked down to her hip, then nipped there. She felt his mouth move down the top of her thigh, hot and wet.

"Open your legs," he said.

Her breath caught. Surely he wouldn't bite her—

"Do it," he commanded.

She hesitantly spread her feet, just a few inches apart. He buried his face between her legs, rubbing his mouth back and forth, and she opened her legs further, wanting the joy only his talented tongue could give her.

He sucked on her clit hard, and she moaned with the sharp pleasure of it. A finger thrust into her, deep and fast, wriggling against her inside walls while his mouth suckled. Oh, yes. She'd come in a minute...in just a minute...oh, just another minute...

Suddenly he turned his head and bit the inside of her thigh. She cried out in surprise.

And then she felt him smile against her leg.

He'd left her hanging on the edge of orgasm. On purpose. Just to torment her.

Damn him.

He was lucky her hands weren't free.

He moved up and spread his body out against her side, leaving his fingers between her legs, brushing lightly over her clit. Too lightly. Far too lightly to make her climax.

She wriggled her hips, and his touch grew even lighter. More teasing. "Jake, please."

"Please what?"

She groaned. "You know."

"Maybe. But I won't do it until you ask nicely."

"Please…I want you inside me."

He pressed a finger deep inside her. "There."

She clenched down on him, moaning. "You know what I mean."

He kissed her, filling her mouth with his tongue. When he pulled back, she could barely focus on his face through the haze of her need.

A second long, hot finger joined the first, stretching her open, thrusting in a devious rhythm. "I'm inside you. Isn't that what you asked for?"

God, he'd tease her to death. "Please, Jake. Please."

His hand moved in slow, steady thrusts, brushing her clit with every stroke. She bit her lip to stop a moan.

"This isn't what you wanted?"

She shook her head.

"Tell me."

You know, damn it.

Say it.

She closed her eyes, hiding from his knowing gaze. "Your cock," she whispered. "I want your cock inside me."

He lifted away from her, and then she felt the mattress sag under her head. Something warm, hard and hot brushed her lips. She gasped and opened her eyes.

He was kneeling over her head, his cock against her mouth.

"Here," he said. "Take my cock inside. Just like you asked."

She could refuse. But need rolled off of him in waves, the need to have her pleasure him like this, the need to dominate her. And she needed to please him just as much.

So she opened her mouth and took the head of his cock inside, sucking gently, swirling her tongue around him.

God, yes.

She couldn't tell whose thought that was.

He touched her jaw with one strong hand, feeling her mouth move on him. His hips rocked back and forth, shallow thrusts that made her wish she could take him deeper, made her wish she could grab his hips and hold him hard against her.

She'd never enjoyed this so much. Sensing exactly what he needed, feeling his pleasure…it was almost like she was pleasing herself. And even if she hadn't felt how much he loved this, his gasps and moans would have told her. She sucked harder, making little noises of her own around his cock.

He groaned. Her mouth made a soft sucking sound as he pulled his cock away…pulled it away just an instant before he came. She sensed that, too.

He lay next to her, pressing against her full length, and his hand found her pussy again, dipping and teasing.

He knew just how to keep her on the brink. No doubt he could sense it, just like she was reading things from him.

Maybe he could sense how damned desperate she was. *Fuck me.*

"I can't hear you," he said.

Damn his arrogance. "I know you did."

"Say it," he demanded.

Fine. Whatever it took, she'd do it. "Fuck me," she said.

He kissed her cheek. "You're blushing."

No doubt. "I've never said that to a man before," she admitted.

He brushed his mouth over hers in the lightest of kisses. "I know. That's why I wanted you to say it to me."

How sweet. If she could have moved, she'd have kissed him back.

He kept stroking her sex with his hand, sliding into her with his fingers. He made no move to cover her.

"Aren't you going to…" She couldn't say it again.

"Patience."

How could he be patient? She was dying from his teasing…aching, squirming, all but screaming. If her hands were free, she'd make him just as crazy. Next time.

He propped his head up on one hand, gazing down at her face while his fingers tortured her. Looking into those glinting blue eyes while his hand drove her crazy — it was too much. Too much intimacy. She had to close her eyes.

But even with her eyes closed, she read his thoughts, his feelings. He loved teasing her like this. He wanted her to beg. To beg him to dominate her. He wanted her to talk dirty to him.

She took a deep, shuddering breath and opened her eyes. "Fuck me, damn it! Fuck me or make me come with your hand."

He flicked her clit with the tip of a finger, making her gasp. "So demanding," he murmured. "I think you've forgotten who's the master here."

He lifted his hand from between her legs, then rose to his knees beside her. "Maybe I won't fuck you at all."

An idle threat. But she couldn't bear not having him touch her. "Please," she begged, straining against the ties, turning as far as she could to face him. "I'm sorry. Please…touch me again."

"Punishment first." His tone was harsh. But she knew he wasn't really angry. He just wanted to…play with her.

He pulled at her hip, turning her on her side so that she faced away from him. The ties pulled at her wrists, straining her arms. He pushed her closer to the headboard, relieving some of the pressure on her shoulders. He must have sensed her discomfort.

Yet he still intended to punish her.

His hand slid over the curve of her ass. "You have the hottest ass I've ever seen."

Great. He was comparing her to other women.

A sharp bite on her ass made her gasp and try to pull away from him. Then a hard slap stung her. "I'm going to make it even hotter."

He slapped her again. And again. Lightly stinging, warming her skin. He knew just how hard to hit…hard enough to make her tingle, hard enough to make her want more.

And she knew what he wanted, too. She pulled away, whimpering in pretend pain, and his strokes got lighter. He had to know he wasn't really hurting her.

He stopped and pressed his front against her back, pressed his cock into the warm crease of her ass. "You liked that," he whispered in her ear.

She nodded, even though he didn't need the confirmation.

"Naughty Faith," he murmured. "I'll have to punish you for enjoying it."

He pulled away, then tugged on her hip until she was lying on her back again. She couldn't see exactly what he had in mind. She probed more insistently, and there it was—his head between her legs...

"Spread your legs," he demanded.

Oh, yes. Now she saw exactly what he wanted. She obediently bent her knees and spread them wide, exposing herself as blatantly as a woman could.

He moved until he was kneeling between her spread legs, staring down at her sex. She stared at him in return. God, if only she could touch that magnificent cock.

He grasped his cock with one hand, exactly as she'd just imagined doing. "I'll make you beg for this," he said.

Her hands reached for him reflexively, and her shoulder muscles ached in protest. Damned ties. "I've already begged."

In another minute, she'd use the safe word and get him to untie her. And then she'd jump *his* bones.

He groaned, then let go of his cock and fell forward over her. He kept most of his weight on his forearms, but his chest rubbed against her sensitive nipples. And his cock, oh, his cock pressed against her sex perfectly, the tip nudging her clit. She tried to move under him, to drive his cock against her harder, but his hips had her pinned down tight.

"Don't say it," he murmured in her ear.

"What?"

"The safe word. Don't say the safe word."

Ah, he'd picked up on that. Now *he* was the one begging. Good. "If you don't make me come within a minute, I'm going to *scream* your damned safe word," she threatened.

"You want me that bad?" he whispered.

She squirmed, trying to press his cock against her more firmly. "Yes. Please. *Please.*"

His hips moved, his cock sliding, seeking her entrance.

God damn it. His thought startled her. Before she could ask what was wrong, he lifted off of her.

He'd nearly forgotten a condom. Something he *never* forgot.

She smiled. At least he was as lust-crazed as she was.

It only took him a second to find the box. She heard the cardboard tearing, heard the crinkling of a foil wrapper. Then he was back on top of her, hard and hot and strong.

He filled her with a quick, savage thrust.

She cried out. He groaned.

He stopped, stopped with his cock buried deep inside her. She felt him panting against her neck. And the connection between them grew even stronger. Their thoughts flew almost simultaneously.

Good?

The best.

Yeah.

Move. Move.

Like this?

Yes, yes!

She couldn't even think anymore. The hard thrust of his body on hers felt too good.

But she didn't have to think. He knew what she needed, knew it intuitively. Knew exactly how to angle his hips...how fast to thrust...how hard to grind against her aching clit. He bit her earlobe an instant after she imagined it. She wrapped her legs around his the moment the thought formed in his head.

And they moaned together, moaned and gasped and cried out, speaking to each other with wordless, shameless noises. She felt her climax build—felt *his* climax build—she couldn't tell the difference anymore. It didn't matter. *Just don't stop, don't stop, don't ever stop...*

She pushed up against him, straining to get closer to his pounding hips, struggling to match his impatient rhythm. Every thrust took her higher...closer. She opened her eyes and saw his head thrown back, his jaw clenched with aching force as he moved.

Mine, he thought fiercely. *Mine*. Without missing a thrust, he dropped his head and bit her neck, hard. She gave a sharp cry before her pain merged into his savage need. The need to brand her.

The thrill of feeling his desire, of driving him to such frantic heights, pushed her over the edge. Her passion burst into a savage climax, and he was right there with her, matching her spasm for spasm, groan for groan. She *felt* him come, felt it deep in her psyche, in her bones, as though she was a part of him. And he was a part of her.

They cried out together, trembling and shaking together as the passion drained away into aching satisfaction. Jake collapsed on top of her, a heavy, protective weight. God, she wanted to hold him.

He nuzzled his face in the crook of her neck as they both gasped for breath. After a minute, he lifted his head and looked down at her with a bemused, tender expression on his face. "Wow," he said.

She smiled up into his handsome face. "You said it."

He lifted off of her, leaving her sweat-sheened body chilled. She felt him fumbling with the ties that bound her wrists. Her very sore wrists. And her arms were a bit numb; she couldn't lower her hands.

He rubbed her tingling biceps. "Do they hurt?"

"Just a little."

"I hope it was worth it."

He looked concerned. She smiled and draped her arm over his shoulders, pulling him close. "You know it was."

"You're still reading my mind?"

She probed gently, verifying her suspicions. The connection between them had dissipated. "No." Perhaps it had only been so intense because they'd wanted each other so desperately. But that was no excuse for what she'd allowed to happen. She'd read his most intimate thoughts…at his most unguarded moments. "I owe you an apology, Jake. I'm sorry I read you without your permission."

He smiled and brushed a lock of hair behind her ear. "Thanks, but I did challenge you to read me. So it's not like I was unwilling."

"Yes, but I'll try to be more careful in the future. I don't want to invade your privacy."

He winked at her. "I'd say the invasion went both ways."

"I guess that's true."

His expression grew serious. "I'm not afraid of anything you might see from me, Faith."

Lying here with his strong arm wrapped around her, she felt safe and secure. "I'll try not to be afraid, too."

"Good." He turned away and trashed the condom, then rolled to face her again. A warm hand stroked down her arm. "Are you cold?"

She was shivering a little, but hadn't noticed. "Yes."

He pulled the side of the bedspread over them both, then wrapped his arm around her waist. "I suppose if you can't read my mind anymore, I'll have to resort to mundane methods like speaking to share my thoughts with you."

"Yes, speaking will have to do."

His hand wandered to her hip. "Tonight…having a strong, sexy woman at my mercy…it was like a dream come true."

He really could be disarmingly sweet. She smiled against his shoulder. "It was a fantasy I never knew I had," she admitted.

He moved back a little, until they were lying face to face. He seemed oddly serious. Unsmiling. "Well…it was great, but it's not something I'd like to do all the time. Maybe on occasion, but…"

He trailed off. Was he trying to tell her this was just a one-night stand? Was he trying to find a way to get rid of her?

She could read him to find out, but she'd just promised not to probe without his consent. She put a finger over his lips. "You don't need to make excuses, Jake. Do you want me to leave now?"

He frowned. "Do you want to leave?"

Communication sure was easier when they were reading each other. "No. I thought you were trying to let me down gently."

"God, no." He grinned. "If you could read my mind, you'd know I'm already thinking about next time."

He had to be kidding. She forced herself not to lift the bedspread and look at his cock. "You're ready for next time?"

He laughed. "Not yet. Give me an hour." He stroked her arm, brought her hand to his mouth, and tenderly kissed her sore wrist. "I'll be so gentle with you, you'll feel like a virgin."

God, he was sweet. She felt sentimental tears in her eyes. She must look like an idiot, grinning through her tears.

He pulled back just a little, to where she could focus more easily on his face. "About this psychic stuff…"

She stiffened. Now that she wasn't reading him, she had no idea what to expect.

"I thought it was just a game," he went on. "Nothing but tricks. Easy guesses. I thought that people believed it because they wanted to."

"And now?"

"Now I don't know what to think." He brushed his hair out of his eyes with one hand, then cupped her cheek. "But I know you have a gift that I can't explain."

At least he didn't think she was a charlatan anymore.

"And I know that I've never experienced anything even remotely similar to what I felt tonight," he said.

"Neither have I."

His brow furrowed. "But you can read other people all the time. Other men."

He sounded so jealous, she nearly smiled. "I've never..." She felt a blush heat her cheeks. "I've never done it in bed before."

He raised an eyebrow—his trademark skeptic's gesture.

"Really," she assured him. She wouldn't tell him how unique their connection had been, or that she'd never read anyone so easily. Or that she'd never had anyone else read *her*. She didn't want to scare him off. "Usually I have a lot more control."

He smiled. "So you really were out of control."

She nodded. "Jake..." She didn't want to spoil the tender mood, but she had to know. "About the grant..."

He kissed her, a quick brush of warmth that stopped her speech. "You've held up your end of the bargain, Faith. You've more than proved that psychic—that *intuitive*—abilities are real."

"That's not why I came to bed with you."

"I know. And I still have concerns about the university's reputation. But I can't explain what happened between us tonight, and that's what research is all about. Studying the unexplainable."

She kissed him back. "Thank you."

"There's something I have to ask you." He seemed to struggle with his thoughts for a moment. "Do you live here in San Francisco?"

He'd been so serious, so intent, she hadn't expected such a mundane question. "Yes."

He stroked along her arm. "It's not so very far from Monterey."

And he'd mentioned earlier that he lived in Monterey. "No, it isn't."

"I might be in the city more often in the near future."

She wasn't sure where he was heading with this, but she'd play along. "Really? That's nice."

"So, the next time I'm in the city, do you think you might want to see me?"

This was the man who'd tied her up? This man looking at her so cautiously, asking so diffidently if she wanted to see him again?

"I don't mean for sex," he said quickly. "Well…not *only* for sex."

She laughed. "I'd love to see you again. For sex or anything else you have in mind."

He grinned wickedly. "Oh, I have a lot of things in mind." He leaned closer for a deep kiss.

She sighed against his mouth. "I'll never be bored with you, Jake."

He chuckled. "You just read my mind."

As their lips parted, a vivid image came to her. Jake on his hands and knees, a blonde-haired toddler riding on his back, tiny fingers pulling at his hair…and an identical baby reaching up to him, giggling as Jake bent his head and planted a sloppy wet raspberry-kiss on her belly.

Her breath caught.

Twins. *Their* twins.

She nuzzled her face against his shoulder to hide her dreamy smile. No, she'd never be bored with Jake.

About the author:

A lifelong daydreamer, Doreen DeSalvo sold her first short story at the age of eight. Her payment was a candy bar. Over thirty years later, her passion for writing—and chocolate—remains. She currently lives in a Victorian house in San Francisco with the man she fell in love with as a teenager. Having experienced her own personal fairy tale, she can think of no career more rewarding than writing passionate love stories.

Doreen welcomes mail from readers. You can write to her c/o Ellora's Cave Publishing at P.O. Box 787, Hudson, Ohio 44236-0787.

Also by Doreen DeSalvo:

For the Love of Rigah
Passionate Hearts

TIME-SHARE: AMELIA'S JOURNEY

Lora Leigh

Prologue
Venus 2245

"What the hell is this? We've lost stabilization, Commander. Guidance is gone and radar is offline."

"Steering is shot all to hell." Commander Saber Madison struggled against the resistance in the manual guidance column, his hands clenching on the wheel as he fought the turbulence threatening to rip the small shuttle apart.

"We're heating up!" Major Mike Tennison furiously yelled as he fought to re-engage system electronics. "Control. Control. This is East Eden. This is East Eden. We have total system loss. Repeat, total system loss."

Static answered.

"Communications are gone, Commander," Tennison barked as the shuttled continued to drop from the sky.

The air inside the small craft was heating up, sweat building on their bodies as instinct kicked in to cool them down. Commander Madison was fighting the steering, pulling the wheel up and out as he tried to force the nose higher and activate the emergency gliding system.

Amelia Collins sat behind the co-pilot tightly strapped into her seat, her eyes locked on the commander as he struggled with the wheel. Desperation filled the cockpit as they dropped from the sky, gravity catching the spacecraft and pulling it at an enormous speed to the planet waiting below.

Lora Leigh

"Just a little more." Saber's voice was strained, the muscles in his arms bulging so tight his shirt bit into his arms as he pulled back on the wheel. "Almost there."

The emergency gliding system was just that. It required the complete failure of all on board systems, which meant steering. Pulling the column up manually was next to impossible, as the system electronics were said to be failure proof. Someone had evidently been wrong because every light and switch on the pilot and co-pilot's console was black and the air inside the craft was becoming increasingly thin.

"Got it!" Elation filled the dark voice as the column locked in place and the emergency power flickered around the cockpit.

The shuttle jerked, shuddered, the force outside breaking dramatically as the emergency stabilizers began to retract and lock in place. The craft groaned in protest as the direction changed, fighting to nose up, slow down and ease to the surface rather than being thrown into it.

"Control. Control. We have complete systems failure. Are you there, control?" Tennison continued his call to the space station as he fought to manually rebalance the oxygen and bring radar back online. "Dammit, Saber, where the fuck are we?"

Cloud cover was thinning, but there was still no way to tell exactly how far they had slid from their projected heading. Radar was shot, and the GPS silent.

"We're coming out of cloud cover. Shit. We got ocean under us." Saber was fighting with the steering to turn the craft in another direction, hopefully one with land beneath it. If they crashed in the ocean, there wouldn't be a hope of salvaging the onboard communications or their link to

276

control. The mission was slated to be so perfectly safe that only the basic equipment had been included in the survival packs.

"We're turning. We're turning," Saber gritted out as Amelia felt the craft change direction. "We have potential landing at a heading of three o' clock. I'm heading in."

How he managed to wrestle the manual steering from a twelve o' clock position to three, Amelia had no idea. The shuttle turned, though, amazingly, descending without aid of the breaking system at a fast, though hopefully survivable, rate.

"We're going to hit hard!" Saber yelled over the sound of the craft's stress. "Brace in and expect to bounce."

And bounce they did. Amelia wondered if bones had managed to break as she was thrown time and again against the harness as the shuttle hit the ground and began moving across it at breakneck speed. Saber and Mike were involved in a long string of vitriolic curses as they fought to get the craft under control and stopped while still relatively intact.

"Fuck. We're gonna hit!" Mike suddenly screamed.

Amelia fought to stay conscious as fear overwhelmed her. She wasn't supposed to die on this mission. It was supposed to be safe.

"We're gonna clip." Saber was still fighting the steering as the shuttle groaned, howled, but once again shifted direction. A second later the air seemed to explode as the craft jerked, bounced hard and the sound of tearing metal filled their ears.

"Shit. We lost the wings." The wings, but not their lives. The rate of speed had slowed dramatically, enough that when the shuttle plowed into something seconds later it shuddered to a stop rather than bouncing over it.

At that second, Amelia's harness snapped on the right, throwing her heavily into the other side. As she bounced into it, the left side gave as well and pitched her into the pilot's area.

She cried in shock as she pitched forward, her head clipping the back of the pilot's seat and rendering her mercilessly unaware as her body flew toward the glass shields ahead.

He caught her. Saber had only a second's warning that Amelia was being tossed headlong into the forward section of the cockpit. Only a breath of time reach to out, break her flight and jerk her into his arms.

The force of speed nearly ripped his arms out of their sockets as he braced his body and pulled her sideways, sprawling her across his lap rather than head first into the shield before them.

The shuttle was still rocking, shuddering. Steam erupted from the panels beneath his feet and sparks flew from the control console around them before they fizzled to dust at his feet.

His heart was racing, sweat pouring down his body as he trembled from the exertion it had taken to maintain control of the small craft. Beside him, Mike was slumped in his seat, breathing harshly as well, muttering every curse the other man must have learned during his years in the Air Force. And that was quite a vocabulary.

Across his lap, the little botanist he had been forced to accept on the mission was unconscious, her hair having been torn from the neat braided knot she kept it in and flowing around her body.

The first thing he thought of was sex. Damn. They had nearly hurled to their deaths and now that they were safely on land, his cock was engorging, his entire body so hyper that for one tense minute he thought of nothing but stripping her uniform from her body and stuffing her pussy full of the cock surging beneath his own clothes.

Adrenaline was a bitch. And the woman in his arms was a weakness; he had known it the minute she had been assigned to the crew.

"Is she alive?" Mike was breathless, gasping, his short brown hair dripping with moisture as he leaned back in his seat and looked over at them.

Evidently, Saber thought, he wasn't the only one with sex on his mind. Mike's pants were straining at the seams as well.

"Damn. I'm glad she's unconscious," he sighed as he hastily checked the wound at her temple, her vitals, and pupils. "Possible concussion. But hell, she's alive."

Her ass was right over his cock, a soft, tempting pad of flesh. He shook his head, cursing, not for the first time, his more than heated attraction to the little botanist. Now wasn't the time for it. They were in a hell of a situation and sex should be last on his list of priorities.

"Let's get out of here. See how bad it is." He released the catch on his harness, wrapped his arms around Amelia's small body and rose to his feet. "Let's pray we can at least keep warm."

Chapter 1
Two Months Later

It was so much like Earth.

Amelia Collins stood beneath the thick tent awning Major Madison had set up for her lab and stared into the lush valley stretching out before her. The humidity had peaked; thick and heavy for midday, causing her to strip off the outer uniform shirt she normally wore. The light gray undershirt was much cooler, more comfortable in the growing heat. She wished she could strip off the uniform pants as well.

She stared around the deserted area of the camp they had set up. Saber and Mike would be gone for hours yet, searching the surrounding forest and hoping to meet up with other members of the four teams that had entered the atmosphere with them weeks before.

The magnetic disturbances from the planet weren't apparent from space, but the minute they had entered the atmosphere all electronics had gone haywire. It was an unexpected development, as there had been no problems with the unmanned robotics sent in for years to take samples from the planet.

It was still creating havoc with their communications equipment. Amelia had managed to get the lab equipment working, though, and ran her tests daily as required on varied vegetation the men brought in. The tests were proving surprising. It was almost identical to Earth. There were still unknown properties she hadn't been able to identify in the vegetation, water and, to a lesser degree, in the oxygen. But habitation was looking more and more promising. If only the heat would ease.

Setting aside the reports she was writing, Amelia stripped the hated pants from her body and draped them over the back of the chair with her shirt. Relief. The breeze that flowed through the opened sides of the tent caressed her moist flesh and sent a cooling kiss over her body. Several long strands of dark brown hair had fallen from the careless ponytail she had pinned it into it, it caressed her shoulders, making her shudder with the pleasurable sensations.

It made her think of sex. Made her think of Saber. Tall, broad shouldered, his body muscular and fit, he had become the center of her most erotic fantasies. Fantasies she had never considered during her hectic, boring life on Earth. It was becoming harder and harder to maintain the cool distance established at the beginning of training.

It was obvious he was at least interested in her, even if he rarely looked at her. But there was no mistaking the way his pants filled out when he watched her, the bulge that would press hard and demanding against the usually loose-fitting uniform. And at night…

Her eyes flickered closed as she thought of their sleeping conditions. Wedged between the two men in the less than private atmosphere of the shared bed they had created for safety and warmth during the cold nights, her body hummed with arousal, with no relief. There wasn't even the privacy required to masturbate.

Instead, there were two broad male bodies backed against her, heated warmth penetrating her uniform and stroking a fire in her pussy that was becoming harder by the day to ignore. The nights were just hell.

But, the men were gone now. They were gone, her tests were completed for the day, and several hours stretched ahead of her before they returned. She could feel her pussy pulsing in hot, hungry demand for attention. She had never been so hot, so damned in need, in her entire life. Her hands ran over the material of the T-shirt at her stomach. Her fingers created a wake of sensation as she sat down on the metal chair beside her, considering her options. Her options—and the thick cream dampening her panties.

Slouching back in the chair, she stared off into the direction Saber and Mike should return. Her fingers ran over her crotch, her breath hitching in despair. She had seen both men naked on more than one occasion. Both were very well endowed, their cocks thick and long even at rest. Aroused, a trembling moan escaped her lips as her fingers inched beneath her panties. They would be hard thick stalks of flesh that could more than fill her hungry cunt. But Saber. She whimpered. He was larger than Mike by at least an inch and thicker. He would fill her to overflowing, stretch her until she screamed.

Her fingers danced over her clit, sliding down the narrow slit between the slick lips and circling her sensitive entrance. Her head fell back, neck resting against the metal back of the chair as she gave in to a need she had fought for so long.

She had never been particularly sexual, which had worried her at times. Her work had consumed her. Her attraction to Saber Madison during training had been almost instantaneous, but until their enforced isolation on the planet, had not filled her every waking minute. Now, all she could think about was fucking him. Of spreading her thighs, which she did now, and watching that thick, long cock sink into the folds of flesh.

Licking her lips, the fingers of her other hand fumbled on the table beside her until she gripped the cool weight of the Pyrex pestle she used to grind plants and various substances for testing. She had just finished sterilizing it once again. The thick blunt-tipped end and thinner shaft suddenly seemed her best bet to fill the aching depths of her pussy.

She gripped it, pulling her panties over the small mound and running the thick knob along her aching slit. She shuddered. It wasn't as thick as she knew Saber's cock would be, but it had been years since anything larger than one of her fingers had invaded the portal.

She rested the ball-shaped tip at the weeping entrance to her pussy. Did she dare? Of course she did. She was so greedy for fucking she would take whatever she could get.

She whimpered as the thick bulb began to press inside her. Her cunt rippled in a sharp spasm of pleasure as the pinching pain vibrated through the channel. She was so tight. It had been so long. Her mouth opened as she panted for breath and worked the pestle deeper, hissing in pleasure. The thick knob forced her muscles open, parting her, stroking nerve endings that hadn't been caressed in so long she couldn't remember the last time.

Her other hand pushed her shirt above her breasts, her fingers cupping the hard swollen mound, her forefinger and thumb gripping her nipple and pinching it hard. Her hips nearly came off the chair as she plunged the makeshift dildo deeper up her cunt at the same time.

"Oh yes." Her whimpering moan shattered the stillness of the area as she began to move the pestle in rapid strokes between her thighs. She fucked herself deep, her thighs tightening, straining, as her muscles gripped the thick ball-shaped device digging into it.

She was going to come. She could feel it. The coil of heat was building in her belly, white-hot sparks of volcanic heat rippling from her pussy and up her spine as the sounds of moist thrusts and panting moans wrapped around her.

"Fuck me. Fuck me." Her eyes were closed as she imagined Saber between her thighs, his cock working inside her, stretching her pussy, fucking her with strokes that left her screaming.

The pad of her hand rubbed against her clit. Her fingers sank the pestle up her fist-tight channel in rapidly building thrusts until she tightened, her body arching as her orgasm began to rip through her stomach, tearing through her nerve endings and sizzling across her flesh in near violent streaks of pleasure.

Her cunt tightly locked on the smooth device invading her, clenching and convulsing before releasing a flood of thick, syrupy juices that coated it and dripped from the sides. Her hips jerked several times before the euphoria, hollow though it was, began to ease through her body. Her moans of completion echoed in the air around her as she gasped for breath.

It wasn't a hard, hot cock, but it was enough to still the rapidly building hunger tormenting her body. She would content herself with that and pray for rescue. Because if she didn't get off this damned planet soon, she was going to be begging Saber to fuck her.

And she knew, beyond a shadow of a doubt, if Saber managed to get his cock inside her, Mike wouldn't be far behind.

Chapter 2

"This isn't going to work." Mike's voice was tortured as they stood atop the small rise over the clearing, both men training their binoculars on Amelia as she fucked herself to peak in the clearing below.

Her fingers were saturated with her glistening cream, her little mound swollen, the folds reddened from the fucking she was giving it. The pestle was obviously less than satisfactory, but she was making due with amazing efficiency. Sweat gleamed over her body, her sweet juice coating her fingers and her pussy. Slick. Slippery. How easy it would be, he thought, to slam every inch of his cock up that sweet, tight little sheath.

"Damn, when is she going to stop?" Mike's voice was tormented as they watched the thick-knobbed tip of the device ease from her gripping muscles then stroke along the slit.

Saber was silent. His cock ached like a vicious wound, but he knew if he didn't allow the woman time to ease her hungers then her restless twisting against his body at night was going to end up getting her fucked eventually.

It was too cold to consider sleeping alone with their meager supplies. They needed the body heat to survive the frigid temperatures. They hadn't expected with such lush greenery that the nights could be so hellishly cold. Only one large thermal survival blanket had been included in their supplies because of this. That and their body heat kept them warm enough, but the soft female body between the two men was driving them both insane.

Jacking off wasn't helping much. Saber had given Mike the order days ago to relieve his need before night fell. They took turns escaping the camp and finding the privacy to achieve the relief. But it flared instantly back to life the minute Amelia slipped into sleep and began rubbing that sweet body against their backs. Small mewling sounds of arousal would escape her lips. Her hands would wander, slipping between his thighs, delicate silken fingertips finding his balls. Jacking off inside the blanket had become a habit now. She was killing them both. And watching her finally masturbate was making him insane.

Seeing the blunt tip of that pestle opening her up, sinking inside the silky, hot entrance as her fingers erotically pinched her nipples was making him crazy. Sometimes she would even rub the device around her little puckered anus, making the two men hold their breath in anticipation, wondering if she would invade that tight little hole. But she never did. She obviously wanted to.

Finally, mercifully, she seemed to tire out. She was flushed from head to toe, her breathing harsh as trembling fingers dropped the device. Then, glistening with her juice, the tips disappeared inside her mouth as she tasted herself.

Saber's cock jerked; his mouth watered. How much longer were they going to be stranded on this forsaken planet? Much longer and he was going to lose the battle over his lusts and fuck the hot little scientist. And if he did, there was no way he could deny Mike the same pleasure.

Problem was, the thought of that wasn't eating him alive. Saber had always considered himself a possessive man and he had been attracted to Amelia from first sight of her. That possessiveness seemed to be slowly easing, though. His dreams were haunted with the vision of sandwiching her between him and Mike, both of them pleasuring her, fucking her until their cocks finally eased the desperate erections that were making them mad to devour her.

"We're fighting a losing battle." Mike was doing no more than expressing Saber's own fears. Both men were tormented by the hunger and their own sense of honor where she was concerned.

"We fight as long as we can, Mike," he growled as he eased the binoculars down and took a deep breath. "We'll give her a while to compose herself then go in. Dark will be coming soon."

It would be time to pack into the bed he had made, drawing the survival blanket over them, feeling her heat soaking into his skin.

Chapter 3

Something wasn't right. Amelia stared into the microscope, advancing it further to get a birds-eye view into the pollination she had forced on one of the plants. It was amazing. The little microorganisms were screwing themselves silly. And it wasn't just in the plants. She had tracked the pollen-like organism through the water, fruits, and the air around them, too. The planet was one big biological orgy in progress.

She shook her head in confusion. These readings hadn't been present while the mission was being prepped. She knew it wasn't. She, herself, had tested the samples the unmanned bots had brought back. This was something new. Something that had only begun in the course of a few months.

She took a deep breath as she straightened, staring down at the small array of plants she had arranged around the table. She had run tests until she was blue in the face, had worked tirelessly to figure it out, and she was damned if she could. Of course, the heat building in the air around her wasn't helping.

Mike and Saber were working around the camp in only their uniform pants, sweat soaking on their bodies as the heat continued to build. It was like this every afternoon. The temperature readings never changed, but the humidity shot up to nearly intolerable levels.

She had ditched her shirt hours ago, just as the men had, leaving her clad in the small, damp undershirt. It clung to her breasts, drawing attention to the hard nipples poking against the cloth. And Saber had noticed. When he came to the tent earlier to bring in more samples, his gray eyes had gone immediately to the hard little points.

Amelia pushed back the fringe of sweat-dampened hair that escaped her ponytail and tucked her glasses more firmly on her nose as she thought. The planet was growing at a very rapid rate. Oxygen, cloud cover, vegetation and, amazingly enough, small insects. There had been no sign of any insects or animals when the previous unmanned samples had been taken. But there was no sign of any chemical influence at work. No supernatural aphrodisiac, nothing except the fact that it seemed to be at its height during the sweltering heat of midday. The process then seemed to cool as evening and night descended. The next morning, the growth rate could be noted. Not a lot of growth, but more than normal.

Amelia was starting to fear that it affected more than the plant life. She noticed her own arousal peaking at midday, then seeming to settle down until she drifted into sleep. As her mind relaxed, it appeared her body was becoming more active.

More than once she had awakened herself, her fingers desperately searching along Saber's body, searching for the source of satisfaction she knew could be found between his thighs. At the same time, she would find herself relishing the head of Mike behind her, longing to have him touch her, rubbing against him as her arousal built. She was growing so desperately heated in her sleep, with her dreams spurring her on, that she knew the men's control was going to snap soon.

"Saber." She called out to him as he and Mike stared into the guts of the communications equipment. He shot her a questioning look. "Could you come here a minute?"

He frowned before rising to his feet and moving with long, powerful strides to the tent. Dark muscles gleamed with a moist sheen, rippling in movement. Her cunt rippled in response.

"What's wrong, doctor?" His gaze flickered to her swollen breasts then back to her eyes.

Amelia drew in a deep breath, feeling her face flush. "We might have a problem."

He lifted a black brow a bit sardonically.

"Okay, we have another problem then." She grabbed hold of her temper as she stared up at him in frustration.

He roughly sighed, running his hands over his close-cropped black hair as he closely watched her.

"What's the problem?"

"I need blood and cell samples from you and Mike as well as," she cleared her throat, "semen samples."

He blinked down at her, his gaze becoming flat and cold. "I must have misunderstood you." He shook his head. "Could you repeat that last part?"

She cleared her throat again, ignoring her own blush. "I need semen samples," she hissed, knowing he had to have heard her.

He didn't say a word for long moments. His gaze flickered back to her breasts, making her nipples throb at the flare of heat in his gaze.

"For what?" he finally asked with studied calm.

Licking her lips, she quickly explained the results of the tests she had been running and her conclusions.

"I need blood, cell and semen samples to see if our bodies are experiencing the same reactions," she finished.

He didn't say a word during the explanation. When she finished, his eyes had that hard, determined look that made her more than nervous.

"You don't need the samples," he finally grunted. "It's obvious we are. Now find a cure."

He turned to stomp off.

"Excuse me." She jumped from the tent, gripping his muscled arm to bring him to a stop as she moved in front of him. "I need those samples. And what do you mean, 'find a cure'? What the hell do you think I've been working my ass off on for twelve hours a day?"

His face flushed. "Use the time you're spending masturbating through the day and maybe you'll get an answer. Better yet, use your equipment for your studies rather than filling your pussy and it might do more good that way."

Amelia's eyes widened as she felt herself suddenly pale. Her hand jerked back from his arm as humiliation tore through her body.

"You were watching me?" She barely breathed at the thought. Hot color flooded her body as horror rose inside her. The things she had done. The desperation that had pulsed through her.

She moved back from him in a quick step, turning. She needed to put enough distance between them now that she could find a way to deal with the fact that she had totally humiliated herself in front of her commander.

"Dammit. Amelia." Saber caught up with her as she rushed into the shuttle, intent on grabbing her survival jacket and heading into the surrounding forest. His arm caught hold of her as she passed the bed, gripping it hard and swinging her around. She lost her balance, stumbling then falling to her back as she gazed up at him in shock.

"Do you think you're the only one?" he snarled as he came down on top of her, his thighs spreading hers, the hot wedge of his cock burning between their clothes to sear the mound of her pussy. "Damn you. I'm so jealous of the fact that something besides my cock is filling that tight pussy that I can't stand it. But I'll be damned if I'll take you. Because when I take you, I won't be able to order Mike away from you anymore. Do you hear me? If I fuck you, then I have no choice but to leave you open, filled with my seed and ready for him to fuck. Is that what you want?"

"Saber." She moaned his name, her hips arching against him, barely hearing his furious words now that he was touching her.

She didn't care. Whatever he wanted she would give him if he would just ease the driving heat filling her body. To be honest, the more she slept between the two men, the more she craved both their hands touching her, their cocks digging into her. The planet wasn't the only thing that was an orgy in the making.

His hands were pushing under her top, baring her breasts, enclosing the hard globes in his calloused hands. Ahh yes, it felt so good. She arched into the hold, her hips pressing tighter against the heavy erection nudging against her cunt.

Her hands gripped his arms as his eyes went to her breasts. Then with a hungry growl his head lowered, his mouth attaching to one tight peak and firmly drawing on it.

"Oh God." The wet caress was a shattering relief against her tortured nipple.

His tongue stroked over it, his teeth rasping it, his mouth sucking on her so hard and strong that the rough caress nearly drove her to orgasm.

Her legs lifted, knees gripping his hard flanks as he began to rock against her, grinding his cock against her, causing the cloth of her panties and her pants to rasp against her clit with nearly destructive results. All the while his lips drew on her breast, going from one to the other, licking fire from peak to peak before pressing the two mounds tightly together, his mouth enveloping both nipples at the same time.

"Saber." Her head rolled back on the mattress as she writhed beneath him, on fire, so damned aroused now she could barely breathe.

"Damn you," he growled as his head rose. "I've watched you fucking yourself with that damned pestle to the point that I want to destroy it with my bare hands, Amelia. So help me, you shove anything else up that tight little cunt and I won't be responsible for my actions."

His lips came down over hers, his tongue spearing between her lips, kissing with a starving greed that sent her tumbling into such erotic sensations she wondered if she would survive them. His hands continued to palm her breasts, his thumbs heatedly rasping her nipples .

"Saber." It was Mike's voice that had Saber's big body tensing, a warning, almost animalistic, growl issuing from his throat as Saber possessively lay over Amelia's body.

"I'm not going to fight you, man," Mike finally sighed, though Amelia saw the hunger on his face. "But I won't lay back and suffer, either. You take her, and I'll have my turn. Eventually."

Amelia's pussy shamefully pulsed at the hard tone of the other man's voice, the determination in it. Both men were at a breaking point now and Amelia knew that she alone held the key to their survival or their destruction. The question was, would taking that final step save their lives, only to destroy her heart?

The heart she had given to Saber before ever making this journey.

Chapter 4

Okay, it wasn't an aphrodisiac for sure. It wasn't a chemical reaction. It wasn't a biological malfunction. So what was left?

Two days later, Amelia stood hunched over the microscope, dressed once again in only her undershirt and panties. The heat was sweltering.

She had finally convinced Saber and Mike to give her the samples she needed to run the tests. Blood, sweat, semen and skin tests showed several variances, though. Almost—she searched for a way of describing it—a time-share. As though their bodies were suddenly caught in a switch or relay. Normal responses were being interrupted and priority being given to the sexual. She was attracted to both men, had known it all along, though it was Saber she had been falling in love with.

There were two men and she was the sole woman. Two potential baby-makers and her hormones were ready to mate. Somehow, the planet itself was making a way to ensure population. It had created a perfect paradise and now seemed to throb with the need to see it filled with life. Now, Amelia how to figure out exactly how Venus was doing this.

It had to have something to do with the unidentified chemical she had found within the plants, air and water system. It was acting as the switch to trigger that aggressive sexuality of the two men, as well as her own submissive desires and sexual fantasies.

She was a woman. Created to mate, to fit the male. She had been created to submit to him sexually, in every way. Her body was reinforcing the basic principles upon which she knew women had lived under since recorded history. As men, both Saber and Mike understood the call to mate. Understood there was only one of her, two of them. Saber, as their leader, was beginning to feel possessiveness and ownership. Mike, no less dominant but more than aware of Saber's leadership, would take a less dominant role, but no less sexual. A time-share. And they eventually would share , she knew, if rescue didn't come soon.

Standing, she paced to the end of the tent, feeling the crawling, pervasive need that had sent her masturbating several days before. She was aware now that the two men had known of her efforts to relieve herself. As though in agreement that if they couldn't fill her body nothing would, they no longer left her alone in camp.

After the episode in the shuttle the day before, the two men had also seemed to come to an almost unspoken decision. They were both needed to ensure their survival. There could be no battle to claim her. They weren't animals. But Amelia was starting to feel like little else. Her body was clamoring for release, her pussy sticky with need and throbbing in arousal.

"Saber said to rest when it gets this hot." Mike was suddenly behind her, watching with hot, hungry eyes. "You should go into the shuttle where it's cooler."

"I still have work to do." She shook her head, careful to stay behind the low shelves that she hoped shielded the fact that she no longer wore her pants.

"Saber's orders." He stepped around the shelf before coming to an abrupt stop.

Amelia trembled. She kept her back turned to him, terrified to face him. He was the weaker of the two men. She knew he wouldn't deny what he wanted if she acted willing.

"Damn, you're pretty," he sighed as he moved closer.

"Mike. Saber won't like you being in here like this." She fought to keep her voice from trembling.

"Saber's terrified I'm going to mark that little pussy before he does," Mike grunted as one hand gripped her hip, the other pushed at her shoulders.

Amelia whimpered as he flattened her upper body against the table in front of her. His hand pressed firmly between her shoulder blades as his fingers dipped into the back of her panties.

"Mike. Saber will be here any minute."

He didn't listen. His fingers grazed through the syrup he found along the lips of her pussy, drawing the essence back between the cleft of her buttocks.

"I'll make you a deal," he whispered. "I know you only want our commander up that tight little cunt. And I don't blame you, being half in love with him like you are. But I'm going to have you too, Amelia. Be really nice to me right now, and I promise, I'll keep my cock confined to this…"

A high shriek tore from her lips as she felt his finger penetrate the tight entrance to her anus. Knuckle deep, his finger slick from her juices as he claimed the tender passage.

"You give me this when I want it and Saber won't have to worry—and neither will you—about that sweet cunt. I just need to fuck, baby. I don't need to love you. That's for you and Saber to fight through."

His finger stretched her anal tissue, rasping against it in erotic demand as she trembled on the edge of an almost insane arousal. He could have her now. Her body trembled, her rectum relaxing around his finger as he groaned in relief. His fingers retreated. He gathered more of her juices, returned, eased inside her again. Amelia whimpered, her muscles clamping on the invading digit desperately.

"Mike. Get the hell out here!" Saber's big body moved out of the forest across from them, his eyes blazing, his voice cold.

Amelia whimpered as the finger eased from her ass.

"It's a promise, Amelia," he whispered then. "Say yes or no now. You won't get another chance."

She watched as Saber came toward them, the front of his pants filled with his erection, his eyes glowing dangerous.

"Hurry. Time's running out, baby."

"Yes." She watched Saber, knowing she couldn't bear for anyone else to take what she knew was his, but also knowing her body was so greedy for a fucking that even that would be a relief.

"Good girl." He patted her buttocks before letting her up.

"Amelia." Saber stepped into the tent. "Are you okay?"

She straightened up, aware of the guilt, the hunger, swirling around them.

"He wasn't…" She shook her head. "We weren't…"

He stepped closer, his hand cupping her cheek. "As long as it's not rape," he whispered. "Whatever you decide

I'll abide by, Amelia. Anything but force, baby." He gave Mike a hard look.

Behind her, Mike cursed. "I wouldn't force her, Saber."

"Stop." She held her hand up at both of them. "Go away. Both of you. I have work to do."

"You need to rest," Saber protested.

"No." She shook her head, afraid to stop. Afraid of her own weakness. "I need to figure this out. Now both of you go away."

Surprisingly, they did just that as Amelia trembled as her body weakened. She could still feel Mike's finger in her rectum, feel the greed in which her body had taken it. Damn. Was there a cure?

* * * * *

"There isn't a cure."

She stood before them fully dressed, pausing as she paced the length of the shuttle. "It's like animal instinct. Deserted planet, lush and ready to support life, like a fertile woman. From the instant male and female entered the atmosphere, it went crazy. Our bodies went crazy with it. Biological instinct. Breed and procreate. Fuck me, fill me, impregnate me." Her hands rose as she paced, unaware of the effect her description was having on the two men.

Cocks that were already hard pulsed in demand. Fill me. Fuck me. Impregnate me. Yeah, they thought separately, they could do that. They watched her, hunger blooming inside them.

"Get your heads out of your dicks!" she snapped as she turned back, seeing their almost dazed greed. "Are you paying any attention to me at all?"

"So the cure is to get the hell off this planet?" Saber shook his head. "Damn, Amelia, it's not like we haven't been trying."

Frustration was eating them alive. She could see it. Feel it. Her gaze connected with Mike's. Saber's control was legendary. He would die before he would force a decision on her. It was eating them all alive.

Amelia pushed her fingers through her hair, shivering in the late evening air. Her body was still damp from her earlier shower, though the cold did little to still the heat flaring within her.

"Look. We need to sleep. Tomorrow we'll try to figure it out," Mike suggested evenly, though Amelia could see the anticipation in his face. "Let's get ready for bed and maybe tomorrow we'll have some answers."

Saber sighed as weariness seemed to overcome him. "Yeah. We can hope."

They entered the shuttle, then the cramped sleeping area. Fully dressed except for shoes, they took their places on their sides as Saber lowered the thermal blanket from the supports and tied them down. His back was to her, his body tense. Mike was facing the other way. Amelia shook her head. It was becoming too hard, too frustrating, to deny the hunger sizzling between them. One of them, she knew, would make his move soon.

She just hoped Mike fulfilled his promise.

Chapter 5

Amelia shifted restlessly in her sleep, slipping into a drowsy haze as she felt her shirt loosening, then being drawn slowly from her body. Slowly, so that she wasn't certain if it was real or a dream. Just as carefully, the undershirt was discarded before hands moved to the clasp of her pants. She was on her back. How? There shouldn't be room.

Her eyes opened, blinking in the soft glow of the low heat lamp above them. Mike was drawing her pants from her body, his gaze hard, a reminder. He had promised her. Her heart raced as her panties came next, leaving her naked, her body laid out for him.

His lips kicked up in a grin as he motioned for her to turn back to Saber. She rolled back to her side, barely containing her moan as the tips of her breasts brushed against his back.

"Amelia." Saber whispered her name as her arm came over his waist. He wasn't asleep, but she knew he would fight it, knew he couldn't give in first.

Behind her she felt Mike's fingers part her buttocks, his hands demanding as he moved lower in the bed. She gasped, tightening as she felt his tongue lick down the narrow valley until it came to her puckered anal opening. What was he doing? Indescribable sensations swept through her body as his tongue began to circle the little hole, alternately probing against it and licking around it sensually.

His fingers pulled her buttocks farther apart, his tongue fucking in shallow strokes into the sensitive opening as she gasped, her hips bucking, frantic cries building in her chest. He didn't touch her pussy. Didn't lick it, or draw on the thick juices flowing from it. It was Saber's. They both knew that. He wouldn't cross that line.

Long minutes later he moved again, kissing his way up her back until he was fully behind her once again. Then his fingers, cool and slick, pressed against her anus as he pushed at her legs until one lifted over Saber's. She heard Saber's indrawn breath at the same time she felt the fingers working up her anus. She was breathing roughly; small moans escaping her throat now.

"Saber." She whispered his name as Mike filled her with two, broad fingers, reaching in deep, filling her ass with fire.

Did he know what Mike was doing? She could feel him harshly breathing, his body tense, so rigidly controlled she was afraid he did. She bit her lip, her forehead pressing against Saber's shoulder as Mike's fingers pulled back, stretching her, preparing her, working three rather than two fingers up the tight, heated hole.

She could feel her flesh parting for him, the muscles of her anus milking his digits as he fucked her slow and easy, getting her ready, making her burn for him. Then he moved back, pulling at her, placing her on her stomach before raising her hips to allow the head of his cock to nudge at her anal opening.

"Saber." She was almost sobbing his name now, so aroused, so filled with heat, she felt she would ignite into flames at any minute.

Mike's fingers parted her buttocks. His cock pressed against the opening, making it flare over the slick, hard contours of the bulging head. She moaned in desperation, feeling the pain sear her insides as it rode the back of a pleasure so intense she could barely breathe.

"Now," she heard him whisper a second before the full, erect length surged hard and hot inside her rectum, wringing a hard scream of pleasure and pain from her mouth.

Sleep had barely drifted over him when Saber felt the movements behind him. Amelia had been rubbing her swollen, cloth-covered breasts over his back, driving him crazy as he fought to tamp down his arousal. As he neared sleep, though, he felt Mike moving. Undressing her. Turning her. A soft moan whispered around him as he felt the movements behind him before she lay against him again, fully nude now, her nipples like brands in his back.

Her choice, he reminded himself as he fought to keep from turning to her. It had to be her choice. She had to do this without fear of emotion, fear or reprisals from him. His conscience couldn't stand it otherwise.

Saber could almost see the couple behind him in his mind's eye: movement at his hips as her leg was lifted atop his, a strangled, sleep-thick growl of pleasure from Amelia. Was Mike fingering her pussy? Sinking his fingers inside the hot depths? Saber knew Mike was going to fuck her.

Saber tried to force himself to halt the act, but he couldn't. He couldn't order the other man not to touch her. He felt Amelia being shifted to lie on her stomach, her hips raised as Mike moved behind her. Saber's cock jerked in hunger. He wanted that pussy. He wanted to fuck it first. Needed to fuck it first.

The air within the shelter was steamy now, the scent of delicate aroused cunt thickening the atmosphere. Amelia moaned his name. A strangled, almost pained, gasp as Mike continued to work his fingers inside her. Saber imagined them sinking up her pussy, stretching her little entrance.

He knew when the other man went for the kill. Felt both bodies still, then Mike moving his hips in a hard, surging thrust. But rather than a cry of pleasure, a scream tore from Amelia's throat.

Saber turned, moving to his knees, his eyes wide in the dim light of the shelter as the sight before him shocked his senses. He was a man of varied sexual tastes, had thought nothing could shock him, nothing could arouse him to greater heights than he had seen already.

There was Mike, fully naked, his hands gripping Amelia's buttocks, pulling them apart, his head thrown back in sublime pleasure with his cock buried thick and hard up the botanist's tight little back entrance. He wasn't fucking her pussy, wasn't taking the sweet channel Saber thought of as being his. Rather, he was taking her anally and groaning desperately at the ultra snug fit as Amelia writhed against the impalement.

"Saber." Her voice was high, thready, mixed with pleasure, pain and shock. Her shoulders were flat against the mattress, her head turned, her eyes staring up at him in blinding arousal as Mike kept her hips elevated, his cock tight up her ass.

Mike moved then, drawing Saber's attention back to the sexual act taking place. As his cock withdrew to the dark, purpled head, it glistened with a thick coating of the lubrication they had been using to find their own relief. It caused his cock to shimmer, drawing attention to the flesh stretched tightly around it.

"Damn, she's tight, Saber." Mike was panting for breath, sweat gleaming on his face, his eyes glittering with lust. "So fucking tight I can't stand it."

Saber watched, almost in a daze as the other man thrust back up the snug chute, drawing a strangled cry from the woman he impaled. Mike was fucking her ass with slow, deliberate thrusts, letting her feel every stretched tissue, every nerve his cock stroked over.

"Saber." She was whimpering his name, staring up at him as lust contorted her features. "I'm sorry. I'm sorry."

Hunger was eating her alive. He could see it in her eyes, in the hard ripples that attacked her body as Mike claimed her tender back hole. And she was sorry? It was the most erotic sight he had ever seen, watching her being impaled, skewered on the thick erection plowing up her tight ass. His cock was so damned hard, his own lust rising so sharp, he could barely breathe.

He lay down beside her, his hand going to her sweat-dampened hair, his face level with hers.

"Is it good?" he asked her softly, knowing she was loving it, the pleasure and the pain contorting her features into a mask of desperate, agonizing lust.

"Hurts," she panted, though her hips were moving back each time Mike withdrew.

"Good hurt?" he asked her gently, knowing there was a difference. "Or a bad hurt, baby? I'll make him stop. Tell me if you want him to stop."

Tears glistened in her eyes as she stared up at him. Innocent. Damn, he could tell by her eyes she had never been taken anally, never had anything fucking her ass with so much as tentative thrusts, let alone the hungry strokes Mike was using to plow into her.

Her hands were clawing at the mattress under them, mewling sounds of need escaping her lips. He licked his lips, surprised at his own arousal, his own need now. Mike was fucking her harder, his thrusts shuddering through her body as she watched Saber with guilty emotion. She was loving every stroke, but he knew the emotions that had been building inside her for him were flaying her.

"It's so sexy," he whispered against her lips, watching her eyes widen in surprise. "Watching him stretch you. Seeing his cock take you as you cry out, Amelia. I've never seen anything so arousing in my life." His lips were brushing hers with each word. He was breathing each puff of air shuddering from her body as she was taking his breath.

"Needed you." She was dazed, flying now on the pain and pleasure Mike was filling her with.

Yes, she had, he thought. Her lush little body had been moving against his back while her tight ass must have been moving against Mike's. He smiled tightly, his cock jerking in his pants.

"You'll get me," he promised her then, seeing lusty greed overtake her expression. "I'll take you, baby. Give you everything you need and more. Mike and I both will."

Mike was fucking her in abandon, thrusting hard and fast inside her as she fought to breathe, her body tightening, the intensity of emotion causing her to tense, to prepare to fight. He could see the fear starting to fill her eyes as her body began to shudder with the approaching storm.

"No." He held her still as her shoulders flexed to try to rise. "Stay still, Amelia. Relax, baby. Just relax. I'll hold you. I promise, I'll hold you here."

The sound of slapping flesh and sucking sex filled the small shelter as Mike began to give her every ounce of strength left in his body. Powering into her, taking her like she had been born to be ass-fucked, throwing her body into a sensual storm that Saber could only watch with rapidly rising excitement.

As Mike plowed in a final time, his body twitching, his voice hoarse, thin, as he announced his explosion, Saber watched Amelia flame. Shudders tore through her body, jerking her as though electricity had been sent straight into her rectum rather than Mike's hot seed.

She screamed out Saber's name as he held her down, her mouth opening helplessly as she writhed against the explosions tearing through her. Her orgasm was a beautiful thing to witness, tightening his chest with emotion; filling his cock with a hot hunger, driving him insane.

Finally, long minutes later, Mike eased his shaft from the clenching hole as Saber came to his knees and released his own straining erection. As the other man collapsed beside Amelia, Saber turned her to her back.

Mike's come was still easing from that snug back hole as Saber tucked the head of his straining erection at the portal of her swollen pussy. She trembled then, tears glittering in her eyes as she stared up at him.

He wanted to take her easy. Had wanted soft kisses and a slow buildup to a heat that would live in her memory forever. But lust was riding him like a demon, making it impossible to give her what he knew they both wanted. Later, he promised them both silently. Later.

Working his cock into the snug, hot little channel of her pussy was the most pleasure Saber had ever known. She was too tight, too hot and slick. Easing inside her was killing him when all he wanted to do was thrust in hard and deep. But he was larger than Mike. His cock thicker, longer, and above all things, he didn't want to hurt her.

Amelia prayed she wasn't dreaming again. She could feel the tenderness in her rectum, but even more, she could feel Saber working his thick cock inside her greedy depths, stretching her, making her scream out at the sensations as Mike had been unable to do, even buried in her ass.

Saber touched a part of her no man ever had. As she knew no man ever would. He stared down at her, his gray eyes almost glowing with lust and approval as his erection worked inside her slowly, parting her, filling her with agonizing pleasure.

"There, baby," he whispered down at her as he finally worked every straining thick inch up her desperate cunt. "So tight and hot. Nothing has ever wrapped my dick like this."

She shuddered at the explicit words. Beside her, Mike had moved, lifting her arm, his head lowering, his mouth enclosing the peak of her breast, his teeth and tongue rasping the sensitized nipple.

Amelia jerked at the added sensation, her hips surging against Saber, driving his cock deeper inside her weeping pussy.

Saber fought to hold onto his control now. He watched Mike with narrowed eyes as Mike nursed hungrily at Amelia's full peak. His eyes were closed, his cheeks flexing tightly, hands wrapped around the full mound as he plumped it up tighter.

"Saber," she cried out as her muscles flexed around his cock, her eyes darkening, cheeks flushing brighter. "Please." Her hips jerked again. "Oh God, Saber. Fuck me. Fuck me hard."

He couldn't hold back. His hands gripped her thighs as he began to pump hard and deep inside her, forcing past the resistant tissue, her screams echoing around him with every hard, driving stroke. Pain and pleasure mixed, just as it had been for Mike. But Saber heard something more now. Heard her chanting his name, begging as she hadn't begged the other man, staring into his eyes, her own widening as he felt the hard contractions begin within the snug channel he was stroking so roughly.

Her orgasm was the most beautiful thing he had ever witnessed. Her slender body arching to him, her mouth opening, head thrown back as a thin cry shattered a part of his soul and he felt her juices sear his cock. There was no holding back then. He slammed in hard and deep as his cock jerked then exploded with his own release. Hard, hot streams of seed shot deep inside the blistering depths, dragging a cry from his throat and opening a part of his heart.

Chapter 6

They emerged from the shuttle the next morning, each going to their jobs automatically, nothing being said about the events of the night before. They had work to do. An assignment to complete until they were rescued. Saber had no doubt that eventually they would be rescued. He just hoped it was soon. Amelia was a little thing and his own sex drive, strong at the best of times, seemed to have taken a surprising leap. And Mike wasn't in much better shape. He was terribly afraid she wasn't strong enough to take their hungry needs, and he'd be damned if he would see her hurt.

Nothing could ease the memory of watching his friend piercing Amelia's tight little butt. Seeing his erection drawing back, sinking inside her, had nearly had Saber coming from that sight alone. Seeing Amelia lost in the haze of sensations that the act caused had been even better.

He had known when he first met her that she would fulfill every sexual fantasy in his life. He would own her. He would prove that ownership today. He had allowed Mike to take her first because he knew Amelia had no emotional involvement in the other man. It was sexual, pure and simple. The strange infection of biological needs and natural lusts were filling them all. Because of it, Saber refused to make that first move, refused to take the choice out of her hands. Her acceptance the night before had his instincts screaming now.

When they had awoken, Saber'd handed her a clean T-shirt and panties, throwing her shirt and pants out of reach. She had stared at him, her brown eyes surprised, her soft hair falling around her face in a halo of silk. Mike had watched the byplay with curious eyes.

Amelia had taken a deep breath, moved to the bathroom to wash up and dress and returned wearing only the skimpy shirt and panties. She'd moved out of the shuttle then and headed to work. Saber had then turned to Mike.

The other man had looked tense, prepared for Saber's anger.

"We're stuck here," Saber finally sighed. "We agreed what would happen if it came to this. I won't let my emotions interfere. But if she says no, it means no, by God. You hear me?" he questioned the other man, his voice harsh.

"Will you ask her to say no?" Mike asked then.

Saber could only shake his head. He wouldn't ask her to say no. Wouldn't demand it. Hell, he didn't even want her to. Strangely enough, the thought of sharing her was more erotic than it was painful. He had seen her eyes; saw her fear and her love for him the night before. But he had known all along that Amelia was different. The biological urges caused by this planet be damned. His Amelia was a sweet little submissive ready and eager to give him anything that turned him on. And she had known, had seen his arousal the day before, when he caught Mike spearing her tight ass with his fingers.

Mike nodded with a sharp, abrupt movement. "Time-share," he muttered. "Son of a bitch, more like a wet dream come to life."

* * * * *

And that was exactly what Amelia was. A wet dream come to life. When the heat built and midday came fully upon them, they looked up from the receiver they were working on to see Amelia standing before them.

"I've been bad," she whispered in a soft little voice that had Saber's cock jerking beneath his pants.

"You have?" He rose to his feet then, aware of Mike's slowly building excitement. "What did you do?"

He could see the excitement sparkling in her eyes as she moved her hand behind her back and showed him the glass pestle. It was streaked from her cream, the juice lying thick and steamy along the knob.

Saber narrowed his eyes on her. "Very bad," he growled, his hands going to his pants to release the snaps. "You know what happens to bad little girls, don't you, Amelia?"

Her eyes were drowsy, her cheeks flushed with arousal.

"Their daddies spank them," she said, her eyes sparkling with excitement.

"Son of a bitch," Mike whispered in growing arousal behind him.

"Clean the pestle, Amelia." He kept his voice hard. "With your mouth. Suck it clean."

Frantic blistering heat filled her eyes. Her mouth opened as she took the thick device into her mouth. The knob disappeared past her lips as she began to lick and suck her cream from the pestle. Saber shed his pants quickly, his cock hanging thick and hard from between his thighs as she showed him the now cream-free pestle.

"You are a very bad girl," he whispered. "Come over here and suck my dick, bad girl, then I'm going to punish you."

She went gracefully to her knees, her mouth opening in hunger as he sank one hand into her hair and with the other guided his throbbing erection to her lips. She enclosed it instantly, sucking it into her mouth as her tongue began to caress it with fiery licks.

"Saber," Mike groaned behind him with muttered excitement.

Saber growled. This was his. The other man could have his turn later, after Saber's seed filled every orifice where her body could take a cock.

She was sucking him with deep, hot strokes, her fingers cupping his balls, caressing them gently as she moaned around his flesh. Saber could feel his scrotum tightening, drawing up at the base of his cock as he fought to hold back his release.

He thrust slowly in and out of her mouth, enjoying the heat and moist suckling, determined to make it last. Damn, she was good. Her mouth was pure delight. His hands held her still as she took him nearly to her throat, moaning around the hard, throbbing flesh as she sucked him with hungry abandon.

"I'm going to come," he warned her as he gritted his teeth against the pleasure. "Remember, little girl, good girls swallow."

She groaned, her need only rising now , her lips drawing on him, moving over him in a greedy motion as he began to fuck her mouth harder. He would fill her mouth, then see about taking that hot, tight little ass.

His hands tightened in her hair, a groan ripping past his throat as his cock jerked then exploded, filling her mouth with his semen. Hot, hard jets filled her mouth as she fought desperately to swallow every drop he was spilling down her throat. And he was still hard.

"Saber." Mike's voice was more insistent now, hungrier.

"Wait your fucking turn!" Saber snapped as he drew his flesh back from her lips, staring down at her wild eyes.

"You swallowed it all," he muttered, his voice rasping, thick. "But you were still a bad girl, fucking yourself like that. Daddy has to spank you now."

"Don't spank me, daddy," she whispered as he drew her to her feet. "I'll do better next time."

"Too late," he growled, pulling her into the shuttle. "That pestle went up your pretty pussy when I told you no. Now you have to pay."

He had never spanked a woman in his life. He had dreamed of it. Craved it, but had never done it. He sat down on the large mattress in the sleeping area, jerked her over his lap and ripped her panties from her plump ass.

Mike had followed, naked now, his cock jutting out, jerking each time Saber's hand landed on the pert cheeks.

Amelia was bucking against him, crying out at each pounding slap as her taut little ass turned pink, her pussy grinding against his leg as he paddled her. He felt her skin heat, heard her cries rising and still he struck her. He as fascinated, growing so damned horny from the sight of her blushing cheeks that his cock throbbed like an open wound.

He smoothed his hand over her burning butt then, his fingers tucking between her thighs.

"Hand me the lube, Mike," he ordered the other man.

The tube was there instantly.

He opened her blushing cheeks, ignoring her little pleas, her vows to be 'a good girl' from now on. He laid a line of the gel down her cleft, set the tube aside and began to work it up her little hole.

"My cock is bigger than Mike's, little girl," he warned her. Desperate to fuck her tight ass, he opened her up. "It's going to hurt, baby. Hurt so bad you're going to scream and beg me for more."

He was getting a very deep suspicion that the little botanist liked the pain.

"I'll be good." She was panting, then crying out, as two fingers sank up the little pink entrance. The muscles gripped his fingers, tugging and sucking at them as he pulled back. He screwed them inside her again, grimacing as he felt her juices dripping on his thigh.

Finally, he had three fingers worked inside her, scissoring them as he thrust them hard and deep inside the little portal. She was crying out in desperation now and Saber was ready to explode.

He flipped her on the bed, moving behind her quickly, holding her in place as he parted her cheeks . Mike had moved to her head, his hand lifting her face, his cock nudging at her lips. She enclosed it instantly.

Saber couldn't stand it any longer. He pressed the head of his erection against the reddened opening and pushed in slowly. When the crest cleared the tight ring of muscles there, he ignored her frantic moans and worked his cock deep inside the fist-tight grip of her ass, watching her take every inch.

Mike was almost buried to his balls in her mouth, his expression one of rapture as she tried to scream around his fucking cock.

"See what happens to bad little girls who fuck themselves?" Saber pulled back slowly, paused, then sent his cock tunneling hard and deep up the hot little hole.

Her back arched, a muffled scream echoing around Mike's cock as Saber held her hips tight and fucked her with greedy abandon. She had the hottest little hole he had ever sunk a cock into. He increased his thrusts, determined to imprint each stroke on her body before filling her so full of his semen that her flesh never acknowledged another's. Even Mike's. Especially Mike's.

She was nursing on the other man's cock now, sucking it deep in her mouth as Saber began leading her through new plateaus of pleasure and pain. She was shrieking around the other man's erection, bucking into every thrust Saber threw into her rectum until she began to tighten with her building orgasm.

He felt it crash over her. Felt her muscles tighten around his cock, heard her strangled cry as Mike jerked, obviously spilling his seed down her greedy throat as Saber groaned and gave her his as well. He thrust in to the hilt, fire racing over his body, licking over his erection and releasing his semen up the tight, shuddering depths of her anus.

Chapter 7

"Okay, explain this time-share thing again," Saber demanded as they sat around their dinner later that evening.

Amelia sighed. "Okay, it's like this. Time-share is when one thing makes way to allow another program or event to work, right?"

He and Mike nodded.

"In this instance, the planet is incorporating an unknown substance, hell if I can identify it, into the air, the water, the plants, everything. That's why we've seen so many odd plants that seem familiar. Like the palm tree with the oak leaves. The date-like fruits growing on the rose bushes. It's not so much odd as it is a biological mating effect. To see what will work where the best. In the course of two months I've watched one tree that closely resembles a palm shed and re-grow several different varieties of leaves. A mix and match and process of elimination."

"How does this explain...this?" Saber circled his finger between the three of them.

"One female. Two males." She shrugged. "As I said before, it's a process of fill it, fuck it, breed it and see what happens. But in our case, it wasn't so much biological as it worked against us psychologically. What is a woman's greatest fantasy?" She grinned. "Two men servicing her every desire. And basically, men have many of the same fantasies. The effect of the compound worked to increase the natural desires spurred by those fantasies, which increased the chances of us giving into them."

"And when the biological thing goes away?" Saber asked, his eyes narrowing.

Amelia shrugged. "I don't know. It doesn't affect emotions. At least it hasn't mine. I knew how I felt before we ever landed here, Saber." Her voice softened as she watched him. "I knew where my heart belonged."

"Would you have done this before landing here?" He nodded at Mike then.

Amelia caught the careful control in his voice. If he wanted guilt from her, he wasn't about to get it. She flashed him a cheeky grin instead. "Well, Saber, I have to admit, it was one of my biggest fantasies."

His eyes lit up, a sheepish expression crossing his face as he rubbed at his jaw a bit uncomfortably. "Yeah. Mine too." He pulled her into his arms, snuggling her close and kissing her hair gently. "More than you know, baby."

* * * * *

Amelia was back at work later that day on the samples she had to continue her study of the strange reactions on the planet. The quest for life. As she had said, like a fertile woman, every resource she had focused on populating her world.

Unfortunately, the women who had come from Earth were rendered temporarily sterile, just in case of sexual contact with the men they accompanied. It didn't look good when female officers returned from a mission pregnant. The chances of sexual misconduct were high, too. Their superiors had warned them of that.

The atmosphere within the camp eased quite a bit, though. Saber had asserted his dominance over her, as well as Mike. Amelia's body was his, sexually, emotionally, however and whenever he wanted it. But her pussy was his exclusively. Mike could take her anally, or orally, but he was forbidden to invade territory Saber had staked for himself alone.

The effects of whatever biological reaction had infected them upon their entrance into this planet slowly disappeared. Like a nasty little virus, Amelia tracked its peak and ebb and finally its disappearance. But the needs between the three crew members never waned.

They kept warm at night as they always did, with Amelia cushioned between them. Except now, in most cases, they were fucking her long into the night, Saber buried inside her snug pussy, Mike pushing into her hot ass. Locked in a battle of passion that none of them won or lost. And they were content.

Rescue would come soon, Saber assured himself, but he admitted the time was slowly growing near that they would have to abandon their camp and begin looking for the others. Radio reception was still blocked. There had, in over two months, been no contact with the other crew members. They were beginning to lose hope, but not their will to live or to survive.

Amelia awoke late one morning, stretching as Saber licked at her nipple, his mouth drawing it in, suckling at her gently as Mike watched from beside her. Saber's hands coasted over her body, caressing her, stroking her tenderly. Seconds later, Mike's hand reached out, pulling on her neglected nipple, sending a tidal wave of contradictory sensations racing through her. Saber's teeth and tongue were tormenting one tip, Mike's fingers the other, and heat was racing through her system, burning past every nerve ending as she allowed herself to drown in the pleasure.

The feel of Saber's mouth on her breast had her straining toward him, her back arching as her thighs shifted apart. His hand was there instantly, cupping the mound, one finger surging into the sticky wetness there. At the same time, Mike's mouth covered the hard peak he had gripped, sucking on it deeply as both hands cupped the hard mound.

Amelia's head twisted on the mattress as shudders of pleasure raced over her flesh. She could feel the fire building in her belly, in her pussy, wrapping around her body.

They hadn't taken the time to truly torment her before taking her before. Eager lust had driven the encounters until now. Amelia was still more than eager, but each time a hot tongue licked a sensitive nipple, or teeth nipped at the tender tip, rockets exploded inside her head. She was greedy. She wanted it all. Every touch, every lick, every stroke.

The men were humming their pleasure as they suckled her. Greedy draws of their mouths, slow hot licks of their tongues, and she could feel herself dissolving into a puddle of such intense ecstasy it was unreal. They feasted at her breasts. Sipped and suckled, nibbled and licked, until she was screaming from the fiery need prickling over her body.

The swollen mounds of flesh became so sensitive that each breath of air over the hard peaks nearly threw her into orgasm. Her cunt spasmed in exquisite longing, her juices sliding from it, soaking Saber's fingers as he caressed her .

Then they were moving, turning her to her side. Saber's lips feathered down her stomach, one hard hand lifting her thigh as his mouth went to her clit.

Okay. That was good. Rapturous. Sending splintering heat racing through her womb to rocket over the rest of her body. But then Mike was behind her, long fingers parting her buttocks, his hand urging Saber to lift her leg higher as he moved behind her.

"Oh God! Oh God! Saber…" Her eyes widened in shock as she felt Mike's tongue begin to caress the tight, forbidden entrance to her ass.

Saber hummed against her clit, evidently uncaring what Mike was doing behind her. His tongue circled the little bud slowly, his lips capping over it to suckle it into the heat of his mouth as Mike probed languidly at the entrance he had claimed behind her.

Her hands were buried in the short strands of Saber's hair, her world centering to this moment in time, and the mouths eating her with hungry abandon. Mike licked at her roughly, drawing the cream that spilled from her pussy into his mouth, then his wicked flesh was digging into the entrance of her anus once again.

Amelia was begging, screaming, her body on fire, her hips undulating against the separate mouths tormenting her. Then Saber intensified the caresses. He suckled the little bud tighter into his mouth, his tongue flickering fast, hot, a whiplash of fire, of demand. Amelia exploded, her strangled cry echoing around them as her orgasm tore through her body.

The hard waves had yet to diminish before he moved again, going to his back and dragging her over his hard body. Mike eagerly followed, his hands gripping her hips as Saber positioned her, then pushed her hard and fast down on the straining erection awaiting her.

"Saber." She was shuddering with pleasure, with pain, both sensations tearing through her body at the same time as she felt the wide girth of Saber's cock sinking into her greedy vagina.

His arms came around her, holding her shoulders to his chest as his lips whispered against her ear. "Mine. I love you, Melia," he whispered, his voice rough

Her heart rocked in her chest as her hands buried in his hair, her body opening for him, a whimper escaping her lips as Mike's slippery fingers slid into her anus, preparing her.

"I love you," she panted back as the other man nudged the hot head of his cock against her back entrance. "Oh God. Saber. Saber. I love you."

She nearly tore free of his hold as Mike pushed his cock slow and easy up the tender back channel. It stretched her, setting her anus aflame as he worked his length up her tight ass.

Her pussy was filled with Saber. Overfilled. Stretched tight and hot around his straining shaft. It left little room behind. Room Mike was stretching, straining, filling with his flesh as she screamed and shuddered in Saber's arms.

"There, baby," Saber's voice was a dark moan at her ear. "So tight, Melia. So tight and hot and creamy. I can feel your pussy gushing around me, baby. There you go. Let him in. All the way in."

Mike groaned behind her; Amelia cried out at the fiery pleasure/pain of the penetration and the dark eroticism of the act. They were claiming her together now.

Pushing into her, taking her, marking her in ways she knew she would never forget.

Then they were moving. Two powerful cocks. Mike slid back until only the tip of the broad head stretched her open. He pushed forcefully back in as Saber retreated. On and on it went. Strokes of steel impaled her as the dual penetration threw her into a state of fiery, excessive lust.

She moved desperately on the two shafts penetrating the sensitive entrances to her body. Shuddering, crying out with each hard stroke as they fucked her into a state of complete, pleasure-filled mindlessness.

"Good, baby," Saber moaned as he held her tightly to his chest, his hips moving, his cock thrusting into her with hard, rapid strokes as Mike timed him exactly. "Sweet, baby. Yeah..." He held her tighter as she gasped and tensed harder.

It was building. The fire and heat they were filling her with was building. She could feel it, electricity coiling in her womb, painful, tight...

"Now, Amelia," he growled as the strokes increased, driving into her, fucking her so hard and deep she swore they were reaching her soul. "Come for me, baby. Come for me now."

As though on command, she shattered. Wailing, bucking against his hold as brutal convulsions began to tear through her, tightening her vagina, her anus, locking the two men inside her as they began to shudder, spilling hot, surging jets of rich thick semen into her body.

Gasps, shattered moans and whispered vows echoed around her. Calloused hands smoothed over her body; she didn't know whose was whose, as they gentled her past the tearing orgasm that consumed her.

Saber was still locked inside her as Mike slid free of her tight ass. Saber's hands held her close, coasting over her sweat-dampened back, his lips against her forehead as he caressed her with soft, silken kisses.

Her body was heavy and languid, replete. Satiated.

Seconds later, a dark, broad shadow filled the entrance of the shuttle's sleeping area.

"Well hell, Commander, no wonder we couldn't reach you. You were too damned busy having fun," Rich said with amusement and relief. Major Rick Rockland's voice boomed through the interior, shocking them apart, leaving them gaping as the other man neared them. "Get your asses out of bed, boys and girl. The cavalry has arrived."

About the author:

Lora Leigh is a 36-year-old wife and mother living in Kentucky. She dreams in bright, vivid images of the characters intent on taking over her writing life, and fights a constant battle to put them on the hard drive of her computer before they can disappear as fast as they appeared.

Lora's family, and her writing life co-exist, if not in harmony, in relative peace with each other. An understanding husband is the key to late nights with difficult scenes, and stubborn characters. His insights into human nature, and the workings of the male psyche provide her hours of laughter, and innumerable romantic ideas that she works tirelessly to put into effect.

Lora welcomes mail from readers. You can write to her c/o Ellora's Cave Publishing at P.O. Box 787, Hudson, Ohio 44236-0787.

Also by Lora Leigh:

Bound Hearts 1: Surrender

Bound Hearts 2: Submission

Dragon Prime

Elemental Desires

Elizabeth's Wolf

Feline Breeds 1: Tempting The Beast

Feline Breeds 2: The Man Within

Law And Disorder 1: Moving Violations

Legacies 1: Shattered Legacy

Legacies 2: Shadowed Legacy

Men Of August 1: Marly's Choice

Men Of August 2: Sarah's Seduction

Men Of August 3: Heather's Gift

Men Of August 4: August Heat (12 Quickies of Christmas)

Ménage a Magick

Seduction

Wolf Breeds 1: Wolfe's Hope

Wolf Breeds 2: Jacob's Faith

Wolf Breeds 3: Aiden's Charity

Why an electronic book?

We live in the Information Age—an exciting time in the history of human civilization in which technology rules supreme and continues to progress in leaps and bounds every minute of every hour of every day. For a multitude of reasons, more and more avid literary fans are opting to purchase e-books instead of paperbacks. The question to those not yet initiated to the world of electronic reading is simply: *why?*

1. *Price.* An electronic title at Ellora's Cave Publishing runs anywhere from 40-75% less than the cover price of the <u>exact same title</u> in paperback format. Why? Cold mathematics. It is less expensive to publish an e-book than it is to publish a paperback, so the savings are passed along to the consumer.

2. *Space.* Running out of room to house your paperback books? That is one worry you will never have with electronic novels. For a low one-time cost, you can purchase a handheld computer designed specifically for e-reading purposes. Many e-readers are larger than the average handheld, giving you plenty of screen room. Better yet, hundreds of titles can be stored within your new library—a single microchip. (Please note that Ellora's Cave does not endorse any specific brands. You can check our website at www.ellorascave.com for customer recommendations we make available to new consumers.)

3. *Mobility.* Because your new library now consists of only a microchip, your entire cache of books can be taken with you wherever you go.

4. *Personal preferences are accounted for.* Are the words you are currently reading too small? Too large? Too...**ANNOYING**? Paperback books cannot be modified according to personal preferences, but e-books can.

5. *Innovation.* The way you read a book is not the only advancement the Information Age has gifted the literary community with. There is also the factor of what you can read. Ellora's Cave Publishing will be introducing a new line of interactive titles that are available in e-book format only.

6. *Instant gratification.* Is it the middle of the night and all the bookstores are closed? Are you tired of waiting days—sometimes weeks—for online and offline bookstores to ship the novels you bought? Ellora's Cave Publishing sells instantaneous downloads 24 hours a day, 7 days a week, 365 days a year. Our e-book delivery system is 100% automated, meaning your order is filled as soon as you pay for it.

Those are a few of the top reasons why electronic novels are displacing paperbacks for many an avid reader. As always, Ellora's Cave Publishing welcomes your questions and comments. We invite you to email us at service@ellorascave.com or write to us directly at: P.O. Box 787, Hudson, Ohio 44236-0787.